WIN, LOSE
OR DIE

Other James Bond Books by John Gardner

SCORPIUS

NO DEALS, MR. BOND

NOBODY LIVES FOREVER

ROLE OF HONOR

ICEBREAKER

FOR SPECIAL SERVICES

LICENSE RENEWED

Also by John Gardner

THE SECRET GENERATIONS

THE SECRET HOUSES

THE SECRET FAMILIES

WIN, LOSE OR DIE

JOHN GARDNER

G. P. PUTNAM'S SONS
New York

G. P. Putnam's Sons
Publishers Since 1838
200 Madison Avenue
New York, NY 10016

Library of Congress Cataloging in Publication Data

Gardner, John E.
    Win, lose or die / John Gardner.
        p.   cm.
    I. Title.
    PR6057.A63W5   1989
    823'.914-dc20   89-8470 CIP
    ISBN 0-399-13436-0

Printed in the United States of America
1 2 3 4 5 6 7 8 9 10

For my three lovely nieces—
Sally, Susan & Sarah, one of whom is disgracefully libeled in
this book

Contents

WIN, LOSE
OR DIE

1

WIN in the Gulf

An hour before dawn, in the Strait of Hormuz: a dark and dangerous time and place. The air was a chill mixture of sea and sweetness, giving no hint of the heat that would be generated once day took over. The massive Japanese-registered oil tanker *Son of Takashani* slowly plowed its way toward the Gulf of Oman and comparative safety. Its vast flat deck rolled gently; the tall superstructure, rising from the stern, looking like an apartment building, appeared to tip more violently than the deck because of its height.

Every officer and rating—enlisted man—aboard could feel a tightening of the stomach muscles, the sense of urgency, and the absurd detached feeling which people experience when they know any minute could bring death by fire, explosion, bullet or water. Many had died of

11

these very things along this stretch of water over the years of the Gulf War.

Both the Americans and British had helped by mine-sweeping, and escorting the oil tankers. But, on this occasion, the *Son of Takashani* had been forced to make the trip without the assistance of either the American Fleet or the Royal Navy. The Japanese did, however, take precautions.

Armed men were on the bridge, at vantage points in the superstructure, and even on the deck. Some were always there during the journey from the Iraqi oil fields through the Gulf, but, at the hours of dawn and dusk, extra hands with weapons kept a lookout. These were the hours of high risk.

On the bridge the men carried small, lethal Beretta 12s—the model S versions, with metal stocks and a cyclic rate of 500-plus rounds per minute. The heavier general-purpose machine guns were set on swivel mountings: two to port, and another pair to starboard on the deck; while four more were set in the superstructure, giving a wide field of fire, both fore and aft. These were all .50 caliber Browning M2 HBs, unequaled in their class for both range and firepower, their ammunition belts sprinkled with tracer.

The *Son of Takashani*'s Master, Kiyoshi Akashi, never missed being on the bridge at this time of day. He rather enjoyed the sense of tension and danger.

The radar on the bridge searched the sea for other shipping, and the air for any hostile planes. They could do little against mines, but at least they stood a chance if the so-called Iranian Revolutionaries made one of their hit-and-run attacks in small motorized craft.

Reaching upward, this same radar could pinpoint aircraft up to ten miles away at around ten thousand feet. Above that height the invisible beams could not reach, but that did not matter as aircraft attacks in the Gulf usually came in low. It was unfortunate that, on this particular dawn, the attack would come from the unexpected height of around 25,000 feet.

Unknown to the officers and men of the *Son of Takashani,* a giant C-130 Hercules transport aircraft was flying through the dawn sky some fifty miles east of them. The Hercules was painted an overall matt black, and bore no markings: neither serial numbers nor insignia. On the flight deck the navigator gave a terse instruction to the pilot. The turboprop engines were throttled back, and the 136,000 pounds of airplane began to descend from 30,000 to 25,000 feet.

The navigator put a hand to his earphones, straining to hear the constant voice which came in on their frequency, giving vital information on wind strength and direction through the various heights right down to sea level. These reports came via an oceangoing yacht equipped with the most sophisticated meteorological equipment and radio as the vessel cruised off Khaimah, on the coast of the United Arab Emirates. The data was rapidly fed into the navigator's computer. Seconds later he was able to tell the pilot the precise points at which they should release their load. "Exactly twenty-five thousand feet. First stick fifteen miles behind target; second stick two points to starboard, third stick four points port."

The pilot acknowledged, leveled out at 25,000 feet and repeated the instructions to the jumpmaster in the cargo bay, who, like the twenty other men in the cargo bay, wore a woolen helmet, goggles and an oxygen mask. A throat mike carried his query to the pilot. "How long, skipper?"

"Five minutes. Opening cargo doors now." There was a whine of hydraulics as the doors slid back and the loading bay went down like a drawbridge. At 25,000 feet dawn had already broken, the pink pearly light visible behind them. Below there was still darkness, while at the Hercules' altitude it was freezing cold in the thin air. Every man in the cargo bay had any bare flesh covered against frostbite.

The jumpmaster gave a signal, and the twenty men who sat facing inward on the hard metal benches stood up. They were dressed in black: black jump suits, boots, gloves, helmets and the oxygen masks and goggles, together with an assortment of weaponry, including AK47 Kalashnikovs, Galil automatic assault rifles, and Skorpion submachine guns; grenades and, in two cases, clumsy grenade launchers, all firmly clamped onto black webbing covering their chests.

Above them, running the length of the cargo bay, what looked like huge black bats hung from oiled tracks which ended twenty feet short of the cargo ramp. The men now formed a line under these sinister shapes, which were large hang gliders, unpowered and with near-rigid wings made of strengthened canvas, impregnated with a high-powered, long-lasting solution of de-icing fluid. From each set of wings hung a light alloy framework onto which each man now strapped himself, using a harness specially designed with a quick-release lock, similar to those used on parachutes. The harnesses had been adjusted before takeoff, and allowed for interchangeable hanging and sitting positions on the light frameworks.

These men had rehearsed and practiced with the craft over deserts and lonely tracts of land in all kinds and conditions of weather. They were a handpicked and well-trained band who could, after their six months of hard testing, launch themselves from heights of 25,000 feet and spiral down to land within a carefully marked and prescribed area.

The cargo bay was filled with noise, the clamor of the engines and the rush of air filtering back through the open doors. Instructions were reduced to hand signals and the jumpmaster banged his right palm flat on his chest, then lifted both hands, spreading the fingers wide—ten; then another ten; followed by five.

The men, standing in the framework of their hang gliders, bent their heads to the small altimeters attached to their right wrists, setting them to 25,000 feet. In a minute or so their lives would depend on the accurate settings above sea level. Most of them also glanced at the small compasses attached to their left wrists. This pair of simple instruments were the only devices that would assist them in the long glide down to the sea, and what they had dubbed Operation **WIN**.

"Prepare for stick one." The pilot's voice filled the jumpmaster's ears, and he signaled for the first group of ten men to stand by. They walked steadily toward the open doors at the rear of the aircraft, their gliders moving above them smoothly on the twin tracks of rail.

"All sticks stand by," the pilot said. Again the jumpmaster signaled and the further two groups of five men took up their places.

"Stand by stick one. Stick one go."

The jumpmaster's hand came down and the first ten men launched themselves, at ten-second intervals, into space.

The Hercules banked sharply to the left.

"Standby stick two. Stick two go."

Another signal and five men glided down toward the film

of darkness below as the Hercules banked right. Stick three went out smack on time, at the jumpmaster's signal. The cargo doors closed as the aircraft turned and climbed steeply, heading back to its secret home.

The hang gliders fell away, dropping for a thousand feet or so until the wings bit into the air, and their pilots shifted their bodies so that they slowed, made contact with other members of their particular stick, then, in a loose formation, began to glide toward the first streaks of dawn below. The men's bodies seemed to hang motionless in the thin air, and, during the early stages of the descent they were all forced to bring up their gloved hands to wipe the ice and rime from their goggles, altimeters and compasses. It was an exhilarating business, but they were hardly aware of the motion until they passed through the ten-thousand-feet level. There, the air thickened and they all had greater control of their flimsy craft.

The *Son of Takashani* had no warning. True, the radar operator caught a sprinkle of minute blips on his screen, but they meant nothing to him. Birds possibly, or specks of dust or static on the screen.

At exactly a thousand feet above the tanker, the three groups brought their hang gliders into the attack position. The two men armed with grenade launchers were well to the rear of the tanker, hanging in their harnesses, hands free to manipulate weapons. Two grenades arched from the air, one smashing its way into the bridge, the other exploding further down the superstructure, leaving a gaping hole.

The explosion on the bridge was like a sudden blast of white-hot flame. Everyone died instantly.

Seaman Ogawa, one of the gunners on the superstructure, could not believe his eyes and ears. He heard the double explosion, felt the ship quake under him, then saw, for'ard, two creatures that looked like prehistoric birds approaching the bows. Flame leaped from them and he saw one of the deck-gun crews scattered like a nest of mice hit by a shotgun blast. He squeezed the Browning's trigger almost as a reflex action, and his mind registered surprise as he watched the two incoming birds turn to mangled flesh, blood and shattered canvas as the heavy bullets tore them apart.

The two men who had started everything, exactly as planned, by releasing the grenades had also come to grief. Once they had established hits on the superstructure, both men dropped the launchers into the sea and, swinging violently, unclipped Skorpion submachine guns from their chests. In a matter of seconds the pair were streaking down toward the *Son of Takashani*'s stern, maneuvering their gliders, pulling them into a more shallow and slower descent, ready to release their harness the moment their rubber-soled boots struck the deck. They were only some fifty feet away from landing when a short burst of fire from another part of the superstructure took off the legs of the man on the right. He sagged in his harness and the wings above him tilted so that the entire glider sideslipped into his partner.

This second man was thrown to one side, knocked unconscious, swinging out of control so that the angle of attack of his wings increased sharply as he smashed into the stern of the tanker.

The initial shock and surprise was gone in less than two minutes. The gunners who were left, both on deck and in the battered superstructure, were now assessing the situation. The drills that the Master had insisted on paid off. None of the crew of the *Son of Takashani* showed regard for their own safety. Several big hang gliders, spitting flame and death, circled the ship, looking for openings to land on the main deck while desperately trying to maintain height. Two swooped in from starboard, knocking out another heavy-machine-gun crew as they came, only to be mangled and ripped apart from fire directed from the superstructure. Four men actually managed to land safely on the stern, seeking what cover they could abaft the superstructure, unhooking grenades from their webbing equipment. Three more died as they rode the air down onto the port side.

Both the gun crews for'ard on the deck were now out of action, and, with a withering fire, another pair of hang gliders reached the deck. The remainder were now either blasted out of the sky, or killed by smashing into the ship's hull. The seven who remained fought on.

Smoke grenades gave some cover to the trio who had landed on the for'ard part of the deck, while the four men who were attacking from the stern managed, with grenade and gun, to gain a foothold in the superstructure itself.

The fighting lasted for almost half an hour. At the end of that bloody dawn there were several bodies of the glider-borne force strewn around the tanker; eighteen officers and men of the *Son of Takashani* were dead, and a further seven wounded.

The radio officer had continued to put out a distress signal throughout the whole battle, but it was an hour later before a U.S. Navy frigate arrived at the scene, and by then, the Japanese, being an orderly people, had tipped the bodies of the attackers overboard, washed down the deck, seen to their own dead and wounded, and reorganized the tanker so that it could continue on its way.

The most senior officer, twenty-two-year-old Zenzo Yamada, who had taken the place of the dead Master, was able to give the American frigate's captain a graphic, blow-by-blow account of the action. The American officer was perturbed by the lack of evidence left by the Japanese crew, but Yamada did not appear to be worried. "I helped one of them die," he told the frigate's captain.

"How?" The U.S. officer was thirty years of age, a lieutenant commander called Ed Potts, and a man who appreciated order himself.

"He was dying. I finish him off."

The American nodded. "He say anything?"

"One word, only."

"Yeah?"

"He say, *win*." The Japanese officer laughed at the thought.

"Win, huh? Well, he didn't, did he?"

"Man not win. He lost, and died." The Japanese officer laughed again, as though it was the funniest thing he had heard in a long time.

Later, others did not find it so amusing.

2

Voices From the Air

The repercussions which sprang from the strange attack on the tanker *Son of Takashani* were predictable. Japan accused first Iran, then Iraq. Both countries denied complicity. No terrorist organization owned up, though the Intelligence communities of the West kept their eyes and ears open.

Much of the traffic concerning the Japanese tanker passed across James Bond's desk in that faceless building overlooking Regent's Park where he was, to his frustration, chained to an administrative job. He could not know that he would, eventually, become deeply involved in the business.

In these days of high-tech electronics, it is not unusual for people who should know better to claim that

21

HUMINT—the gathering of intelligence by human agents in the field—is either dead, or only lives on borrowed time. Bond had recently laughed aloud when hearing a writer of adventure stories claim that the spy novel was dead, because: "These days, it's all done by satellites."

Certainly those electronic wizards girdling the earth can pluck photographs, and even military transmissions, from the air, but there is far more to it than that. The satellite in war can give armies, navies and air forces the edge, but in peace, when there is more time at the disposal of Intelligence agencies, the backup analysis of photographs and spoken information can be achieved only by the man or woman in the field. Apart from that, there are often delicate covert operations which cannot be accomplished by whole echelons of electronics, only by humans.

In one area, that of ELINT, the collection of intelligence by electronic means, both the human agent, the SATCOMS (Communications Satellites), and ELINT itself were welded together as a team. In recent years the micro bug, used so successfully to tap into telephone and other conversations, was sparingly taken into the field, usually only on close-quarter covert operations.

Indeed, the new buzzword is ELINT. Entire areas of towns, cities, and even the countryside can be monitored, worldwide. No person is safe from the listeners, for eavesdropping has become part of life, necessary because of that other horror with which all countries and peoples are forced to cohabit—terrorism, in its many faces and forms.

Every twenty-four hours, electronic listening devices scan sensitive areas and, as they scan, the giant memories of computers, at hundreds of installations, will strain to pick up particular trigger words and phrases. In parts of certain cities which are considered sensitive, if you talk to your girlfriend about Semtex, or accidentally speak a code word, or phrase, used by known terrorists, your conversation will almost certainly be monitored until the listeners decide your idle chatter is harmless.

Only human beings can install the small, very powerful listening stations, at prescribed points; and other humans insert the key words and phrases into the computer data bases. After that, the machines take over, making decisions to transcribe conversations, pinpoint their locations, even name those who are talking by identifying voiceprints. More human beings analyze these transcripts, sometimes at leisure, more often at speed, lest the advantage be lost.

Just over a month after the *Son of Takashani* incident, two men met in a villa overlooking the Mediterranean. They were smooth-skinned, immaculately turned out, and to all intents and purposes, businessmen taking coffee on a vine-covered patio from which they had an uninterrupted view of spectacular beauty: cypresses, olive groves, rough grazing land for sheep and goats, the twinkling sea, and, in the distance, the baked red and white roofs of a small village. Neither of the men could have known that a powerful receiver was hidden in that village which looked so peaceful and secluded.

The receiver scanned an area of some fifty miles, shooting a million or so words a second, spoken in streets, bars, private houses and on telephones, through one of the COMSATS and on into the computers of two large listening posts. One of the computers picked up an entire phrase, spoken by one of the two men as they drank their sweet coffee. The phrase was, "Health depends on strength." It was spoken as a toast, and the computer

memories metaphorically sat up and took notice as the four
words were repeated. They had only recently been inserted
into the wordscan programs.

"Health depends on strength." The younger, dark-
haired man smiled as he lifted his cup toward his older
companion—a sleek, olive-skinned fellow with broad
shoulders and a distinguished gray flecking his temples.

"**WIN** was a spectacular disaster," the older man said.
There was no hint of criticism in his voice, only a trace of
distaste.

"I apologize." His companion bowed his head slightly. "I
had great confidence. The training was exceptional—"

"And cost a small fortune—"

"True. But it does prove that if we are to take all of them,
when they're aboard what they like to call Birdsnest Two,
we require a much more subtle approach. Even if we had
doubled, or maybe trebled, the force for **WIN** there would
have been carnage. Birdsnest Two is geared for any kind
of attack. They would have taken out our hang gliders long
before they came within five hundred feet of the target.
Also it will probably have to be done in hard winter
weather."

The older man nodded. "Which means the attack can
really only come from within."

"You mean we should have people on board?" The dark-
haired one sounded alarmed.

"Can you think of a better way?"

"It's impossible. How can you infiltrate such a service at
short notice? We've less than twelve months to go. If that
had ever been an option we'd have used it, saved a lot of
time, and also a great deal of money."

On the tapes that were finally studied, the listeners

strained their ears through a long pause. In the distance came the sound of an aircraft high and a long way off. Nearer at hand, a dog barked angrily. Then the older man spoke—

"Ah, my friend, so often we go for a complex solution, how would it be if we made this more simple? *One* man. *One* man aboard Birdsnest Two would be all we need, for one man could unlock the gates, and let others in. Or even someone in the retinue, a discontented flag officer, for instance. One is all we require. A single Trojan horse."

"Even one would be—"

"Difficult? No, not if he is already there, in place."

"But we have nobody who—"

"Maybe we *do* have somebody already in place; and maybe even he does not yet know it. Your people are skilled, surely they could tell who this man is, and bring pressure to bear?"

Again a pause, complete with the barking dog. Then—

"Compromise. Yes, an obvious solution."

"So obvious that you had to waste the lives of twenty mercenaries, not to mention the finance of training and equipping them. Now, go and find the agent we need. Officer, or enlisted man. Crew or visitor. It doesn't matter which. Just find him."

•   •   •

M tossed the transcript back onto his desk and looked up at his Chief of Staff, Bill Tanner, who appeared to be studying the old Admiral's face as a strategist would examine the terrain of battle.

"Well," M said. It was a grunt from the throat rather than

a word clearly spoken. "Well, we know who these people are, and we know the target, what we don't know is the full objective. Any comments, Tanner?"

"Only the obvious, sir."

"Meaning?" M was in an unashamedly bellicose mood today.

"Meaning, sir, that we can have things altered. We can have the brass hats moved at the last moment. Put them on a cruiser instead of Birdsnest Two—"

"Oh, for heaven's sake, Tanner, we know Birdsnest Two's HMS *Invincible,* so say *Invincible.*" HMS *Invincible* is one of the three remaining aircraft carriers—capital ships—of the Royal Navy: in fact three of the largest gas-turbine-powered warships in the world. All are designated as TDCs—Through Deck Cruiser—of the Invincible class, and all had gone through major refits of electronics, weapons and aircraft capabilities since the lessons learned in the Falklands War.

With only the slightest pause, Tanner continued. "Put them in another ship—at the last minute—"

"What other ship? A destroyer, or a frigate? There are *three* of them, Tanner. *Three* top brass, complete with their staff. I'd say around twelve or fifteen bodies at the least. Use your sense, man—they'd have to share bunks on a frigate or destroyer, and that might be all very well for the Russkies, but I cannot see our American friends, or Sir Geoffrey Gould, taking kindly to that."

"Call it off, sir?"

"I think there would be rumblings everywhere, including our wonderful Press and TV Defence Correspondents. They'd be asking 'why?' before we even concocted a story. In any case, *Landsea '89* is *essential.* All our combined exercises are essential, and what with this wretched business of *Glasnost* and *Perestroika*, NATO feels it's doing the decent thing. Letting the Russians in on our war games, eh?"

"We're not supposed to call them war games anymore, sir—"

"I know that!" M thumped his desk heavily. "It's the thin end of the wedge, though, letting the Commander-in-Chief of the Russian Fleet in on a combined exercise as complex as this."

Bill Tanner sighed. "At least our people won't have to dodge their spy ships all the time. You know, sir, even Churchill thought a sharing of information might be a good thing."

"That, Chief of Staff, was before the First World War. It was also a sharing with the Germans. Russians are different creatures. I've made no secret of the fact that I don't approve of it."

"Quite, sir."

"I've been very outspoken with the Joint Intelligence Committee, though a fat lot of good it did me. All friends together, now—so they say. One idiot even quoted Kipling at me: *Sisters under their skins* and that kind of stuff. No, we have to do something positive."

Tanner had walked to the window, and stood looking out at the rain beating down on Regent's Park. "Bodyguards, sir? Well-briefed bodyguards?"

M made a grumbling noise. Then—"We know what these people're after, Tanner, but we don't want to tell the world, if only because we don't know the reason why. Bodyguards would mean widening the circle of knowledge, and as you very well know that's the first rule in our business—keep the circle small." He stopped suddenly, as though struck by a new thought, then said, "No!" loudly, and not to anyone in particular.

The rain continued to fall on the grass, trees and umbrellas below. In his head Tanner had started to try and recite a piece of doggerel somebody had told him. It was a common theme about security and rumor dating back to the Second World War and it always made him smile—

> "Actual evidence I have none,
> But my aunt's charwoman's sister's son,
> Heard a policeman on his beat,
> Say to a nursemaid in Downing Street,
> That he had a cousin, who had a friend,
> Who knew when the war was going to end."

It was not until he reached the last line that Bill Tanner realized he had quoted the lines aloud.

"That's it!" M almost bellowed.

"What, sir?"

"Nursemaid, Chief of Staff. We'll give them a nursemaid. A good Naval man. Sound as a bell. A man willing to put his life before the lives of his charges." M's hand reached for the internal telephone which put him directly in touch with his devoted, though long-suffering private secretary. "Moneypenny," he all but shouted, loud enough for her to hear on the other side of the padded door. "Get Double-O-Seven up here fast."

Within ten minutes, James Bond was sitting in M's Holy of Holies with his old Chief giving him what he thought of as the "fish eye," and Bill Tanner looking a little uneasy.

"It's a job," M announced. "An operation that calls for

more than the usual discretion; and certainly one that'll require you to alter your circumstances a great deal."

"I've worked undercover before, sir." Bond leaned back in the armchair in which M had invited him to sit. It was a chair Bond knew well. If you were asked to sit in this, the most comfortable chair in M's office, the news could only be bad.

"Undercover's one thing, 007, but how would you feel about going back into the Royal Navy?"

"With respect, sir, I've never left the RNVR."

M growled again, and James Bond thought he saw a gleam of unusual malice in the old Chief's eyes. "Really?" M raised his eyes toward the ceiling. "How long is it since you stood a duty watch, 007? Or had to deal with defaulters, or masthead as the U.S. Navy would say; live day and night with the routine and discipline within a capital ship; or even felt a quarterdeck rise and fall sixty feet in a gale?"

"Well, sir—"

"The job, 007, will require you to go back to active duty. In turn that'll mean you'll have to go on a course, several courses in fact, to bring you up to date with life and warfare in our present-day Royal Navy."

The thought struck home. Bond's life in the Service had, many times, caused him to work at full stretch, but on the whole there were long periods of relaxation. To go back to active service in the Royal Navy would be a return to the old disciplines, and a rehoning of skills almost forgotten. A series of pictures flickered through his head. They were rather what he had always imagined a dying man saw: his life many years ago, in the Royal Navy Volunteer Reserve on active service. The images in his brain did not attract him as much as they had done when he was a young midshipman. "Why?" he asked lamely. "I mean why should I go back to active service, sir?"

M smiled and nodded. "Because, 007, in the late winter of next year the Royal Navy, together with elite troops, air forces, and the navies of all the NATO powers, including the United States Navy, will be carrying out an exercise: *Landsea '89*. There will be observers, Admiral of the Fleet, Sir Geoffrey Gould; Admiral Gudeon, United States Navy; and Admiral Sergei Yevgennevich Pauker, Commander-in-Chief of the Soviet Navy—a post unknown in any other navy in the world." M took a deep breath. "The latter has been invited because of the current thawing in relationships between East and West. *Glasnost, Perestroika,* that kind of thing."

"They will be . . . ?" Bond began.

"They will be in *Invincible*. They will have with them, like Gilbert and Sullivan's Sir Joseph Porter, all their sisters and their cousins and their aunts. They will also be in danger. Almost certainly attempted abduction. At worst, murder. You will be there, in *Invincible*, to see it does not happen."

"Can you explain about the danger, sir." The trigger of magnetic interest had been squeezed deep in Bond's mind.

M smiled like a man who has just hooked the biggest fish in the river. "Certainly, James. Bill and I will a tale unfold. It begins with that little problem in the Strait of Hormuz—the Japanese tanker, *Son of Hitachi,* or whatever it's called—"

The Chief of Staff corrected the tanker's name, and for his pains received a venomous glare from M, who barked, "You want to tell it, Tanner?"

"No, sir. You carry on, sir."

"Good of you, Tanner. Thank you." M's mood was not

only bellicose this morning, but sarcastic. He fixed Bond with the same, cold fish-eye look. "Ever heard of BAST?"

"Anagram for STAB, sir?"

"No, 007, I mean BAST. B-A-S-T, and this is no laughing matter."

The smile on Bond's face disappeared quickly. M was being too serious and prickly for jokes. "No, sir. BAST is news to me. What is it?"

With a wave of his hand and a vocal sound meant to signify deep displeasure, M motioned to his Chief of Staff to explain.

"James"—Tanner came over and leaned against the desk—"this really is a very serious and alarming business. BAST is a group; an organization. The name hasn't been circulated as yet, simply because we didn't have many leads or details at first. The name's pretty puerile, that's why nobody took it very seriously to begin with. But BAST appears to be an acronym for Brotherhood of Anarchy and Secret Terror."

"Sounds like a poor-man's SPECTRE to me." Bond's brow wrinkled and there was concern in his eyes.

"At first we thought it might be a splinter group of the old SPECTRE, but it appears this is something new, and oddly unpleasant," Tanner continued. "You recall the small bomb incidents in October of '87? All on one day; all coordinated? There were firebombs in a couple of London stores—"

"The ones put down to animal rights activists?"

Tanner nodded. "But the others were not so easily explained. One small plastique near the Vatican; another one which destroyed an American military transport—on the ground at Edwards Air Force Base: no casualties; one in

31

Madrid; another, a car bomb, premature, shattering the French Minister of Defense's car; and a large one in Moscow: near the Kremlin Gate, and not generally reported."

"Yes, I saw the file."

"Then you know the file said it was coordinated, but nobody had taken responsibility."

Bond nodded.

"The file was lying by omission." Tanner sounded grave now. "There was a long letter, circulated to all the countries concerned. In brief it said the incidents had been coordinated by the Brotherhood of Anarchy and Secret Terror, to be referred to as BAST. Everyone did some backtracking, because these kind of groups do have a tendency to choose highfalutin names. The damage from those first incidents was small and there were no deaths, but those who advise on international terrorism told us to take them damned seriously, if only because BAST is a Demonic name. BAST, it seems, is a word that comes from Ancient Egypt: sometimes known as Aini or Aym. BAST is said to appear as a three-headed demon—head of a snake, head of cat, head of a man—mounted on a viper. The demon BAST is connected with incendiarism, and we now have little doubt that the Brotherhood chose the name because of its Demonic connotations."

"Demons?" Bond raised his eyes toward the ceiling.

"Yes, demons." M, who was far from being a superstitious man, appeared to be taking the entire thing very seriously. "A lot of research has been done on this. Now we know that there are indeed three leaders—like the snake, man and cat—and a prime leader upon which they all ride and exist. The viper, if you like, comes by the name of Bassam Baradj, a former ranking member of the

PLO, a former friend of Arafat's, and a wealthy man in his own right. Baradj is certainly paymaster and mastermind."

Tanner nodded and said that other intelligence had pinpointed three associates of Baradj, all one-time members of Middle Eastern paramilitary political groups. "Abou Hamarik; Ali Al Adwan; and a young woman, Saphii Boudai—the man, the snake and the cat. Apparently those are their key names: street names. They're all experienced in the arts of terrorism, they're also disenchanted with all the old causes.

"They've embraced the idea of anarchy with one thought only. They believe that Napoleon's definition of anarchy is the one and only true definition—'Anarchy is the stepping-stone to absolute power.' "

Bond felt a tingling chill down his spine. He had fought against fanatical shadows before.

"Y'see, James"—M appeared to have softened—"these people who sound so childish with their BAST signature are far from childish. Baradj can lay his hands on billions; he is also a shrewd and cunning strategist. The other leaders are trained soldiers in the terrorist wars. They can teach skills, and, through Baradj, they can buy and sell as many mercenaries as they need. Mad as it might seem, these people are pledged against practically all political and religious ideologies. They have their own ideal—to gain absolute power. What they do with that power once they've won it, heaven only knows. But that's what they're after, and, if recent activities are anything to go by, they're going to be a nasty poisoned thorn in the sides of all nations and all types and conditions of government for some time to come."

33

"And how do we know they're after the little band of naval brass?" Bond asked.

M explained. He spoke at length about the voiceprints they had on three of the leading members of BAST; how they had also stumbled across the organization's call sign or password: "Health depends on strength."

"The problem is," M went on, "that these people appear to be so flaky, as our American brothers-in-arms would say, that one is inclined not to take them seriously. We *have* to take them seriously. That strange and almost ridiculous attack on the Japanese tanker was their doing, and that was a rehearsal, carried out in cold blood. A supertanker, James, is not altogether unlike an aircraft carrier. They wanted to see if they could take out a tanker, in order to test the feasibility of a similar assault on *Invincible*."

"But how do we know that?" Bond pressed.

"We plucked two voices from the air." M smiled for the first time since Bond had entered the room. "We got voiceprints on Baradj and Abou Hamarik. It appears the latter organized the event—they coded it Operation **WIN,** incidentally—and Hamarik's trying to plant or compromise someone either already serving in *Invincible* or on the staff of one of our visiting admirals. The ones to whom you, 007, will act as Nanny."

"Delighted, sir." Bond's lips curved into one of the cruelest smiles M had ever seen. Later the Chief was to say that, to use the Biblical expression, "Iron had entered into 007's soul." He was not far wrong.

Bond thought to himself that while Napoleon had certainly maintained that anarchy was the stepping-stone to absolute power, he had also said, "A love of country, a spirit of enthusiasm, and a sense of honor will operate upon young soldiers with advantage." Not only young soldiers, James Bond considered, but Naval officers with a history of matters secret as well.

Many people in the Intelligence world who knew Bond were surprised a month later to read in *The London Gazette*—

BOND, James. Commander RNVR. Relieved of current liaison duties at the Foreign Office. Promoted to the substantive rank of Captain RN and returned to active service forthwith.

3

Reflections in a Harrier

The Sea Harrier taxied to the foot of the so-called ski ramp—a wide metal hill, sweeping upward at 12°—and the nose wheel rolled into perfect alignment with the dark painted strip that was the centerline.

The legendary V/STOL (Vertical/Short Take-Off & Landing)—pronounced "Veestol"—aircraft responded to the tiny throttle movement and climbed so that the entire fuselage became positioned into the upward configuration.

Bond went through the takeoff checks for the last time: brakes on, flaps OUT, ASI (Air Speed Indicator) "bug" to liftoff speed. The aircraft was alive, trembling to the idling of the Rolls-Royce (Bristol) Pegasus 104 turbofan which could generate an impressive 21,500 pounds of thrust.

On the Sea Harrier that thrust is channeled through two

engine propulsion nozzles, set at port and starboard, capable of being rotated, from the aft horizontal position, through some 98.5°. This is the Harrier's great advantage over conventional fixed-wing aircraft, for the jet nozzles allow vertical lift plus horizontal flight, together with all the other variables in between, such as hover and backward flight.

Bond's hand moved to the nozzle lever, and he glanced down to confirm that it was set to short takeoff position at the 50° stop mark. He lifted his right hand into the clear thumbs-up position, which would be seen by the deck control handling officer in his "bubble" on the starboard side, and whom Bond, strapped into the cockpit and angled toward a squally gray sky, could not see. At the same moment he heard the Commander (Air) give him the "Go"—"Bluebird cleared for takeoff."

Bond opened the throttle to 55% RPM, released the brakes, then slammed the throttle hard into fully open. The Pegasus engine roared behind him, and he could feel himself pushed back against the padded metal seat as though a pair of giant hands were pressing his chest and face.

The Sea Harrier rocketed from the ramp, and as it did so, Bond flipped the gear into the "Up" position, hardly noticing the whine and thump as the wheels came up into their housings, for in the first fifteen seconds or so of the ramp takeoff the Harrier was not actually flying, but was shot, ballistically, into a high, fast trajectory. Only when the ASI "bug" flashed and beeped did Bond set the nozzles to horizontal flight, and click flaps to IN. The Head-Up-Display (HUD) showed that he was climbing at an angle of almost 60° at a speed in excess of 640 knots.

If the takeoff had been from a carrier, or similar ship, the sea would lie directly below, but this, Bond's first real take-off from the ski ramp, was from the Royal Naval Air Station, Yeovilton in Somerset, among some of the West Country's most beautiful landscapes. Not that he had any view of the ground now, for his Harrier had shot above the mile-high cloud base and was still climbing as he set course for the bombing range in the Irish Sea, not far from the Isle of Man.

Though this was his first real ski-run takeoff, Bond had already done it a couple of dozen times on the simulator. He was now into the third week of his Harrier conversion course, and eight months into his return to active duty with the Royal Navy.

His promotion to captain was a quantum leap, as it is for any Naval officer. Not that the new rank had made much difference over the past months. On all the courses Bond had taken, rank was well-nigh forgotten, and a captain under instruction rated at about the same level as a sub-lieutenant.

Since starting the courses, he had studied the new advanced strategies of Naval warfare which seemed to alter at alarming speed; another course on communications; a third on ciphers and an important fourth concerning advanced weaponry, including hands-on experience with the latest 3D radar, Sea Darts and SAM missiles, together with new electronic weapons control systems operating the American Phalanx and Goalkeeper CIWS—Close In Weapon Systems: "sea-whizz" as they are known—which have now become standard following the horrifying lessons learned during the Falklands Campaign.

Bond had always kept up his flying hours and instrument ratings, on jets and helicopters, in order to remain qualified as a Naval pilot, but he had now reached the final and most testing course—conversion to the Sea Harrier.

After some twenty hours in Yeovilton in the flight simulator, he had flown Harriers in normal configuration of rolling takeoffs and landings. The ski-jump takeoff marked the beginning of the air combat and tactical weapons course. The whole thing appealed mightily to Bond, who reveled in learning and honing new skills. In any case, the Sea Harrier was a wonderful machine to fly: exciting and very different.

He now checked the HUD, which showed him on course and cruising at around 600 knots along the military airway. Glancing down at the HDD—the Head-Down-Display—he could see the visual map, the magic eye which gives the modern pilot a ground map view even through the thickest and most murky cloud. He was crossing the coast, just above Southport on the northwest seaboard, right on a heading for the bombing range. Now he would require total concentration as he lowered the Harrier's nose toward the peaceful cloudscape below, the horizontal bars on the HUD sliding upward to show he had the aircraft in a 10° dive. Down the left-hand side of the HUD he watched the speed begin to increase and blipped his air brakes open for a second to control the dive. The altitude figures streamed down the left-hand edge of the HUD showing a steady decrease in height—30,000 . . . 25 . . . 20 . . 15 . . By now he was in cloud, still going fast, his eyes flicking between airspeed, altitude, and the HDD, while his feet on the rudder bars made slight corrections.

He broke cloud at 3,000 feet and clicked on the air-to-ground sights, thumbing down on the button which would arm the pair of 500-pound cluster bombs which hung, one under each wing.

Below, the sea slashed by as he held an altitude of around 500 feet. Far ahead he glimpsed the first anchored marker flashing to lead him onto the bombing range where a series of similar markers were set in a diamond shape, which was the target.

It came up very fast and the HUD flashed the *In Range* signal almost before it had registered from Bond's eyes to his brain. Instinctively he triggered the bombs and pulled up into a 30° climb, pushing the throttle fully open and pulling a hard 5G turn left, then right, so that his body felt like lead for a second before he turned, at speed, but more gently, to see the cluster bombs explode from their small parachutes directly across the diamond of buoys.

"Don't hang about," the young Commander had told them in the briefing room. "There are four of you at five-minute intervals, so just do the job, then get out fast."

Altogether, there were eight Naval pilots on the conversion course: three more Royal Navy men, a U.S. Marine Corps pilot on liaison, two Indian Navy pilots and one from the Spanish Navy. All but Bond had already done several hours on Harriers with their home units and were at Yeovilton to sharpen their skills with some weapons and tactical training. That afternoon, Bond had been first man away and was followed by the Spanish officer—a sullen young man called Felipe Pantano, who kept very much to himself—one of the Royal Navy lieutenants, and the American.

To comply with safety regulations, there was a predetermined flight path to and from the target, and Bond swept his Harrier into a long, climbing turn, then gave her full throttle, stood the airplane on its tail and, looking down at the small radar screen on the starboard side of his cockpit, swept the skies immediately above his return course, to be certain none of the other aircraft had strayed.

The radar showed nothing out of the ordinary, so he dropped the nose to a gentle 20° climb. He had hardly stabilized the Harrier in its climb when a completely unexpected sound seemed to fill the cockpit. So surprised was Bond that it took at least two seconds for him to realize what was happening.

As the sound became louder in his ears, Bond woke to the danger. So far he had only experienced this in the simulator: the harsh, rasping neep-neep-neep quickening all the time. There was a missile locked on to him—judging by its tone, a Sidewinder. Just under thirty pounds of high-explosive fragmentation was being guided toward the engine heat of his Harrier.

Bond had reacted slowly, and that was the way people got blown out of the sky. He pushed the stick forward, putting the Harrier into a power dive, jinking to left and right, pulling about seven Gs to each jink, holding it for a second or two, then going the other way. At the same time he hit the button which would release four flares to confuse the missile's heat-seeking guidance system, then, for luck, followed it with a bundle of chaff—radar-confusing metal strips. It was another safety regulation that all aircraft using the bombing range should carry both flares and chaff, housed in special pods—another lesson of the Falklands where chaff had been stuffed in bundles inside the air brakes.

The neep-neeping was still there, quickening as the missile gained on the Harrier. He lifted the nose, jinked again and, at a thousand feet, performed a rate-five turn, pulling a lot of G, then rolling and putting the Harrier into a second dive. His body felt like lead, his throat was dust-dry and the controls felt stiff and he pushed the Harrier to its limit.

He had the aircraft right down almost to sea level before the growling signal suddenly stopped. There was a flash far off to the starboard, in the direction of the target range. Bond took a deep breath, lifted the Harrier's nose, reset his course and climbed to 30,000 feet with the throttle right forward. As he went up he switched his radio to transmit— "Bluebird to Homespun. Some idiot almost put a Sidewinder up my six." Taking the points of a standard clock, "six" meant directly behind.

"Say again, Bluebird."

Bond repeated and Yeovilton asked him to confirm no damage, which he did, adding that it was more luck than judgment. Of the four aircraft detailed for the bombing range that afternoon, no one carried anything but cluster bombs. The range, however, belonged to the RAF, though its use, and timings, were strictly monitored. It was just possible that a Royal Air Force jet had accidentally been scheduled and had arrived either early or late.

"Bluebird, are you certain it was a missile?"

"Chased me all around the sky. Of course I'm sure."

Bond reached Yeovilton without further incident and, once landed and out of his flying gear, he stormed into the office of Commander (Air)—known to most as Wings—set in the control tower.

"Who was the fool?" Bond snapped, then he stopped, for Commander Bernie Brazier, an experienced officer, looked both angry and shaken. He motioned Bond to sit. "There'll be an investigation, sir." His eyes had the weary look of a man who had seen it all and never really got used to it. "There's a problem. Nobody from here was carrying missiles, and the RAF say they were not using the range today. We're checking your Harrier for possible malfunction of detection electronics."

43

"That wasn't a malfunction, for God's sake. It was a real missile, Bernie. I'm filing a report to that effect and heaven help the cretin who loosed one off in my direction."

Commander Brazier still looked unhappy. Quietly he said, "There's another problem."

"What?"

"We've lost an aircraft."

"Who?"

"Captain Pantano. The Spanish officer. He was second away, bombed on time then went off the radar during his climb-out. Nobody's reported seeing him go down and we've got S and R out looking for him, or wreckage."

"Perhaps a Sidewinder popped him." There was a large segment of sarcasm in Bond's voice.

"There were no missile-carrying aircraft around, sir, as I've already told you."

"Well, what do you think the one up my backside was, Wings? A Scotch mist?" Now, quite angry, James Bond turned on his heel and left.

In the wardroom bar that night before dinner the atmosphere was only slightly subdued. It was always a bit of a shaker losing a pilot, but the strange circumstances surrounding this loss, coupled with the fact that the Spanish pilot had not been a natural mixer, helped to calm what often causes a slight twitch among young pilots.

So, when Bond entered the wardroom, the bar hummed with near enough the usual high-spirited pre-dinner chatter. He was about to go over and join two of the other Navy pilots from the course, when his eyes landed on someone he had been watching from afar since reporting to RNAS Yeovilton. She was tall and very slim; a WRNS First Officer (Women's Royal Naval Service—"Wrens" as they were referred to) who was always much in demand, which was not surprising, as she had the kind of looks and figure that make middle-aged men regret their lost youth: a sloe-eyed combination of self-confidence, together with a hint of complete indifference to the many officers who paid court to her, as one crusty old visiting Admiral commented, "Like hornets around a honeypot." Her name was Clover Pennington, though she was known to many, in spite of her upbringing in the bosom of a well-connected West Country family, as "Irish Penny."

Now this dark-haired, black-eyed beauty had the usual quota of three young lieutenants toasting her, but, on seeing Bond, she stepped away from the bar toward him. "I hear you had a near-miss today, sir." Her smile lacked the cautious deference her rank demanded when approaching a much senior officer.

"Not as close as our Spanish pilot it would seem, Miss . . . er, First Officer . . ." Bond let it trail off. Recently, he had not been given the chance of spending much of his time with women, a fact that would have gladdened M's heart.

"First Officer Pennington, sir. Clover Pennington."

"Well, Miss Pennington, how about joining me for dinner? The name's Bond, by the way, James Bond."

"Delighted, sir." She gave him a dazzling smile and turned toward the wardroom. Daggers were invisibly hurled in Bond's direction from the eyes of the three young officers still at the bar.

Tonight was not a formal wardroom dinner, so Bond seized the chance while it was on offer. "Not here, First Officer Pennington." His hand brushed her uniformed arm with the three blue stripes denoting her rank low on the

45

sleeve. "I know a reasonable restaurant about quarter-of-an-hour's drive away, near Wedmore. Give you ten minutes to change."

Another smile which spoke of a more than usually pleasant evening. "Oh, good, sir. I always feel better out of uniform."

Bond thought unpardonable thoughts and followed her from the bar.

He gave her twenty minutes, knowing the ways of women when changing for an evening out. In any case, Bond also wanted to get into civilian clothes, even though it would have to be almost another kind of uniform, Dunhill slacks and blazer complete with RN crest on the breast pocket.

Before taking up his new duties, M had advised, "Shouldn't take that damned great Bentley with you, 007."

"How am I supposed to get around, sir?" he had asked.

"Oh, take something upmarket from the car pool—they've a nice little BMW 520i in an unobtrusive dark blue free at the moment. Use that as your runabout until you set sail for distant shores." M, Bond would have sworn, was humming "Drake's Drum" as he left the office.

So it was that the dark-blue BMW pulled up in front of the officers' Wrennery, as the women's quarters were known, twenty minutes later. To Bond's surprise she was there, waiting outside wearing a fetching trench coat over civilian clothes. The coat was tightly belted, showing off the neat waist and adding a touch of sensuality. She slid into the passenger seat next to him, her skirt riding up to expose around four inches of thigh. As Bond swung the car out through the Wrennery gates he noticed that she did not even bother to adjust the coat and skirt as she pulled on the obligatory seat belt.

"So where're we going, Captain Bond?" Did he imagine the throatiness of her voice, or had it always been there?

"Little pub I know. Good food. The owner's wife's French and they do a very passable *Boeuf Beauceronne,* almost like the real thing. Off duty, the name's James, by the way."

He heard the smile in her voice. "You have a choice—James. My nickname's 'Irish Penny,' so most of the girls call me Penny. I prefer my real name. Clover."

"Clover it is, then. Nice name. Unusual."

"My father always used to say that mother was frightened by a bull in a clover field when she was carrying me, but I prefer the more romantic version."

"Which was?"

Again, the smile in her voice. "That I was conceived in a patch of clover—and my father a respectable clergyman at that."

"Still a nice name." Bond paused to negotiate a long bend. "Only heard it once before, and *she* was married to someone very big in intelligence matters." The reference to Mrs. Allen Dulles was a calculated come-on: almost a code to attract Clover into the light in case they were both in the same business. M had said there would be other officers around, on this deep-cover assignment. But Clover Pennington did not rise to the bait.

"Is it true about this afternoon, James?"

"Is what true?"

"That someone tried to put a Sidewinder up your six."

"Felt that way. How did you come to hear about it? The incident's supposed to be low-profile."

"Oh, didn't you know? I'm in charge of the girls who maintain the Harriers." On most stone frigates, as shore

47

stations are called by the Royal Navy, maintenance and arming was, to a large extent, performed by Wrens. "Bernie—Wings that is—passed me a curt little memo. He writes memos rather as he speaks, words of one syllable, especially to the Wrens. I always imagine he regards us as having very limited vocabularies. We're checking on all your aircraft's electronics, just to be sure you weren't getting some odd feedback."

"It was a missile, Clover. I've been at the receiving end of those bloody things before today. I know what they sound like."*

"We have to check. You know what the Commander (Air) is like: always accusing us of infesting his precious Harriers with Wrenlins." She laughed. Throaty and infectious, Bond thought, something he would not really mind catching himself.

"Wrenlins," he repeated half aloud. He had almost forgotten that old Fleet Air Arm slang, culled and altered from the RAF's "Gremlins." Today's young people, he presumed, would take for granted that Gremlins were creatures conjured from Spielberg's brain for a popular, if zany, movie.

Fifteen minutes later they were sitting at a table in the quiet, neat restaurant ordering the pâté and the *Boeuf Beauceronne*—that delightful and simple dish of rumpsteak cooked with bacon, potatoes and onions. Within an hour they were talking like old friends, and, indeed knew people

---

*Though it has only been hinted at, and never admitted in print, Bond almost certainly saw action during the Falklands War. It has been said that he was the man landed secretly to assist and help train civilians before the real shooting war started.

in common, for it turned out that, while Clover's father had been what she called "a humble man of the cloth," his elder brother was Sir Arthur Pennington, Sixth Baronet and master of Pennington Nab, a stately home which Bond had enjoyed, in more ways than one. "Oh, you'll know my cousins, Emma and Jane, then?" Clover asked, looking up sharply.

"Intimately," Bond replied flatly, and with a completely straight face.

Clover let it pass and they discussed everything from the hunt balls at Pennington Nab, to life in the Royal Navy, taking in, on the way, jazz—"My bro', Julian, introduced me to trad jazz when he was up at Cambridge and I've been an addict ever since"—fishing in the Caribbean, a favorite for both of them; skiing; and, finally, the novels of Eric Ambler and Graham Greene.

"I feel I've known you for a lifetime, James," she said as they drove slowly back toward the RNAS.

It was, Bond thought, a somewhat trite remark, but possibly one of invitation. He pulled the BMW into a lay-by and cut the engine.

"The feeling's mutual, Clover, my dear." He reached for her in the darkness and she responded to his first rough kiss, though pulled away when he began to move in closer.

"No, James. No, not yet. It might become difficult, particularly as we're going to be shipmates."

"What d'you mean, shipmates?" Bond nuzzled her hair.

"*Invincible,* of course."

"What about *Invincible?*" He gently backed off.

"Well, we're both being drafted there for *Landsea '89,* aren't we?"

"First I've heard of it." Bond's voice remained steady,

while a snake of worry began to curl around his stomach. "First I've heard of Wrens going to sea as well—particularly during an exercise like *Landsea '89.*"

"Well, it's all over the place. In fact I've been told officially. Fifteen of us. Me, and fourteen ratings—apart from the other ladies who'll be on board."

"And what about *me?*" Deep within him, Bond was more than concerned now. If it was common knowledge that he was being drafted to *Invincible* it would not take much intelligence for the unscrupulous to put two and two together, particularly if they had got hold of the information that three senior admirals, including the C-in-C of the Russian Navy, were going to be aboard. His mind jumped back to the near-miss that afternoon, and he wondered if somebody was already trying to take evasive action and cut him out of the baby-sitting business.

Clover continued to talk, saying that she wouldn't have said anything if she did not already know he was involved. "Of course it's classified." She sounded a shade defensive. "But security's for those *without* need-to-know, surely."

"And I have need-to-know?"

"Your name's on the list, James. Of course you have clearance."

"And these *other* women. Who are they?"

"We haven't been told. All I know is that there are to be other women."

"Okay, from the top, you tell me *all* you know, Clover."

Bond listened, and became more concerned. Concerned enough to make a very secure call for a crash meeting with M during the coming weekend.

"I shouldn't go blabbing about this to all and sundry, Clover," he admonished. "Not even good to talk to me about it," he told her when they got back to the Wrennery.

"Well, kiss me goodnight, at least, James," she pouted.

He smiled and gave her a peck on the cheek. "Not just yet," he said solemnly. "Especially if we're going to be shipmates."

Though he laughed as he drove away, the entire events of the day were more than worrying. Bond made his crash call to M from a telephone box a mile up the road, off the base. The duty officer, using a scrambler, arranged the meeting for Sunday.

4

A Sunday in the Country

The search for the Spanish pilot, Felipe Pantano, and his missing Sea Harrier had been called off at dusk, but would be resumed in the morning. Yet, long before the S & R helicopter teams had clattered out to look for wreckage and, possibly, a signal-emitting life raft, Captain Pantano was sitting comfortably in the captain's cabin of a small freighter two hundred miles off the coast of his own country, Spain.

The freighter was registered in Oporto, Portugal. Indeed, Oporto, the harbor city famous for that most clubbable of wines, was where she was headed, and she sported the name *Estado Nôvo* on bows and stern. Low in the water, the *Estado Nôvo* obviously carried a heavy cargo in her hold and a large container secured for'ard took up the bulk of

53

her deck space. On the ship's manifest, the container showed as engineering equipment destined for Gibraltar, from a well-known British firm, and would not be subject to any customs scrutiny in Oporto where they would only stop for twenty-four hours to refuel.

Sitting opposite Pantano in the cabin was not the captain but Abou Hamarik, the strategist of BAST, who sat smiling and nodding as the swarthy little pilot told of how well the plan had gone.

"I'm sure nobody noticed I had gone off the plot," Pantano spoke in rapid Spanish, "and your people were waiting right on time. It took less than five minutes." He had taken off as number two in the quartet of Harriers, climbed to the correct height and had been careful to continue on the obligatory course. The operation had been set up only ten days before, even though there was already a plan to filch the Harrier: in fact that was originally the reason for Pantano being sent on the course. For weeks, through their carefully planted penetration agents within the Spanish Navy, BAST had forced Pantano onto the Harrier course with the elegant expertise of a theatrical magician making a member of the audience take the Ace of Spades from a clean deck of cards. The unscheduled addition, to destroy Captain Bond, had only been slipped into place when another of their agents had confirmed what that officer's role was to be during the all-important *Landsea '89* exercise.

Just north of Shrewsbury, over a densely wooded area, Pantano had literally dropped his Harrier from the sky, using the vectored thrust of his engine and coming down vertically like an express elevator. No pilot would have faulted his skill, for the Harrier had dropped at the exact, planned, point, into a small clearing of trees. Pantano had to make only minor adjustments—moving forward and sideways—to slow down and gently bring the Harrier to rest in the clearing. There was a Land-Rover parked nearby, and four men waiting for him. As Pantano had already suggested, the work of wiring up, fusing and fitting the Sidewinder AIM-9J missile (one of three stolen some four months earlier from an RAF base in West Germany) to the starboard outer pylon would take only a very short time. Five minutes twenty seconds later Pantano's Sea Harrier was rising fast from the trees, putting on forward speed and climbing away, back on course, but increasing his airspeed, going flat-out. It was essential for him to catch up with the lead aircraft, piloted by Bond, and stay well ahead of the number three.

"I think we'd have heard if the radar at Yeovilton actually lost me at any point." He smiled confidently at Hamarik, who gave a gentle nod.

The Spaniard's Harrier had come within three miles of Bond just as the latter was making his bombing run. "I locked on to him, and let the missile go," he told Hamarik. "After that I was busy with my own bombing run and the little bit of deviousness which followed."

Hamarik shrugged, making an open-handed gesture. "I fear friend Bond escaped." He smiled, as if to say, "It is difficult to win every battle."

Pantano gave a heavy sigh, obviously annoyed with himself. "I'm sorry. I did all I could. Damn. Damn the man."

"Please do not concern yourself. There is plenty of time for us to deal with Captain Bond. A pity we could not combine two birds with the one proverbial stone. But, I promise you, Felipe, he will go. In fact *that* is essential."

Pantano smiled, showing a small gold mine of fillings,

before he went through the final phase. His bombing run had been normal up to the time when he climbed away. "I simply pulled into a thirty-degree climb to show myself to the radar. At one thousand feet I let all the flares go, switched off my radar and banged on the ECM [the Electronic Counter Measures Pod]." The ECM is used to confuse ground radar and missiles. "This was not foolproof, of course, but I went down to zero feet and set the course you had given me. It was pretty exciting, I can tell you. I was just feet above the water. There were times when I was getting salt spray on the windshield, and even with the heater and wipers going full blast I couldn't budge all of it. Also, I had the throttle banged wide open and the altimeter 'bug' was screaming at me. I had it set to minimum—one hundred feet—and it went crazy. It was more like a boat ride than flying."

The Harrier had run right out into the Atlantic, then turned toward the Bay of Biscay. Two hundred miles later, Pantano had slowed to a hover beside the waiting *Estado Nôvo.* There was ample room to make a vertical landing, and almost before he was out of the cockpit, the crew had started to erect false sides which eventually made up the huge container standing on the forward deck.

"Good." Hamarik's oily smile greased over his face. "You have done well. Now, all we have to do is make certain the machine is fully gassed up, overhauled, and fitted with the other weapons. Then, you will be ready for stage two of your part in the operation we are to call **LOSE.** There is meant to be humor in that. Operation **LOSE** means that the major powers lose all that is dear to them, for what country can function without their personal gyroscopes?"

"I don't follow that part of it." Pantano did not press the point, though he was obviously intrigued.

"You don't follow it because you do not know what is really at stake." The greased smile again. Then Hamarik rose from his chair. "Come, let us eat and talk of good things. We have a small gift for you on board. She is from Egypt and, I am told, enjoys the same kind of trivial pursuit as yourself. Food first, for you will require energy."

•   •   •

James Bond was flying for most of Saturday, and the wardroom was almost empty when he went in to dine at around eight in the evening. He entered the anteroom and was surprised to see Clover, in a smart, almost military-looking dress—beige with brass buttons and darker beige piping around the shoulders and collar.

"How are you tonight, then, Clover?" He smiled, as though the fencing of the previous evening was now well forgotten.

"I'm fine, sir." She returned the smile though she spoke formally. "I was waiting to try and get a word with you."

"Right. How about dinner?"

"That's really nice. I'll get my coat, can we . . . ?"

Bond shook his head, putting an arm out to stop her. "There are few people in the wardroom on a Saturday night, Clover. Let's see what they have for us there. I seem to remember that on the ratings' messdecks of a Saturday evening, it was always 'Herrings in.' " He recalled it well enough from the days when, as officer of the watch, he had to do rounds of the messdecks. "Herrings in" was the name they always gave to the large tins of herrings in tomato sauce, a favorite among both ratings and Petty Officers. Bond could never understand it. The food looked and smelled revolting to him, but there were never any complaints on Saturday nights. He presumed things had changed since then.

The only people dining in at that time were the officer of the watch and the Royal Marines duty officer, who both nodded deferentially to Bond as he led Clover to a couple of chairs distant to the other two officers. The Wren stewards served them with the only choice on the Saturday-night menu—smoked salmon, followed by grilled steak. Bond took his steak rare and, refusing the pommes frites, ordered a small green salad.

They talked idly, circling the problem both knew existed, until the main course had been served. It was Clover Pennington who took the lead—

"I wanted to apologize for last night." She turned her eyes away and blushed as she spoke.

"Apologize for what?" Bond stared at her until she had to make eye contact.

"I broke all security regulations, sir. I shouldn't have mentioned either *Invincible* or *Landsea '89.* I'm sorry, it just seemed natural, particularly as I knew you were being drafted as well."

"You're quite right." Bond was almost sharp with her. "To have gained the rank of First Officer you should really have learned all the lessons of security by now. I have to be honest with you, Clover, I've always had great reservations about young women with either loud voices, or runaway tongues. The Royal Navy isn't known as the Silent Service for nothing. We've an almost unblemished reputation for keeping mouths closed and ears open."

"I know, sir. I'm sorry. I just thought that, if I got my apology out of the way, perhaps—"

Bond could not make up his mind whether she was just a garrulous woman or an upper-class gold digger.

"Perhaps what?"

"Well, last night we—"

"I think you'd do well to forget about last night. At least until the matters on your conscience are over." In case he was being too harsh, Bond gave her a tight smile. "Let's see how it all goes. After that, anything's possible. We could meet socially. No problem there."

Clover Pennington looked suitably crestfallen, pushed her plate away, made a muttered excuse and left the ward-room. Bond quietly finished his meal, went into the ante-room, took a small brandy with his coffee, then headed back to his quarters. Tomorrow was a free day, but for him it would be a full one.

•   •   •

He left the Royal Naval Air Station just after eight, having eaten his usual breakfast. Bond was beginning to realize what had attracted him to the Navy in the first place. He was a man of routine, and enjoyed the privileges that came with rank. But now, rank was put to one side. He wore civilian clothes, and drove the BMW with caution, keeping his eyes on the rearview mirror. Even though he was in England, this was an operation and any contact with his real Service was a clandestine matter where Field Rules applied.

He drove to Cheddar, pleased that on this late-autumn Sunday there were few other people on the road. Certainly he appeared to be free of any surveillance as he turned off the main road and headed toward a modern house on the edge of an upmarket estate.

The double garage doors were open and Bill Tanner stood by the crimson Lancia already drawn back from the automatic doors. It took Bond less than a minute to change cars, reversing the Lancia out while Tanner nodded and drove the BMW into the garage. No other cars came near and Bond crammed an unlikely fishing hat on his head and slipped dark glasses over his eyes. No words were exchanged, but, as he turned the Lancia back toward the main road, Bond saw the garage door coming down to hide his own car.

An hour later he had negotiated the M5 Motorway, and taken the M4 fork which led him toward London. It took about fifty minutes for him to reach the Windsor exit, after which he circled the smaller roads, still watching for a possible tail. It was a lengthy, painstaking, business so he did not reach his destination until after eleven, purring across the Windsor-Bagshot road and looking out for the Squirrel public house on his left, then the gateway of simple stone on the right.

He turned the Lancia through the gateway to see the familiar, well-manicured drive, the screen of silver birch, beech, pine and oak trees which stood guard over the rectangular Regency manor house of weathered Bath stone.

He pulled the Lancia around the side of the main house, parking so that it would also be screened by the trees which, as he knew from the past, were not the only protection that guarded M's beautiful country house called, nostalgically, Quarterdeck.

His feet crunched on the gravel as he approached the portico and grasped the thong attached to the gleaming brass bell, once that of some long-forgotten ship, and clanged it to and fro. Seconds later the stout door was unbolted from the inside and opened to reveal M's servant, Davison, who had replaced the faithful ex–Chief Petty Officer Hammond.

"And Mrs. Davison? She well?" Bond stepped into the

hall, taking in the familiar scene—the smell of polish from the pine paneling; the Victorian hall stand, with M's old ulster hanging from it, and Wellington boots set nearby; the table with its wonderfully detailed $\frac{1}{144}$ scale model of the battle cruiser *Repulse,* M's last command.

"Mrs. Davison's fit as a flea, sir—and twice as nippy, if you follow my drift."

"Indeed I do, Davison." Bond inclined his head toward the model. "Much more beautiful than the present one, eh?"

"Don't know what to make of the Andrew anymore, sir. Carriers that aren't carriers, and no real ships. Not like in the old days, anyhow."*

The present *Repulse* is the S23, one of the Royal Navy's first Resolution class SSBN, Polaris-armed submarines.

"Hanyway, sir, the Hadmiral is expecting you."

"Good. Lead the way, Davison."

The former CPO knocked loudly on the thick, heavy Spanish mahogany door and M's voice sounded, sharp, from behind it—"Come."

"Captain James Bond, sir."

"Permission to come aboard, sir?" Bond smiled, but immediately realized that his smile was not returned.

M did not open the conversation until the door was closed behind them but, in those few seconds, Bond took in the entire room. It was still as neat as ever. The table near the window, with watercolor material laid out in what looked like a parade-ground precision; the old Naval prints, neatly aligned along the walls and M's desk, with papers, an old inkstand, leather blotter, calendar, the two telephones, one ivory the other red, all in perfect order.

---

*"The Andrew" is naval slang for the Royal Navy, and has been since the mid-19th century. Before that the word usually described one ship.

"Well," M began, "this had better be good, Bond. There was a specific arrangement. No contacts unless you fired a distress signal."

"Sir, I was—"

"If you're going to tell me someone had a potshot at you with a missile, I know about that; just as I know it could have been an electronic fault in your aircraft—"

"With respect, sir. That was no electronic fault. There are other matters also. I wouldn't break Field Rules if there was no reason."

M motioned to an armchair. Bond sat, and M took his usual place behind the desk. "You'd better—" He was cut short by the red telephone purring. He lifted it to his ear, saying nothing. Then M grunted twice, nodded at the receiver and recradled it. "There was nobody on your back, anyway. We're sure of that. Now, if you're certain about the missile—and I'm not—what did you come to talk about?"

Bond started at the beginning—the Sidewinder doing its best to blow him out of the sky, then, without a pause he went on with the story of First Officer Clover Pennington. "She says there are fifteen Wrens slated for attachment in *Invincible*, says it's common knowledge, just as she says it's common knowledge that I'm going to be there as well. I felt it vital that I talk directly to you, sir. This is a security matter, and I don't like details being known to all and sundry. Particularly as you were so adamant that we kept to strict Field Rules, and I was to operate under deep cover. If a Wren First Officer's blabbing about it, how do we know these BAST people haven't got everything already? Knowledge that the three Admirals are going to be in *Invincible*, knowing I'm their Nanny, responsible for their safety? Damn it, sir, they can take me out any time they want. For all we know that Sidewinder was an attempt to remove me."

M remained silent for a full minute, then cleared his throat. "The best thing would be to remove young First Officer Pennington from the draft," he growled. "But, if she's not on the side of the angels, it might be best to keep her in play, where you can keep an eye on her. It's all very interesting though, especially in view of this." He opened a plain buff file and carefully removed two stapled pages, handing them over to Bond.

They were a standard maintenance form, dated the previous day and referring to a detailed examination of the Harrier in which he had flown on the day of the missile incident. Bond's eyes moved down the pages, taking in the technical detail as he went. Most of it referred to a pair of faulty transponders, part of the internal warning system. The summary and conclusion were written in a neat hand toward the bottom of the second page.

While it is quite possible for Captain Bond's aircraft to have developed the trouble in the transponders after some accidental firing of the missile, it appears more likely that the faults were triggered, either before or during his bombing run. Pilots have been known to report missiles closing, or at least fired in their direction after failure in one or both of the transponders mentioned in the report above, and, bearing in mind the absence of any missiles aboard aircraft in the vicinity, this appears to be the only adequate reason in this case.

C. Pennington (First Officer WRNS)

"Nice to know who's on your side, sir. I can assure you there was *no* transponder failure. That was a missile, and First Officer Pennington seems to be doing her best to play it down. To cover her own pretty little backside do you think, sir?"

M grunted, took back the report then looked at Bond with his unflinching damnably clear gray eyes. "You are *absolutely,* one hundred percent certain, 007?"

"Stake my life on it, sir."

M nodded. "In the circumstances, while it would appear to be normal security to have this young woman removed from the draft going to *Invincible,* I prefer to leave things as they are. At least you're alerted."

A tap at the door brought Davison in to announce that luncheon was served. "Nothing much, even for a Sunday." M pulled himself from his chair. "Kind of thing you like though, 007. Cold roast beef, new potatoes and a little salad. That do you?"

"Make a change from wardroom food, sir."

"I'll be bound." M gave an imitation which came as near to a laugh as you would ever get from him. "Good for you. Get all the more unpleasant chemicals out of your bloodstream. Those chi-chi meals you're always eating'll be the death of you yet."

Mrs. Davison assisted her husband to serve the modest meal which was very much to Bond's taste—particularly the horseradish sauce, rough-cut and made by Mrs. Davison herself. "Calculated to clear the sinuses," M commented. "Can't do with that namby-pamby creamed stuff they're always serving these days. Sans taste, sans bite, sans everything horseradish should be."

When they were alone once more, Bond slowly intro-

duced the question that had been most on his mind—
"Might I know, sir, exactly why we have to put up with
fifteen Wrens in *Invincible?* I'm only as superstitious as the
next sailor, so I personally think of it as bad luck—women
on a naval vessel."

"Not simply superstitious, but a solid male chauvinist
pig, I'd say, Bond—whatever male chauvinist pig means,
dratted bad use of language if you ask me. But you've asked
me something more tricky. Something you shouldn't even
know, and I'm not sure if this is the right time to tell you.
I was going to do it before you went on draft to *Invincible,*
of course." He helped himself to more of the beef and a
large spoonful of the horseradish. "My story was going to
be that the Russkies're bringing at least one female naval
attaché with them. But one Russian woman does not equal
fifteen Wrens, does it?"

"Hardly." Bond followed his Chief's lead and took some
more beef.

"Then here goes, 007, and remember, this really *is* high-
security stuff, classified possibly as nothing has ever been
classified before—not in time of peace anyway."

He talked for over half an hour, and Bond's initial surprise at what M said turned into a whole world of churning worries which were to haunt him for many weeks to
come.

At six o'clock that evening, James Bond made the return
journey to the RNAS at Yeovilton, via a small car-changing
charade in Cheddar. Now he knew the entire thing and
could see that the covert action which appeared to be in
motion via BAST had pushed him into one of the most
difficult and dangerous assignments he had ever been
forced to undertake.

•   •   •

While Bond and M were meeting in the house near Windsor Great Park, another fortuitous meeting was taking place in Plymouth. A Petty Officer Engineer, on twenty-four-hour leave, spent the lunchtime in an unfamiliar public house. It was Sunday and drinking men often go over the limit during a normal pre-lunch session, but this particular man took only his usual number of pints. When it was time to leave, he was, if anything, only slightly "merry," full of good cheer, and not given to making an exhibition of himself.

He had also made two new friends.

The Petty Officer did not live in Plymouth, but knew the city well, like many a sailor before him. Plymouth on a Sunday can often be lonely for a sailor without a girl in port and this particular man's girl was his wife of fifteen years, and she lived in London because she had a good job there. The new friends were a pair of civilians who started to make conversation with him at the bar of the pub. One, called Harry, was the representative for a firm that provided some essential components for turbines, so he had something in common with the Petty Officer; the other, Bill, was also a rep—for a company that specialized in fiber optics. Harry and Bill were old friends, for they often met at the same hotel when work brought them to Plymouth.

The Petty Officer was glad of their company, and found the conversation, mainly of wine, women and ships, exceptionally stimulating. So much so that he invited the two men to have a bite to eat with him. "After that, me old mates, I'm going to find a good-looking young pusher." Freely translated, a "pusher" had nothing to do with drugs.

The term was old Navy for girl; usually one of easy virtue and who did most things for money. Professional or amateur.

"Now, there we can really help you," said Harry. "Bill and me, we stay here often. And guess what our hobby is?"

They lunched well, their conversation rarely straying from matters below the navel. "What'd your wife say if she ever caught you at it?" Bill asked the Petty Officer.

"Give me bloody 'ell. She'd set her brothers on me, that's for sure, and they're big bastards."

They took him to a small private club where they both had membership. There, the Petty Officer was shown a series of young girls, all of whom were highly desirable. So much so that the PO commented on the fact that he had never seen pushers like that in clubs or on the streets of Plymouth in the whole of his life.

"That's because you don't know the right places to go," Harry said with a smile. "Take your pick, Blackie. Any one of them. . . ."

"Or more if you're feeling greedy. This is on us, mate." Bill laughed.

The Petty Officer chose a blonde who looked about sixteen, but had the credentials of someone far more experienced than any teenager.

The cameras were hidden behind a pair of two-way mirrors, often used in this particular establishment. The PO spent nearly two hours with the girl and left, as he said, "suitably impressed."

Harry and Bill invited him to dinner at their hotel. Over dinner they all planned to spend the following Sunday together. Then the conversation turned to the big Naval turbine engines, on which the Petty Officer was an expert.

5

The Christmas Horse

The phrase "Health depends on strength" was picked up once more by the listening posts toward the end of November. The computers locked on and the transcript was on M's desk within twenty-four hours.

Again it was Bassam Baradj and Abou Hamarik who spoke.

"Surely you don't think this Naval man, Bond, will be any threat to an operation as complex as ours?" Baradj said.

"I like to be sure of my enemies." Hamarik's voice was almost a whisper. "Bond isn't merely a simple officer of the Royal Navy: not that there are any simple Royal Naval officers. This man has a curious and impressive record, and my informants tell me he is to be drafted to the ship as a special liaison officer."

"Head of a select bodyguard section?"

"Possibly."

"And you thought he was enough of a threat to warrant removing, even in the midst of something vital to the final plan?"

"I saw it as a military opportunity. The chance was there. It failed."

There was a long pause, then Baradj spoke again. "Well, Abou, I trust the other part of our **Operation Lose** goes well and will not be compromised. Apart from the general political aims of the Brotherhood, I have a great deal of hard currency tied up. I've never disguised the fact that there are financial issues here. While I believe ardently in the Brotherhood, and see it as the only way a new, and more just world, can be established, I am also concerned with creating a financial buffer for myself, and, of course, the Brotherhood, which would be nothing without my support. Pray the next segment of the plan goes without any hitches."

"This coming weekend will see the completion of that phase. We have our man neatly sewn up. You need not be concerned about that part. All will go well."

"And the Bond fellow?"

"Maybe it would be a good idea to remove him from the scene. He was formerly a member of the British Secret Intelligence Service, at one time a skilled assassin until the British had no more stomach for such things. But he is experienced, a good leader, and a man to be reckoned with. He will, doubtless, have people under his command guarding the trio who will be aboard Birdsnest Two."

"If we get rid of him before the event?" Baradj paused. "*If* we dispose of him, will they bring in someone of his quality as a replacement?"

"They will replace him." Hamarik sounded a shade diffident. "But not with a man of like caliber. Bond is, shall we say, unique."

Once more there was one of those long pauses, when the listening devices picked up stray noises, a goatherd or shepherd on the slopes below; people, probably servants or bodyguards, arguing.

"They have their feast of Christmas next month." Baradj sounded suddenly hard, and threatening. "Find out where this man is to spend Christmas. I'll give him to the Cat. That will lessen our chances of failure."

M, in his office overlooking Regent's Park, watched Bill Tanner reading the transcript. Tanner was a quick reader, but M was impatient, drumming his fingers on the leather skivers inlaid in his desk top.

"Well?" he asked sharply when his Chief of Staff had finished.

"They're too well informed," Tanner spoke decisively. "It's become uncontrollable. I think you should advise a rethink. Call the whole thing off."

M grunted. "Mmm. But, Chief of Staff, can you see our advice being taken? Knowing what's involved, there are risks in trying to have the thing called off."

It was Bill Tanner's turn to grunt as he moved to his favorite place, by the window, looking down into the Park below. "I understand the problem, sir. But if the worst happens—"

"Our best chance is to stop it happening at all. Keep Bond in play. You heard what Baradj said about Christmas. Why don't we flush 'em out? Make 'em vulnerable by letting them show their hand."

"You mean use Bond as a tethered goat?"

"More a stalking horse, Tanner. Have to ask him first, of

course. Yes, set up a meeting, and make sure it's absolutely one hundred percent sterile. Got me?"

"I understand, sir."

"The Cat." M was almost musing to himself. "BAST, the three-headed monster riding on a viper. The heads of a man, a snake and a cat. The Cat, Tanner."

"Saphii Boudai, yes?"

"What's on file?"

"Precious little, sir. We know she was PLO at one time. There is a possibility that she spent a few years as a penetration agent within Mossad, but they're either too coy, or tied too tightly into their own vengeance plans, to release any photographs. Boudai, we know, is around twenty-nine or thirty years of age; we also know she is attractive and an expert in many things clandestine. But we have no photographs and no real description."

M gave another grunt. "They have Bond well assessed. His weak point has always been women. He's going to have to be briefed fully. Try and get more information on the Boudai woman, even if you have to lean on your Mossad contacts. They're a touchy lot, I know, but do your best—and set up that meeting with more than usual care."

Tanner nodded and left the office looking grim and determined.

•   •   •

The Harrier conversion course at Yeovilton had become even more demanding. Each day Bond flew, and each day they stretched him to new limits—not just on the bombing range but also in the role of fighter pilot.

First in the simulator, then later in the more dangerous

environment of reality, he practiced dogfight techniques—sometimes with other aircraft flown by instructors, or his coursemates.

In one day he would go through the high-speed, stomach-churning maneuvers like the High G Yo Yo, Flip Yo Yo, Low G Yo Yo, and the old, tried and true Immelmann, modified for jet aircraft so that you changed direction by rolling the airplane, not at the top of a loop, as in the classic Immelmann turn, but as you shot up in a vertical climb.

There was also the maneuver unique to the Harrier—thrust Vectored In Forward Flight, or VIFF as it is known. The Harrier has the ability to rise vertically, or move sideways from its normal flight path. This was a technique thought to be absolutely revolutionary in air combat, but the conversion course pilots, having learned how to perform the VIFF, were put in the true picture by a veteran pilot of the Falklands Campaign.

"The Press made a big deal out of Viffing," the pilot told them in a closed lecture. "But I don't think any of us used it. I've seen articles and drawings in magazines showing Harriers allowing an enemy aircraft to position himself for an attack directly behind their six, then whizzing upwards and blasting the attacker as he overshot." The pilot, a young lieutenant commander, gave a rueful smile. "You just don't let anyone calmly place himself at six o'clock, it's just too bloody dangerous. Also the VIFF slows you down—that's its one great use. Personally, I'd only use it to alter the position of my nose so that I could get a good shot at my opponent. Forget about heroic leaps upwards, and letting enemy aircraft overshoot you. If there's someone on your six, he'll probably get you whatever you do—

73

unless he fires a missile a long way out of range. These days aerial combat is still mainly Battle of Britain stuff at speed, and at a longer separation. Rely on your radar and lock-on. A well-placed heat-seeker fired from even the outer limits of range will do the job—on him, or *you*."

So, they added Viffing to their stockpile of maneuvers, knowing its limits, just as they all began to feel out their own limits. Bond knew he had not operated under such stress for a long time, and was particularly concerned about Clover Pennington, who, instead of being put off by his own cold-shouldering, appeared to have become more and more interested. She would wait for him, lingering in the anteroom, or seek him out at meals, showing an unusual concern for his well-being, but careful not to overstep the mark.

"That spectacular Wren three-ringer's really got the hots for you," the U.S. Navy pilot remarked one day at lunch.

"Really?" Bond gave him a surprised look. "Well, if she has, I suggest that someone tells her to take a cold shower."

"Know what you mean, Captain. After a day chasing around the sky in these birds, I doubt if I could put on a performance, even for the most desirable two-legged bird. These Harriers sap it all out of you."

"True," Bond said with a tight smile as he rose and left the table.

A couple of days later he received a postcard picturing the Martyrs' Memorial in Oxford. He did not recognize the writing, but presumed it had been done by one of the cleared secretaries back at the Regent's Park office. It was neat, short, and to the point.

Completed twenty-two pages of notes on bear-baiting in the 16th century; visited Blenheim Palace to take a look at the archives which kept me busy over the weekend. Hope to see you soon. Love as ever — Judith

Anyone with common sense could have deciphered it. Judith was the code for a crash meeting. The text told Bond exactly when and where. The Bear Hotel, Woodstock, near Oxford. Room 22 at eight o'clock on Sunday night—the room number was exact, the time was 16:00 hours plus four: that was the add-on code. Either something was up, or—as the course was nearing completion—plans had been altered.

The Bear Hotel, Woodstock, lies in the main square of that crowded little town, which stands a few minutes' walk from the grounds leading to Blenheim Palace, that gorgeous gift to the First Duke of Marlborough from a grateful sovereign. The palace was designed by Vanbrugh, and the magnificent grounds landscaped by Capability Brown. The main palace doors contain a replica of the intricate locks which once graced the main gates of the city of Warsaw, and these days people travel to see it in its historic context, for one of the great leaders of the twentieth century, Winston Churchill, was not only born in the palace, but also lies buried in nearby Blaydon. Bond had often come here, driving from London on a Saturday, spending the day walking in the grounds, simply enjoying the breathtaking views. He remembered one Saturday in October, some years before, standing on the bridge which spans the main lake, and watching the autumn sun draw a golden spear in the water.

The spear often returned to him in a dream, as though it was some kind of omen.

Blenheim and Woodstock are magnets for tourists from all over the world, and though the palace is closed in November, the inordinately beautiful grounds and parkland remain open for part of the day, and now, on the Sunday, with woodsmoke in the air and the paths sprinkled with the gold and red leaves of autumn, Bond once more stood on that same bridge, watching the same red sun, low in the sky, produce a similar effect—a spear of light pointing directly at him. Now he wondered if that spear reflected on water was indeed an omen.

He had taken a room for the night at the nearby Feathers Hotel, partly for security and partly because he preferred it to the more famous Bear.

He completed his walk and returned to The Feathers where he put his feet up for a few hours before taking the short stroll to The Bear. It was with some distaste he noted that the whiff of oil and potato chips hung heavy in the evening air, coming from pubs that advertised "Pub Grub" or "Good Food," a pair of terms Bond would have liked to see banned from the English language, just as he would, if pushed, like to see the countless young people crowding those very bars banished to some kind of National Service—preferably in the armed forces. That, he considered, would take violence off the streets of country towns, and make men out of the louts who littered pavements and got drunk at the sniff of a barmaid's apron.

He dodged into the front entrance of The Bear, neatly keeping clear of the reception area at the rear of the narrow passage leading through from the entrance hall, and squeezing into the small elevator that would take him to Room 22.

Both M and his Chief of Staff were waiting.

"Q Branch have just swept the place," M said as a form of greeting. "It appears to be clean, though nowadays who's to know?"

Bond gave both his Chief and his closest friend within the Service friendly smiles then waited for what would doubtless be laid on him. Judging by their faces, the news was not good.

M waved to a chair, and 007 sat, still waiting until M asked, "You remember BAST?"

"How could I forget, sir. After all they seem to be our main opponents."

"After your hide, 007. Out to get you, take you out, ice you, buy the farm for you. At least that's what the doomsayers would have us believe."

"I would have thought the missile incident had already pointed us in that general direction."

"Yes." M flapped his hand as though trying to waft bad air away from his nostrils. "But this time we have a chance to lay our hands on at least one of them. We know when they're going to set you up and who's going to do it. What we don't know is where."

"Then, with due respect, sir, I would have thought we should get cracking and find out exactly where."

Bill Tanner rubbed his hands together. "That's really anywhere of your own choosing, James."

"Mine?"

"Yes." M's clear gray eyes were locked on to Bond's face. "We would like to send you away for a Christmas holiday, 007."

"Tethered goat," said Bond.

"Stalking horse," Tanner corrected him. "Sort of Christmas horse, so that BAST can come down your chimney and knock your socks off. In this case BAST will take on the human shape of a woman."

"Ah," said Bond with a wry smile. "You want me to play slow horses and fast women."

"Something you've been known to do before this, 007." M did not even twinkle, let alone return the smile.

"I have any option?"

M shook his head. "None whatsoever. BAST already know far too much; they're going to have a go during *Landsea '89*, and they regard you as a mild threat. Mind you, they don't yet seem to know all the details: such as the six SAS people you'll be commanding for the bodyguard operation."

"Funny, I hadn't heard about them either, sir." Bond paused, then looked from M to Tanner and back again. "If you know all this, why can't you deal with BAST on its own terms? Take them out before they do their bit?"

M sighed. "We know the names of their ringleaders; we have descriptions of two of them, but we have no idea how large their Brotherhood is, or really how fanatical they are. The four or so leaders are fanatical enough, though the mastermind is, we deduce, more concerned with a return for his capital investment than the political aspect."

"We wouldn't normally put you at risk, James . . ." Tanner began.

"Not much."

"Not with *Landsea '89* coming up," M said firmly. "We would like to get our hands on one of their leading people, though. So what about Christmas?"

"Not my favorite time of the year." Bond looked down his nose. "I can't stand all that bonhomie, and families getting together around the festive board, but that's probably because I have no real family." Tracy, his dead wife of only a few hours, flashed through his mind. Christmases would have been good if she had lived, he thought. Even an uncharacteristic picture of the two of them by a log fire with presents and a tree went flickering in and out of his mind. Then he saw the reflected spear of light again and wondered how all this would end. He looked bleakly at M. "I suppose you've already got somewhere lined up, though, sir."

M nodded. "You recall that a few years ago I sent you for some rest and recuperation. A villa on Ischia, in the Bay of Naples?"

"That was in summer . . ." He recalled it vividly. Secluded, beautiful setting, almost idyllic. You only had to drive a couple of miles for food. The rest of the time you were all set up by the pool, with maid service, a cook, if you wanted one, and spectacular surroundings. "The Service paid for it, I know, but they only open them up for the summer."

"I think I can persuade the owner." M had his stubborn look grappled to his face.

After a couple of heartbeats, Bond said—"Christmas on Ischia, then, sir. Just tell me what to do."

"First," M began, "you'll have to run the thing solo. We can give you only modest cover. Nothing fancy, and certainly not the local police. . . ." He went on for the next hour, and as he progressed, Bond realized that, as ever, the whole business would be down to him. Sit there and wait for a woman out to kill him, and who would possibly have a backup; then outwit her; and, finally, bring her back into the UK with everyone, including himself, alive and kicking.

"Run-of-the-mill sort of job really," he said when M stopped talking.

"The kind of thing you should be able to do, armed with a butterfly net and a killing jar, 007."

"I'll settle for the killing jar." Bond smiled. "Preferably 9mm with a lot of kick to it. You know, the kind of thing any Christmas stalking horse carries around."

.   .   .

At just about the same moment as Bond was being apprised of how he would spend a happy Christmas, Harry and Bill were putting some bad news to their old friend the Petty Officer Engineer.

"It's not that we don't like you, Blackie," Bill was saying. "We're under a certain amount of pressure ourselves."

"I mean we didn't know they took photographs in that place, and there's a fair old collection now as you can see." Harry laid out some thirty black and white prints on the table.

They were in Harry's room at his usual Plymouth hotel. The photographs, with their grainy texture, looked almost as dirty as the cavortings they had captured for all time. The PO looked very miserable. "You'd send these to the wife?" It was not so much a question as a shocked statement.

"No, 'course *we* wouldn't." Harry's voice was low, soothing. Oil on troubled waters. "We're in the mire as much as you are, Blackie. We didn't know."

"And there's all that money." Bill tried to look as miserable as his colleague. "I mean we put things on our expense accounts. Now, we're both in the same boat. It's coming to something when two companies, with two different interests, turn down your expenses."

"*And* we always understood that place with the girls was buckshee. They never charged us a penny before."

"How—how much are we talking about?" The Petty Officer was chalk white. He could feel the blood draining from his cheeks.

Harry sighed. "Seven thousand, eight hundred and twenty-five pounds."

"And sixty-two pence," Bill added.

"But I can't . . . There's no way. The wife'll kill me—at best leave me—and there's no way I can get my hands on that kind of money."

"Second mortgage on the house?" Harry asked.

"First bloody mortgage isn't paid off yet." The gloom was almost tangible.

Harry gathered the photographs up into a neat pile. "They *have* offered us a way out, but I said you'd as like do it as fly using your arms."

"What is it? The way out?"

"Well, I don't think you'd want to hear it."

Bill, who had poured them each a stiff whisky, interrupted. "They're offering money *on top,* though. Best tell him."

"Well." Harry sighed again. "Okay—it gets all of us off the hook, and they'll throw in one hundred K for you, Blackie, seeing as how you'd be taking the biggest risk."

"A hundred grand? For *me?* Who've I got to kill?"

"It's not a matter of killing." Harry moved closer, and began to make the Petty Officer the offer which, in the circumstances, he could not afford to refuse.

6

See Naples and . . .

Naples was not James Bond's favorite city. Now, sitting in a bumper-to-bumper, horn-hooting, yelling traffic jam, cramming one of the narrow streets leading down to the harbor, he placed it almost at the bottom of his list. The double-lane freeway from the airport had not been too bad, but, as ever, the city streets were crowded and in a state of chaos. To make matters worse it was raining: that fine, soaking misty rain that is even more unpleasant than an out-and-out downpour.

This was a city that time had forgotten, Bond reflected, as he eased the uncertain hired Fiat behind an unsteady lorry overloaded with bottled water. Naples had never regained its status as a tourist resort. Instead it had become a transit point. People arrived at the airport, maybe stayed a couple of nights to "do" Pompeii, and were either whisked off to Sorrento, or made this journey down to the ferries for Capri or Ischia, the two islands that form the gate to the Bay of Naples.

Constantly the two islands were regarded as *passé* or outdated, yet that was where the tourists or socialites went. The only people who stayed were the Neapolitans, or NATO sailors from the various naval vessels which tied up off the coast, in the safety of the bay. For sailors it was one hell of a city with its blatant red light district, and the area running down the foothills, between the Castel Sant'Elmo, and the Municipal Building. This last was crowded with bars, clip joints and gaudy fleeting pleasures. It was known, like George V Street in the old Malta days, as The Gut. The Gut saw every possible depravity. It was, Bond thought, near enough like some parts of Pompeii must have been before Vesuvius slammed its lava down over the city. The traffic moved about six feet, and again ground to a halt, while shouts from drivers and police filtered back through the closed, steamy windows of the car.

In summer the earth-red houses and terra-cotta roofs of Naples soaked up the sun and filled the streets with dust; in winter the same walls seemed to blot up the rain, so that the buildings took on an even more crumbling look, as though they might turn to sludge and slide into the sea. Over it all, threatening Vesuvius glowered.

At the Ischia and Capri ferry points, cars and ramshackle wagons stretched back, clogging the restricted space. A large black limo tried to jump the line, and Bond watched, amused, as a police officer leaned into the car and backhanded the uniformed chauffeur. In London the cop would have been in big trouble. Here, the driver probably knew he would never work in Naples again if he complained.

After the frustration of the slow journey from the airport, the waiting cars and wagons boarded the ferry with relative speed, though with much shouting, waving of arms and protestations to God and the Blessed Virgin.

Bond left the car on the vehicle deck and climbed through the crowd of passengers to seek out a reasonably sheltered part of the ferry. Shouldering his way to the little bar, he reluctantly bought a plastic beaker of what was supposed to be coffee. The liquid tasted like sweet colored water but at least it moistened his throat. Once at the Villa Capricciani he would be able to pick and choose for himself.

As the ferry began to move out into the bay, Bond looked back across the black oily water, wondering what Naples had looked like in its days of glory. Once its beauty was inspirational. Parthenope the Siren had thrown herself into the sea for love of Ulysses, and was washed up on the golden shore that became the Bay of Naples. "See Naples and die." Bond smiled to himself. The old Italian saying had a double edge at one time: see Naples and die for its beauty; then the second edge when the seaport had become the focal point of typhoid and cholera. Now? Well, there had been slums and depravity here for decades, with an increase since the end of World War II. He decided that the old phrase could become triple-edged now that AIDS was spreading across the world like the new Black Death. But the same was true of most ancient ports.

Perhaps it was the thought of age and decay, of lost glory and the current world tensions, that plunged Bond into feelings of concern and anxiety as the coastline shrank in the ferry's wake. Undercover once more, he knew the risks for he had gambled his life in this way on many occasions before. He was aware that the day could easily come when the odds would be stacked too heavily against him. The last time he had made this trip had been on a glorious summer day, when he was looking forward to rest and healing relaxation. This time—see Naples and . . . what? Die or live? Win or lose?

So, it was in a somewhat somber mood that, an hour later, he looked out over the sea on the port beam toward the brooding Aragonese Castle, shaped like a small-scale model of Gibraltar, with its umbilical road reaching toward Ischia. Within ten minutes they were docking at Porta d'Ischia, and the whole shouting, jostling and yelling match began again. The cars and lorries made their way onto the very restricted area around the berthing point, to the accompaniment of horn blasts and more shouting. Planks were laid down to assist some of the heavier vehicles and the entire operation was made even more hazardous by the slick of rain on quayside and ramp, while the throng of pedestrians seemed to delight in walking directly in front of the slow-moving vehicles.

He had carefully checked the car before getting behind the wheel, for these people of BAST did not care about the lives of innocent victims. Then, after what seemed an eternity, he finally negotiated the Fiat off the ferry, around some makeshift stalls still selling tourist junk on the off-chance of catching some gullible holidaymaker who had left home and hearth to spend the festive season here on the undeniably beautiful shambles that was Ischia, the peaceful island that had known the crack and blast of history, and seen much violent death as well as happiness in its time.

He drove west, feeling at his most vulnerable. He had carefully salted the ground for whoever was supplying BAST with information, declaring to a lot of people, in and out of the wardroom at Yeovilton RNAS, that he was heading for the Bay of Naples, to spend a quiet Christmas alone.

They knew that BAST was filching information from Yeovilton; just as they knew that the oily Baradj had fingered him, putting the Cat—Saphii Boudai—in charge. As with Baradj, Hamarik, and Adwan, there were no photographic descriptions available. At best the pictures were blurred, photofits provided by people who had caught fleeting glimpses of the quartet which formed the leadership of BAST. All Bond knew for sure was that the Cat was a woman, variously reported to be short and tall, fat and thin, beautiful and repellent. The only matching feature was that she had very dark hair.

He was traveling in a rented car, which was bad security to start with, and, until he reached the Villa Capricciani, he was unarmed. It was only after M had given the final instructions that Bond had also realized, from memory, that the villa itself was a security nightmare. As he drove the narrow, dangerous roads he constantly scanned the rearview mirror: catching sight of vehicles that had been on the ferry—a Volvo here, a VW there. But none seemed to linger, or take any interest in him.

On the road between Lacco and Forio, respectively on the northwest and west of the island, he turned off, down the very narrow metaled road which led to the villa. Nothing seemed to have changed on the island, everything was how he remembered it, from the destructive, near suicidal driving, to the sudden beautiful views that came, unexpectedly, at a turn in the road. There were also other aspects:

handfuls of peeling buildings, the open front of a cluttered shop, a dowdy gas station. In summer these last would seem romantic. In winter they came into clear, depressing focus. Now he looked for the gates set into the high gray stone wall to the right, hoping that nothing at the villa had fundamentally altered.

The gates were open, and he swung the Fiat into the tight turning circle inside, cut the engine and got out. In front of him was a large and beautiful lily pond, bordered on the right by another gate which in turn led to steps overhung with vines and greenery. He could see the white dome of the villa above, and was halfway up the steps when a voice called—

"Signor Bond?"

He shouted back an affirmative, and, as he reached the top, a young girl appeared. She was dressed in a tank top and jeans that were not so much cutoffs as ripoffs, making her look as though a pair of gorgeous legs had been grafted onto a small, exquisite body. Her face could only be described as cheeky. Dark eyes danced above a snub nose and wide smiling mouth, the whole topped by a bubbly black tight-curled foam of hair.

She had come out of the big sliding glass doors of the villa and now stood, smiling, by the poolside. In the palms and tropical fronds to her right a short, white statue of a young satyr thumbed its mouth and produced almost a mirror-image of the girl.

"Signor Bond," she said again, the voice jolly and bright. "Welcome to Villa Capricciani. I am Beatrice." She pronounced it with almost cassata-flavored Italian—Beé-ah-Treé-che. "I am here to greet you. Also to look after you. I am the maid."

Bond thought he would not like to bet on it, but strode onto the wide terrace which was covered with a green material so that in hot weather you would not barbecue the bare soles of your feet getting to the pool, which was now empty and covered. The villas were never open in the winter, so he wondered how M had pulled off the renting of this one. The answer probably lay in a close, maybe secret, arrangement with the owner. M had high-placed friends the world over, and, Bond suspected, was able to apply pressure when required by circumstances such as this.

As though reading his thoughts, Beatrice stretched out her hand and took his in an unexpectedly firm grasp. "The Signora is away. She go to Milano for the *Natale.* I remain here and guard the house and all the villas entirely."

And I wonder if you guard them for BAST, also? Bond thought.

"Come, I will show you." Beatrice gave his hand a short tug, like a child leading him into the villa, then stopped. "Ah, I forget. Already you know. You have before been here, yes?"

He smiled and nodded, following her into the big white room with arched ceiling and matching sofas and chairs, encased in cream covers. There were three glass-topped tables, four lamps with surrounds of white glass shaped like opening lilies, and four paintings—one in the style of Hockney, an unknown man leaning against the chrome surround of the pool; three others of various garden views which needed no explaining to Bond.

In spite of Beatrice's realization of the fact that he already knew the place, she continued to lead him around, almost at breakneck speed, showing off the three large bedrooms—"You will have trouble in making your mind which to use, hu? Or possibly you use them one at a time. Different each night. You are alone, hu? A pity. One different each night would be enjoyable." This last followed by grandsire triples of laughter.

The villa was on one level: just the main room, with doors off to the three bedrooms, and a narrow passage— neatly contrived to store two refrigerators, food, china, pots, pans and cutlery—leading to the kitchen. The rear of the main room was arched and, in turn, led to the dining area: the whole beautifully furnished with a clever mix of old and new, each room taking on a style of its own. Behind the dining area you passed through a pair of french windows onto a second terrace, on the left of which, steps led up to a flat roof, converted into an open-sided room— simply a wood and rush roof, topped by a weathercock, supported by heavy wooden beams and furnished with a long refectory table, making an excellent dining area in summer. The view looked out toward the little white and gray old town of Forio, with its ancient refurbished church of Our Lady of Succor, brilliant white, built with simple architectural lines, perched on the older gray stone projecting from the headland of Soccorso.

The rain had cleared, and there was a little winter sun which seemed to hit the church, tiny in the distance, then bounce off to sprinkle and glitter on the water. Bond looked back at the town, with its hills rising above, then returned his gaze to the promontory and the church.

"Is beautiful, eh?" Beatrice stood by his side. "This is for the help of fishermen; for all who sail. Our Lady of Soccorso takes care of them."

"We have a hymn," Bond unexpectedly heard himself say. "It is a prayer. *Oh hear us when we cry to Thee, for those in peril on the sea.*"

"Is good."

She was standing close to him, and even in the chill of this winter day he could smell the sunshine on her. A sweetness that seemed to have been trapped in the strong hot weeks of summer, mingled with a scent he could not identify.

He turned and walked back, pausing by the steps to look at this incredible wonder which lay behind the villa.

At one time, the local people had thought the Signora—who, as Beatrice had said, was now in Milan—was mad. Widow of a great artist, she had bought this land: barren rock. She had arranged for some of it to be blasted away, shaping it into a kind of amphitheater. Hard against the side of the rock she had then built a large villa which looked like a gray, buttressed fortress. The four small villas which she rented out in the summer were converted from old structures, once shepherds' huts and barns. But her greatest achievement had been The Garden, which was reflected in some of the pictures back in the Villa Capricciani.

She had gathered together men who loved growing things, as she did, and, with immense toil and frustration had built this incredible, beautiful place, full of cyprus, palm, mountain flowers, flowering shrubs and bushes, shaded walks, ponds and fountains, water tricks which would hurl liquid into great archways over paths, or imitate a mountain stream pouring endlessly from bare rock into a blue pool from whence it was recycled to create the illusion of constant moving water. The ponds were peopled by small turtles and goldfish, and even in winter there was color, from hardy plants. All year round there was some form of natural color, and the beauty of this place stayed in Bond's memory. Once seen, The Garden lived with you,

as though it had been implanted in your mind through
some magic of its own creation.

He looked up along the stone-encrusted ridge at the far
end of the great scooped rock, and allowed his eyes to trace
their way along the zigzag of paths and walks, the trees and
bushes bent, growing at angles determined by the harsh
winds of winter. Indeed, this was a work of great love and
dedication. The local people had long since come to understand that the Signora should be treated with awe and
reverence.

"Is a great genius, the Signora," Beatrice said, as though
speaking of a saint.

"An amazing lady." Bond smiled at her, standing to one
side to allow the girl to descend first, as he looked down at
the rear terrace. Since the moment they had met by the
pool he had been careful to keep Beatrice in view. Even
when she had come close to him on the open, covered
rooftop, he had made sure his body had always been turned
toward her with one hand braced, stiff and tense, to be used
as a cutting edge should she make a wrong move. For all
he knew, the effervescent Beatrice could well be the Cat,
Saphii Boudai, or at least one of her messengers.

Once back in the house, she said she would light the
stove. "It will become cold tonight, and I do not wish an
invalid on my hands." She gave him a sideways glance as
though to imply that she would not mind him on her hands
if he was fit and willing.

Bond merely smiled and said he would go down to the
car and get his luggage. "Have you the keys?" he asked. "I
should lock the gates."

"Of course. They are in the kitchen. In their usual
place." A pause of four or five heartbeats, then, "Every-

thing is in the kitchen as you expect." Another pause, slightly shorter. *"Everything,* Signor Bond."

"Call me James," he threw back over his shoulder. If she was on the side of the devils and not the angels, it would be best to meet her on Christian-name terms. They said that knowing the name of devil or angel always put you at the advantage.

The bunch of seven or eight keys lay on the freestanding kitchen unit. They were attached to a penlight key ring and looked as though they had just been tossed onto the work-top, even though the smallest key stuck out separately and was aligned with the edge of the unit. He picked the whole lot up by the small key, inserting it into the lock on the drawer just below the point where the bunch had been lying. It turned easily.

Inside the drawer lay one 9mm Browning automatic and three spare ammunition clips. The action moved slickly, well oiled, and showed there was a round in the chamber. Later he would strip the weapon down and go through it piece by piece. "There'll be a pistol in the locked kitchen drawer," M had said. Had Beatrice put it there? Or had she merely been inquisitive and found the secret?

Bond hefted the pistol in his hand. The weight seemed right for a fully loaded weapon. The spare magazines also appeared to be correct, but he knew weapons and ammunition could easily be doctored to feel right. If that happened, then the last thing you ever knew was that someone had been clever, spiked the firing pin, mechanism, or even the rounds.

For the time being he simply had to trust, slipping the spare magazines into the pockets of his windbreaker, put-ting the Browning's safety to "on," and pushing it into his waistband, far to the left so that it was hidden, then pulling the butt down so that the muzzle was screwed to the left. This was always advisable. Movie cops and agents so often jammed a pistol straight into the waistband, risking a shot foot, or worse—"testicide" as one leathery weapons instructor had called it.

He locked the drawer again and went out of the kitchen door, which contained a glass panel. On his way down, he went through the whole catastrophe of the Villa Capricciani's security. The main gates, and the gate at the foot of the steps, could be taken out quickly enough, either by scaling, or the use of a lock gun. The pair of sliding doors which led from the villa to the front terrace would be a noisy job, but could be accomplished quickly. The kitchen door was simplicity, particularly with the one pane of glass, while the rear french windows offered easy access using a jimmy. Ninety seconds at the most for any of them, he calculated as he secured the bolts on the main gate, and took his heavy case from the car.

He locked the second gate behind him and went up the stairs and in through the main sliding doors. Beatrice was standing by the telephone, checking the meter which would monitor all outgoing calls. She looked up and gave him her cheeky smile, reading off the numbers and asking him to agree them.

"Now, I show you what food is here." Another smile as she led him toward the kitchen. "You found all you needed?" Over her shoulder with eye contact and the same smile.

Bond nodded. She loves me? She loves me not?

She opened the refrigerator with a flourish, and began to reel off all the provisions she had bought. Chicken, veal, eggs, butter, cheese, milk, three bottles of wine, bacon, sausage, pâté, pasta. In the other small fridge set into the opposite units of cupboards and drawers there were vegetables.

"Is enough until tomorrow?"

"Only if I've got an army staying overnight."

"Tomorrow is last proper shopping before *Natale.*" Tomorrow was Saturday and Christmas Eve.

"Yes," Bond mused. "Christmas is a'coming and the goose is getting fat . . ."

"You wish for goose?"

He shook his head. "Old English children's rhyme. No, Beatrice, I don't know how I'll celebrate Christmas—*Natale.*"

"In England you have snow, yes?"

"Usually only on the Christmas cards. We gather the whole family together, give each other unsuitable gifts, and eat ourselves stupid. Turkey, as a rule. I do not like turkey." He looked at her hard and asked how she would be spending Christmas.

"At the big villa. On my own. I told you. I am in charge. Umberto and Franco, two of the gardeners, will come in to see all is well, and maybe one of the young girls we have to help when the villas are all occupied, or the Signora is at home, will call to see me."

"Well, I'll probably drive into Forio and buy some kind of special feast we can share. How about that?" If she were a devil, then at least he would know where she was; if an angel, it would not matter.

"This is good, Signor Bond—James. This I would like."

"Okay." He found the dark eyes disconcerting, for they locked on to his like radar.

"Now I must go back to the house. The big villa. La Signora she telephones me each day. In"—her slim wrist came up showing her watch—"in about fifteen minutes. I must be there always for her. Otherwise is lot of shouting over the telephone. Is not good."

Bond saw she was wearing a very functional wristwatch. Black metal, with all the bells and whistles Middle Eastern airline pilots liked on their chronometers.

Beatrice paused by the doors leading to the rear terrace. "Look, James. I make good cannelloni. How if I come down tonight and cook for you?"

The temptation went in and out of Bond's mind in the time it takes for an expert to slit a throat. He smiled and shook his head. "Very kind of you, Beatrice. Perhaps tomorrow. I'm tired and want to make it an early night. Need the rest. You know, light meal and bed with a good book."

"You're missing one of the great delights of Ischia," she said, the cheekiness in both face and voice.

"I'll make up for it." But, by the time he said it, she had disappeared. All that remained was the soft patter of her shoes on the path leading back to the main villa.

He chose the bedroom at the back of the house: the one furthest away from any of the doors and windows. It was large with a big, old-fashioned wooden bed, built-in closets fitted with doors and interiors that had once belonged to a pair of beautiful old wardrobes. There was a complicated icon facing the bed—elongated figures, a fussy combination of faith and philosophy that showed the Trinity surrounded by saints and angels. It looked like a genuine product of the Stroganov school, but who would know? A doctor friend of Bond's could have knocked a similar piece off in a matter of weeks, then aged it over twelve months and nobody but an advanced expert would have known.

He hung up the one suit and two spare pairs of slacks, carefully put the shirts, socks and other items in the drawers which formed one side of each closet and laid out the short toweling robe he had brought with him. Lastly he casually threw a heavy rollneck sweater onto the bed, placed a little leather-cased tool kit on the night table, then went into the main room to the telephone.

The number in England picked up on the third ring. "Predator," said Bond.

"Hellkin." The voice was clear from the distant line. "Repeat. Hellkin."

"Acknowledge." Bond put down the receiver. "We will give what cover we can," M had said. "There will be a daily password so that everyone knows what's what." The instructions were that Bond should telephone on arrival. After that he would call at a similar time every twenty-four hours. The word of the day would be given, and that would last until the next contact. "Don't want our own people getting shot up," M had said as though he did not give a damn who got shot up.

In the kitchen, Bond prepared a light meal: a four-egg omelette with a tomato salad. He ate alone, there in the kitchen and confined his drinking to three glasses of the red wine Beatrice had provided. The label said it was a Vino Gran Caruso and he did not doubt it for a minute. He even toyed with the idea of taking a fourth glass, but in view of his situation he left it at three.

After the meal he went around the entire villa to make certain every lock was applied, every bolt closed, and all curtains drawn. Then he sat in the main room, with the tool kit beside him, and stripped the 9mm automatic, examining each part before reassembling it. Then, carefully using two pairs of pliers, he removed the bullets from four rounds of ammunition, each taken at random from the four magazines. Once he checked that they were the real thing Bond disposed of the mutilated shells, filled one magazine and slammed it into the Browning's butt, cocking the mechanism before readjusting the other clips—one full, the other two with a couple of rounds short.

It was almost ten o'clock by the time he was ready for the next move. In the bathroom he showered, then changed into the thick rollneck, heavy cord slacks, and a pair of soft black moccasins. He strapped on a leather shoulder holster from the bottom of his case, then shrugged on his windbreaker before sliding the Browning in place and distributing the spare magazines around his pockets. It was not, he considered, going to be the most comfortable Christmas week he had ever spent.

Finally, Bond moved from room to room, starting at the kitchen, altering the furniture, placing it against doors and near window-entry points before strewing bottles and cans from the kitchen like mines across the floor. He worked back toward his bedroom so that anyone who managed to gain entrance would have to use a flashlight or cause a great deal of noise. Even with a flashlight, a trained man would have problems in not bumping against, or falling over, one of the obstacles. He stretched strings between chairs, tying them to pots and pans. He even fitted simple booby traps, of pans, plastic buckets and cooking utensils near doors or the smaller windows.

He then arranged the pillows in the bed so that the impression to any intruder would be that he was quietly sleeping. It was a very old dodge, but one that worked efficiently on an assassin doing a quick in-and-out job. Lastly, Bond pulled a sleeping bag from the bottom of his case and, still moving furniture and scattering traps, he put out the lights, carefully heading toward the french windows which led from the dining room to the rear terrace.

The sky was clear outside, and the moon not fully up as yet. Silently he closed and locked the windows, making his way slowly and without a sound to the covered rooftop. The night air stung his face with cold, but, once zipped snug inside the sleeping bag, set close to the wall near the steps, James Bond closed his eyes and drifted into a light sleep.

Sleep, for Bond, was always shallow: it came with the job. When he woke it was suddenly, his eyes snapping open, all senses alert, ears straining for sounds. Certainly there was a soft noise, a scraping coming from below, near the french windows.

He quietly unzipped himself from the sleeping bag, rolled away and stood up, Browning out and ready with the safety off—all in a matter of thirty or forty seconds. Crouching, he peered over the parapet at the top of the open steps leading to the rear terrace.

The moon was sinking, but still gave him enough light to see the figure, kneeling and examining the lock.

Hardly breathing, he inched toward the steps. Below, the figure rose and he could see the intruder's shape and form coming up from the kneeling position, straightening and turning carefully. There was a weapon in the crouching figure's hand, an automatic pistol, held with both hands, as the person moved with the proficiency of an expert.

As she turned, Bond stood up, arms stretched out, grasping his own pistol, feet apart in the classic stance.

"Don't even think about it, Beatrice," he said loudly. "Just drop the gun and kick it away."

The figure below turned sharply, giving a sudden little gasp.

"Do as I say! Now!" Bond commanded.

7

Hellkin

She did not drop the pistol, but threw it into the bushes so that it made no noise.

"James. Hellkin," she whispered. "Hellkin. There's someone in the grounds."

Her voice, Bond thought, had lost its broad accent, and she had given him the code, obeyed his orders, but with the care of one who wishes to avoid noise that might just be heard by some third person. He came down the steps quickly, keeping his back to the wall. "Hellkin" was enough for him.

"What did you see or hear?" He was close to her, whispering in her ear.

"A flashlight. Down by the second gate. Five minutes ago. I came straightaway."

"You saw it from where?"

"The main villa. I was on watch: the balcony at the top."

"Find your pistol." Bond cocked his head in the direction of the bushes. "Then follow me down and cover me."

She dropped to her knees and then flattened her body, squirming into the undergrowth while Bond kept his back to the french windows, standing stock-still, waiting for her. Hellkin, he thought. She was on the side of the angels but the intellectuals who still chose cryptos and code names in London were being clever-clever. He seemed to recall that Hellkin was one of the twelve fork-bearing lesser demons of Dante's Inferno. Hellkin—Alchino, the Allurer. Well, Beé-ah-Treé-che was certainly alluring.

She was back with him now, holding up a Browning 9mm similar to his.

"Cover me," he whispered again as he moved along the wall, flattening himself at the corner, then going around it fast, pistol up ready to take out anyone skulking near the kitchen door.

Nobody. He moved on along the wall, back flat to the stucco again, glancing behind to see that Beatrice was following. He could make out the dark shape against the white wall, inching forward, hands locked around the pistol, elbows bent so that the weapon came level with her forehead.

The next turning of the wall would bring them to the front of the villa: to the terrace and winter-covered pool. Bond threw himself forward, rolled across the terrace, arms stretched out and pistol at the ready.

He saw the movement close to the gate at the foot of the steps and shouted, "Halt! Halt, we're armed."

Whoever was on the other side of the gate imagined they

were in with a chance for two bullets ripped through the water lilies and palms, gouging hunks out of the green floor covering of the terrace, all a little close to Bond for comfort. He could see nothing now, but heard the quick double bark of Beatrice's Browning and a little cry, like an animal mewing with pain.

Bond spun around just in time to see Beatrice come pounding out of the shadows in pursuit of whoever had been hit on the other side of the gate. He shouted to her to stop, seeing the dangers that could lurk below the steps. They would not simply send one man to deal with him. Unless he was greatly mistaken a whole hit team would be operational and, if anything, Beatrice had probably winged the locksmith who had not even got through the single, second, gate.

He followed her, trying to keep close to the wall in the darkness, wincing in anticipation of the fatal burst of machine-gun fire that would surely come at any moment. Somewhere from outside, a fair way off, he heard the stutter of a car ignition, then the grind of gears. . . .

Beatrice had reached the gate without any further shots coming out of the night, turning her head and calling, low-voiced, "The keys, James. You have the keys."

He already had them out on the penlight ring in his left hand, running his fingers through them to select the key to the inner gate.

Beatrice had stopped with her back to the wall, trying to find cover in the slim stem of a vine as Bond passed her, fumbling with the keys. It took around twenty seconds which seemed like an hour, but, when the key turned, there was Beatrice at his back, preparing to give covering fire.

Nobody. No movement. No sudden fire slashing through

the night. Only wet spots of blood around the gate, showing dark, like oil, in the small beam from the penlight.

They spread out, Bond moving left to the car, the girl to the right, crouching and ready, heading for the main gates.

It took thirty seconds to give the Fiat a perfunctory going over. It was locked and untouched. They both reached the gates, and saw that they had been breached with a lock pistol, the bolt of which had smashed out the flat oblong mechanism, as it was propelled at high speed by a CO_2 cartridge.

Together they even ventured into the road, Bond crossing first while Beatrice covered him. For ten minutes or so they offered themselves as targets. Nothing. Had the team been frightened off so easily? To the girl he said they should try and secure the gate. She nodded. "I have a chain and padlock. I'll get them now." She moved quickly back into the turning circle within the gates and sped up the steps toward the villa.

Bond looked over the Fiat again, just for the insurance, then leaned against the wall. Why all this trouble for me? he asked himself. Certainly the supposedly undercover job on *Invincible* had responsibilities. But taking out one man, himself, would make no lasting difference: someone would take his place. He recalled M's words about their intelligence-gathering. "They imagine you're unique," the Old Man had said. "They think your presence on *Invincible* is very bad medicine for them." M had made a sarcastic one-note laugh. "I suppose BAST and its leaders are your fan club, 007. You should send them an autographed picture."

Bond shrugged in the dark. That was not the point. He was the stalking horse, the tethered goat who might bring BAST to *him*. It was a pity they had obviously managed to spirit away the member of the team Beatrice had winged. But it was thorough thinking on their part. There was plenty of time and it would be best to move one injured man or woman to safety before they tried again. Later tonight—or morning as it was now? He looked at his watch. Three-thirty on a cold and dangerous morning, and all was not well.

He heard Beatrice come down the steps, two at a time, but wonderfully light on her feet.

Together they wrapped the chain around the gates, securing the ground bolts which went into metal and concrete holes, then clicking the large, strong padlock into place. A last look around and they turned back, through the second gate, which Bond locked, and went around the villa to the rear terrace.

"I'll make coffee." Her tone had something about it that you did not argue with, so he unlocked the rear windows and let her go in first. When he turned the lights on she said something about the place looking as though gypsies had been camping there. "You were being pretty thorough. Anyone coming in here would have made quite a din."

"That was the general idea." Bond smiled. "I didn't know I had a bodyguard so close. Why didn't you tell me?"

"Not in my brief," she said, almost curtly and in perfect English.

"I owe you my life."

"Then you owe me mine." She turned, smiling, putting the pistol down on one of the tables. "How can you ever repay me?"

"We'll think of some way." Bond's mouth was only inches from hers. He hovered, then turned away. "Coffee," he said. "We must stay alert, they could be back."

"It'll be light soon," Beatrice said, busying herself in the kitchen. "I doubt they'll return in the daytime."

"How much do you know?"

"That you're here, and that there's a contract out on you."

"And how much do you know about contracts?"

"I'm fully trained."

"That's not the answer. I asked how much do you know about contracts?"

"I know it's some crazy terrorist organization called BAST. And I've been told that they know where to find you. That they'll go to great lengths—"

"Suicidal lengths, Beatrice. That's why we shouldn't restrict ourselves. They can try to get me on the street, or here, by day or night. I'm the magnet, they are the iron filings. We *want* one of them. Alive if possible. So, we have to keep our guard up twenty-four hours a day."

She remained silent for the few minutes it took her to pour boiling water over the freshly ground coffee in the tall cafetière, adjust the lid and push down on the plunger. "Are you intimidated, James?" Her eyes did not move from the coffeepot.

"How intimidated?"

"Because you were given a woman bodyguard."

Bond laughed. "Far from it. Why do some women automatically think that people in our trade are antifeminist? Well-trained women are sometimes better than men in situations like this. You nearly took one of them out tonight. I didn't get near. You were also quicker than I. No. Not guilty to being intimidated."

"Good." She raised her head, the dark eyes flashing with something which could have been either pride or power.

106

"Good. Because you're in *my* charge. I'm the boss, and you do as *I* say. Understand?"

The smile disappeared from Bond's face. "I have no orders. Just act naturally, they said. We'll have someone watching out for you, they said."

"And that someone is me." Beatrice was pouring the coffee. "Black? Good. Sugar?"

"No."

"Wise choice. If you're worried about taking orders from a woman, why don't you telephone London. Give them the day's code for me and they'll tell you." Her eyes met his again and this time they locked. For half a dozen heartbeats it seemed to be a battle of wills. Then Bond nodded curtly and crossed the room to the telephone. He could not speak in clear language, but there were enough double-talk phrases for him to get at the truth.

They picked up on the third ring. "Predator for Sunray." His anger betrayed itself in his clipped tone. He took field orders from M; or, when necessary, Bill Tanner. For Beatrice to reveal that she, as his bodyguard, was in charge scraped at the nerve ends of his considerable pride.

A second later a voice—that of the duty officer—said, "Sunray. Yes?"

"Contact with Boxcar." This last was an agreed running cipher for BAST.

"Serious?" the DO asked.

"Serious enough. Also contact with Hellkin."

"Good."

"Request order of battle, Sunray."

"Hellkin leads. You follow, Predator."

"Thank you, Sunray." Bond's face was stiff with anger, but turned away from Beatrice as he recradled the telephone. He shrugged. "It appears you're right." He rearranged his face, "So, Beatrice Hellkin, what're your orders?"

She nodded toward the large mug placed on the table in front of him. "First, drink your coffee." She was sitting on one of the big chairs, her body stretched back and a pleasant, friendly smile playing around her lips. She was dressed in black jeans and rollneck, an ensemble that was practical and almost accentuated her figure. The jeans were tight, clinging to her long legs, while the rollneck showed off her breasts, small and firm against the cotton.

"So, you don't think they'll have another go today?"

She shook her head. "Not here. We should watch it when we go out."

"Go out?"

"Weren't you going to get food as a nice surprise for Christmas?"

"Oh, yes. *Natale,* yes. What happened to the Italian accent, Beatrice?" Almost sarcastically he pronounced it "Beé-ah-Treé-che."

"Is gone."

"I noticed. So what're your orders?"

"I think we should rest. Then go and do the shopping—behave normally. They might well try while we're out and about, but I must make a telephone call, to get those damned gates fixed. I also think we should bring in the dogs."

"Dogs?"

"We've got two pairs of Rottweilers at our disposal. They're as vicious as they come, and we can let them loose at night."

"You're well organized as a bodyguard. How long have you worked for La Signora?"

She gave an amused little sniff. "Forty-eight hours. The Chief has some big pull with her. She's a pretty well-connected lady, but she moved out for Christmas as a favor to M. She also moved her staff out. The couple of guys I mentioned—Franco and Umberto—are extra-heavy help. They were around when we had that little brush with the BAST team, but they're only for support if things get really tricky." Franco and Umberto were at the main villa, she said. "That's why you can rest easy. I'll alert them now. They can watch until we're ready to go shopping."

She rose, in a series of very attractive moves, and walked slowly to the telephone. Her conversation was short, to the point and in Italian. The two men should take over the watch, and the dogs should be fed only the minimum this morning. They would be let out tonight. In the meantime, would Franco go down and secure the main gates. New lock and, yes, "put a screamer on it."

She left the telephone and paused behind Bond's chair. "See, I am efficient."

"Didn't doubt it for a minute."

She slid forward and sat on the arm of the chair. Once again Bond smelled that mixture of dry summer and the scent he could not identify. "I still think you don't like having a woman in charge."

"What's your real name?" He disregarded her observation.

"Like I told you. Beatrice," she pronounced the Italian way.

"I believe you, but what else? I mean you're not Dante's angel, Beatrice. You have other names?"

She giggled. "They told me you were just a blunt, well-trained instrument. A hunk. Now you're talking literature and poetry. Full name, Beatrice Maria da Ricci. Italian father, English mother. Educated Benenden and Lady Margaret Hall, Oxford. Father in Italian Foreign Service. Their marriage broke up 1972. I was handed over to Mama, who was a lush."

"You're pretty luscious yourself."

"That's not funny," she bridled. "Have you ever had to live with a lush? It just isn't amusing."

"I apologize, Ms da Ricci." There was no sidestepping her anger.

"Okay, I'm touchy about it. I read modern languages, and took the Foreign Service examination—"

"And failed."

"Yes."

"Don't tell me: a man comes around and says that perhaps they can offer you a job within the Foreign Service, and before you know it you're mixed up with all the paraphernalia of espionage."

She nodded. "More or less, but they wanted me for languages. I took another degree in computer sciences and found myself in Santa's Grotto."

Bond nodded. In the basement, below the underground parking at that building overlooking Regent's Park, there was a great sterile computer room they all called Santa's Grotto. With the advent of the microchip the old Registry had been relegated to a smaller area and people were constantly transferring the paperwork onto a series of giant data bases. Rumor had it that all the work would not be completed from past files until the year 2009, or thereabouts, as the crow flies. "Then they remembered you had languages," he filled in.

"Partly. I got sinus trouble from the air conditioning."

"Better than a touch of Legionnaires' Disease."

"I asked for a transfer to the real world."

"No such thing in our business. We're T. S. Eliot's 'Hollow Men'; we are also rust-stained dinosaurs. Our day has come, and gone. I give us a decade more. After that, well, we could be sitting in front of computer terminals all day and most of the night. It's known as the invasion of the killer tomatoes syndrome."

She nodded gravely. "Yes, the days of the Great Game are numbered."

"The years are numbered. We're not down to days yet. But, Beatrice Maria da Ricci, which is a classy sort of name anyway, how did a nice girl like you end up in a sordid bullet-catcher's job like this?"

She leaned over him, her face a few inches from his. "Because I am very good at it, and part of my job, James Bond, is to keep you relaxed and happy."

"Meaning?"

Their mouths met. Not simply lips brushing, or doing all the things graphically described in romantic novels or those historical things known in the trade as "bodice rippers." This was real mouth-to-mouth resuscitation of other emotions. After a minute their bodies and hands also moved, and five minutes later Beatrice said, with a husky dryness that matched the delightful smell of her, "Would you like to lie down with me, Mr. Bond?"

"You're a pleasure to work for, Ms da Ricci."

"I hope so."

"Do I get a raise in salary?"

"I think you already got one, Mr. Bond."

They barely made it to the bedroom. Outside, the sun had come up. Franco was working on the main gates, fitting a new lock and the electronic sensors that would scream an alarm should anyone tamper with them again. In the rear bedroom of the Villa Capricciani there were low moans and little screams of joy.

In a room high in the main gray, fortresslike villa, the other hood called Umberto stood back in the shadows and scanned the garden and the rocky skyline above them. If anything was going to happen, it would probably come from that direction and not the main gates. A frontal attack had proved dangerous. He wondered if his new boss, the girl who was very much in charge, and whom he had met for the first time a couple of days ago, was vulnerable to a frontal attack. He guessed she was—but not for the hired help.

·　　·　　·

Far away, in Plymouth three men had spent the night indulging in the sins of the flesh. They had drunk a great deal, and one of them had been with a tall black girl who had done things to, and for, him that had until now been only fantasies.

"It's time for the deadline," Harry said to the Petty Officer they called Blackie.

"Time to sell your soul and save all of us," added Bill.

"Oh, Gawd." Blackie had been putting off the evil day. Stalling for time and knowing time was a commodity he had run out of long ago. It was Christmas Eve and he had the rail ticket in his pocket to return to the wife and kids for two weeks' leave.

"It's serious." Bill's face was set, engraved with concern.

"It was serious when we first told you. Now we're all in a mess . . ."

"I know; I know . . ."

"All debts settled and one hundred thousand pictures of her Majesty just for you, Blackie."

"Yeah. I just—"

"Look, Blackie." Bill had wrapped his large strong fingers around the Petty Officer's wrist, making the man wince with pain. "Look, it's not as though you were being asked to steal anything. These people need a few hours, that's all."

"I know . . ." He paused, his bleary eyes moving slowly around the room. "I know, and I ain't got no option, have I?"

"Not really." Harry was quiet, soft-spoken and persuasive.

The Petty Officer nodded. "Okay, I'll do it."

"That's a solemn promise?" from Bill.

"On my mother's grave."

"They'll give you time, place and the equipment before you leave. If it happens, you'll get the money and the slate's wiped clean. If you chicken out . . . well, I wouldn't fancy your chances. Harry and me? Well, we can always do a runner. Tough, but we could do it—just. You have nowhere to hide, Blackie, and they'd come looking fast as a swarm of hornets, and a lot more painful."

"I said I'd do it." The Petty Officer was very convincing. But, then, he was not lying. As far as he was concerned, all other options had run out.

•   •   •

A 9mm Browning automatic pistol is not the easiest thing to conceal about your person. This is why the "close-protection" experts advise smaller, lighter weapons which will do just the same job. Beatrice carried her pistol in a shoulder bag; Bond used the holster, adjusted so that the pistol lay directly behind his left shoulder blade.

Franco and Umberto, who had both stayed well out of sight, were left to look after matters while Bond and Beatrice went off into Forio on their shopping expedition. On this Saturday the little town, with its narrow streets and limited parking facilities, strictly controlled by the local *polizia,* was crowded with people doing their last odds and ends of Christmas shopping.

They found a place to park legally, and Beatrice, who had made a list of food and other good things that would allow them a pleasant, somewhat gluttonous day, led the way to the nearest market where she shuffled Bond from aisle to aisle, knowing instinctively where the various items were to be found. They filled one large wire cart, with a mind of its own, in a matter of twenty minutes and Bond noticed to his pleasure that Beatrice hardly looked at the shelves at all. She would murmur where he should go next and reel off the list of required items, but her eyes were alertly stabbing around the crowded market, and she kept one hand inside her shoulder bag.

Bond felt that he had found the compleat pro in Ms Beatrice Maria da Ricci. Everything she did adhered to best security practice, and she appeared to have eyes in the back of her head. At one point, while facing away from him, she murmured, "No, James. Not the Belgian ones. Take the French, they're a few lire more, but one hundred percent better." Or, again, in similar circumstances, "The bottles, not the tins. Once you open a tin you have to use the whole lot. The bottles will seal again."

114

They even bought a small tree and some gaudy baubles. "A Christmas to remember." She smiled at him, the black eyes inviting him to return immediately to the delights of the morning. It was the one time during the expedition that she actually looked at Bond.

They loaded their purchases into the car, and Bond insisted on going on his own to make a secret transaction. She did not like it, but agreed to stand guard in front of the shop: a jeweler's in which he bought an exquisite gold clasp, shaped like a *scutum*—the old oblong or oval shield used by the early Roman Army—with a large diamond center and an edging of smaller diamonds. It cost a ransom, but they took Amex and he would pay for it with his private money. The little jeweler smiled a lot and gift-wrapped the piece with exaggerated care. It was only when he was back on the street again that Bond realized it had been a long time since he had bought such an extravagant gift for a woman: particularly one he had known for less than twenty-four hours. Could it really happen like this? he wondered. Women had come easily to him, but his own expertise, and the exigencies of his Service life, had usually held him back from any deep involvement. Had he really broken the rule of years?

He drove, with Beatrice giving instructions. They finally reached an intersection where the traffic was blocked, held at bay or waved on by a tall, unhappy-looking police officer.

Beatrice had her pistol on her lap, hand wound around the butt, her eyes moving everywhere at once, darting constantly to the vanity mirror on the sun visor, which she had pulled down.

Slowly the traffic crept toward the white stop marker until it was the little Fiat's turn. Bond had his eyes on the cop, waiting for the quick hand signal that would wave him on, when suddenly he sensed other eyes on him to the right and directly ahead. He moved and saw, with a sense of shock, a girl turn away quickly and start to walk at speed with her back to him. But he recognized her in that one fast glance, and the movement of her body, as she stepped along the pavement.

There was a parping of motor horns, and Beatrice testily snapped, "He's waving you on, James. For heaven's sake, move."

He slid the clutch out and negotiated the turn, the traffic cop making a gesture with his eyes and head which indicated that this driver ought not to be allowed on the road at all.

He drove back to the Villa Capricciani with a troubled mind, wondering what in heaven's name First Officer Clover Pennington, of the RNAS Yeovilton, was doing on Ischia: particularly what she was doing in the town of Forio, not five miles from where he was staying.

8

All the Other Demons

For a few seconds, James Bond wondered if it was guilt gnawing at his conscience. He had certainly shown, at the least, a sexual attraction to Clover, but this had gone cold when she proved to be an uncertain security risk. There had been something not quite right about First Officer Pennington. Now her geographic proximity to him triggered anxiety. He would tell Beatrice when the moment was right, later.

The gates were open at the Villa Capricciani, and a short, stocky young man stood near the steps. He wore jeans and a *passé* T-shirt which proclaimed THE MAN WHO DIES WITH THE MOST TOYS WINS. His hair was golden-bleached by the now departed summer sun, and the muscles visible on his arms were toned to an awesome strength. Take off the

T-shirt, Bond thought, and his body would give an impression of sixteenth-century armor, complete with breastplate, vambraces and pauldrons. Even from this distance you could mark him down as a trained minder. "Franco," Beatrice explained.

He started to unload the car while Beatrice spoke in a soft murmur to Franco, who eventually came down, closed the gates, locked them and, with a conspiratorial wink, handed a key to Bond. He also pointed to a tiny switch set in the wall, all but covered by ivy. In almost tedious dumb show, Franco activated the switch, indicating that if anyone fiddled with the gates or lock, the "screamers" would begin wailing.

Then they all went up to the villa, and Franco disappeared through the rear french windows on his way back to the big villa. He looked like a man who would not need to use the doors, but could walk straight through the walls, pausing only to shake brick dust from his hair.

Leaving Beatrice to deal with the food and drink, Bond went down the steps again, locked the car, made it secure, and returned, locking the inner gate behind him.

"They're not going to like it." Beatrice came to him, holding him gently in her arms and pressing herself against his body.

"They're not going to get it." Bond smiled down at her.

She sighed. "Oh, James, be your age."

"I usually am." He was genuinely surprised to have used such an old schoolboy piece of repartee. Beatrice seemed to have wrought an unexpected change in him.

"Listen to me. Poor old Franco and Umberto will have to spend this Christmas as watchers. The Rottweilers will prowl the grounds, and I'm not going to let you, my darling

James, out of my sight, unless the bloody BAST people have another go."

"Eat your hearts out, Franco and Umberto."

"Mmmm," she nodded. "I'm going up to the big villa now. Give them instructions. Make an obligatory phone call. Then I'll be back and the celebrations can commence." She gave him a gentle kiss on the cheek, and he felt that his face had never yet been kissed like this. Beatrice had the art of kissing a cheek as though it were his mouth, or even his deepest secret being. Kissing, he considered, was a lost art in this crumbling, shock-ridden world. Beatrice had rediscovered it, and now practiced the craft in a way that had been hidden for centuries. He stood on the rear terrace, listening to her footsteps on the stone path, wondering what had happened to him. He had never been one for quick, serious decisions of the heart. Quick, serious decisions were for operational Service matters, not for women. Yet this girl had certainly worked a powerful and potent magic. He felt, after one day, that he had known her for most of his life.

It was untypical, and it worried him, for, in this short space of time, Beatrice had started to command his heart. Bond's discipline was such that this rarely happened. Even the courting of his now dead wife had taken time. Apart from that one instance, he was one of life's natural playboy bachelors as far as women were concerned: one who had so often lived by the three Fs—Find, Fornicate and Forget. It was the safest way in his job, for basically he believed field officers should be married only if they needed the cover. It was a cold and clinical approach, but the right one. Beatrice was turning it upside down.

He thought about this dilemma for some time, then remembered there was a new code word to collect, so he turned back into the villa and dialed London.

The number in England picked up, as usual, on the third ring. "Predator," said Bond. "Day two."

"Dragontooth." The voice was clear from the distant line. "Repeat. Dragontooth."

"Acknowledge." Bond put down the receiver. So some of the intelligentsia who burrowed away in the Regent's Park office *were* trying to be clever. In his extreme youth, Bond had read much, and his memory was almost photographic. He called back the lines now, from Dante Alighieri's *Inferno* in *The Divine Comedy*.

> Front and centre here, Grizzly and Hellkin . . .
> You too, Deaddog . . .
> Curlybeard, take charge of a squad of ten.
> Take Grafter and *Dragontooth* along with you.
> Pigfusk, Catclaw, Cramper and Crazyred. . . .

They were some of the named demons with forked claws and rakes who tended, and goaded, the damned in their cauldron of boiling pitch. So those at headquarters were now deeply influenced by the strange mystic concept of the Brotherhood of Anarchy and Secret Terrorism—BAST, the three-headed monster who rode on a viper.

"Dragontooth, James." He had not even heard her come in through the french windows behind him. She had been as silent as a cat. "Correct. Dragontooth," he said, thinking, Cat. Could the Pennington girl be the Cat of BAST—Saphii Boudai?

"Dragontooth," he said again, giving Beatrice a sad smile. Behind the smile his brain worked at the equation. Saphii Boudai's file showed her as a dedicated terrorist from her teens. The British authorities had been close to her on two occasions, yet she remained, like the other members of the BAST hierarchy, a ghost; an insubstantial, if deadly, figure with no true form or shape, of which there was no real description. The Pennington girl had a history. A good family. He even knew her uncle, Sir Arthur Pennington, Master of Pennington Nab in the West Country. Her cousins had both been close to him at one time or another. The background was impeccable. Or was it? Another thought struck him.

"What's wrong, James?" Beatrice had come to him, wrapping her arms around his neck and looking into his face with her hypnotic black eyes. The eyes seemed almost to weaken him, and their bottomless darkness drew him into her brain so that all he could see was a possible future with her: a future free from danger and responsibility—except to her.

Bond drew back, holding Beatrice at arms' length. "I saw someone in Forio. Someone who shouldn't be there."

Her face underwent a change. Just a slight twitch of concern, but enough to reveal that this delightful girl had the tough inner resources required by people in their mutual trade. She drew him over to the couch and started to question him—her queries all aimed at the heart of the problem, the reason he was here, in the villa on Ischia. It was plain that, as well as everything else, Beatrice was a skilled interrogator.

He told her everything, in its chronological sequence. First Officer Pennington at Yeovilton, her lax sense of security, and the fact that she was to be in charge of a section of Wrens on draft to *Invincible*—something very much out of the norm for the Royal Navy.

"And she knew of your drafting?" Beatrice asked.

"To where?" he countered, still in control of his own sense of need-to-know, the central pin of all security matters.

"*Invincible,* of course. James, you don't think they would have put me in charge of this assignment without a complete briefing. She knew you were to be in *Invincible* for *Landsea '89?*—the Pennington girl, I mean?"

He nodded. "Yes, and she didn't seem to think it was something she had to keep quiet about. Clover had access to all the draft orders. It was like giving classified information to a gossip columnist. She had as much idea of security, and keeping her mouth shut, as a town crier."

"Mmmm." Beatrice frowned, and Bond thought she even looked attractive when her face became repatterned with anxiety. "Look, James." She laid a hand on his thigh, which seemed to pass a current of signals to alert his most basic physical needs. "Look, I have a secure radio link back to the big villa. This is something I should report now, before it's too late. It won't take long. Are you up to some menial chores, like doing vegetables for tomorrow's dinner?"

Bond rarely bothered himself with the preparation of food. For years it had always been something others did for you. But he simply nodded, and went into the little kitchen while Beatrice left the Villa Capricciani, hurrying, her face reflecting the fact that she considered Clover Pennington's presence on the island, and nearby, to be something of grave concern.

In the kitchen, Bond began to prepare the vegetables, smiling wryly and thinking how M would love to see him now. He would not have been surprised to learn that M had given Beatrice Maria da Ricci instructions to "Put Bond in his place." He could hear the Old Man telling her that 007 was sometimes a shade too conscious of his class for his own good. "Get him to do some physical jobs, like swabbing the decks of that villa." It was the kind of devilment in which M would revel.

•   •   •

In England that Christmas Eve, M was down at Quarterdeck, but not at ease. An extra-secure telephone link had been installed so that he could get information concerning Bond and his situation within seconds of its coming in to Headquarters.

Though M was naturally a solitary person, he did have relatives. A daughter, now married to an academic who worked on incomprehensible and obscure pieces of European history at Cambridge. They had provided M with two grandchildren, a boy and girl, whom he adored and spoiled in, for him, a most uncharacteristic manner.

The tree was trimmed, Mrs. Davison had everything ready, and, during the previous week, M had gone, with her husband on a spending spree, most of the purchases being extravagant playthings for the grandchildren. At Christmas, M seemed to turn into the reformed Scrooge—in fact, part of the Quarterdeck Christmas ritual was a reading from Dickens' *Christmas Carol.* But this year M did not seem to have his heart in the preparations. He sat in his study, unmoved by the Nine Lessons and Carols, broadcast live each year from King's College, Cambridge. This in itself was also unusual, for in spite of his crusty, sharp manner, and weatherbeaten features, Christmas usually brought out a drop of sentiment in M.

His hand seemed to leap to the telephone a second before it rang, and he answered with a crisp "M."

Bill Tanner was at the other secure end. "Something's come through, sir."

M nodded, not even speaking into the instrument. There was a brief pause, then Tanner continued. "Today we've had two contacts. The usual change of cipher. Then another one. A Flash."

"Serious?"

"Not sure, sir. It's a report from Dragontooth. It looks as though the Cat, or one of her lieutenants, is there and very much on the prowl. The query is should we pull her, or wait for her to move?"

"No idea how big her team is?"

"Impossible to tell, sir. Maybe three. Possibly more. Certainly one was wounded in the not overzealous attempt we know about."

M sat, silent, for a full minute. "We need hard intelligence, Chief of Staff. Hard as nails. But, if it serves the purpose, tell Dragontooth to be utterly ruthless. Our contacts with the Italians are still holding up?"

"No problem there, sir."

"Right. Ruthless if necessary. And there's another order . . ." He spoke to Tanner for ten minutes, giving him detailed instructions. Then, with a sharp "Keep me informed," M hung up, wondering why, of all the agents under his command, he worried most about 007. Was he the son the Old Man had always wanted? Difficult. Something not to be dwelt upon.

Behind the rise and fall of *Wassail! Wassail!* he heard his daughter's car crunch on the gravel outside. Banishing all thoughts of what was probably going on far away in Ischia, M fashioned a smile of greeting and went to the door.

• • •

They trimmed the little tree with the cheap and gaudy things bought in the Forio market, prepared everything for tomorrow's dinner and settled down for a light snack of a soup that Beatrice had already put together quickly and allowed to simmer while they were dealing with the tree. There was also bread and a choice of a dozen cheeses, washed down with a bottle of good local wine. Afterward, Bond stretched out in an easy chair, with Beatrice resting her back against his legs, while his arm caressed her shoulder, occasionally dropping to finger one of her breasts.

He had purposely not asked her anything about her contact with London. Now he thought the time was right. "What was their reaction?"

"Whose?"

"London's reaction to the Pennington girl being around."

She twisted her body so that she could look up at him. "Better you shouldn't know. It'll all be taken care of, James. It's under control."

He nodded, trying to explain that all this was new to him. "Normally it's me doing the protection and giving the orders."

"Well." Her voice took on the husky tone he had come to know and appreciate from the previous night, and what had passed between them during the morning. "Well, James, there are some orders you can give me."

"I hadn't noticed it. You're a pretty dominant young woman. Even—"

"Even in bed? I know, but I can change all that. You want to try?"

"Soon." He sounded very relaxed. "You know, Beatrice,

125

I think—barring anything going wrong—this is going to be one of the happiest Christmases ever."

She took his hand from her shoulder and drew it down to her mouth, kissing it, nibbling at the vortex between thumb and forefinger, then gently sucking each finger in turn. At last she asked, "Until now, what's the best Christmas you can remember?"

Bond grunted and stretched. "I think the last Christmas I spent with my parents." His voice also changed, the sentences delivered haltingly, as though he found it difficult to discuss. "I'm a mongrel as well, Bea. Scottish father and Swiss mother. Christmas in a little chalet on Lago Lugano." He gave a laugh. "Odd that it was the best, because I was ill—just recovering, anyway. Chickenpox, measles, that sort of thing."

"Why was it the best?"

He gave an almost schoolboyish smile. "I got everything I asked for. They indulged me. There was an air pistol, as I recall it."

"What else?"

"I had to stay in bed, but my father opened the window and put some tin cans on the ledge. Let me pot away at them for half an hour or so. In the evening they both stayed in my room and ate Christmas dinner from trays. It was different. A final taste of love. I'll never forget it."

"Final? Why final?"

"My parents were killed, climbing, a few weeks later."

"Oh, James." She seemed shocked, as though regretting she had asked.

"A long time ago, Beatrice. Your turn. Your best Christmas ever?"

She twisted around and pulled him down from the chair,

close to her, on the floor. "This Christmas. I never had great Christmases, James, and I've never had things happen to me so quickly before. It's . . . it's all strange. I don't entirely believe it." She took his hand and placed it intimately against her.

Bond fumbled in his pocket and brought out the gift-wrapped package. "Merry Christmas, Beatrice."

She opened it like a child, tearing the paper from it as though she could not wait to see what lay beyond. When she lifted the lid of the box she gave a little cry. "Oh. Oh. Oh, my God, James."

"Like it?"

She looked up at him and he could see the tears staining her cheeks.

Later, in the darkness of the bedroom, and at a crucial moment, she whispered, "Merry Christmas, James darling."

Without thinking, Bond whispered, "God bless us, every one."

Franco, Umberto and the dogs must have done their work well. Nothing came suddenly to interrupt a blissful night, and when the lovers dropped into sleep they did so with quiet untroubled dreams.

Waking at ten-thirty, Beatrice proved to be highly domesticated and moved around the kitchen with speed, preparing their meal. Even the Browning 9mm, tucked into her waistband, did not seem out of place.

They ate chicken, not the traditional turkey. But it was a huge bird, cooked in some mystic manner which she said had been a secret of her mother's. The trimmings were in keeping, however, and after the chicken there was a real Christmas pudding, round like those you saw in Victorian drawings, and very rich, with an outrageously alcoholic brandy sauce. Then came mince pies and nuts.

"What about the crackers?" Bond asked with a laugh.

"Sorry, my darling. Couldn't lay my hands on a single Christmas cracker, nor any kind of favor."

"I think I'll sleep for a week." Bond stretched his arms and yawned.

"Well, that's *not* what you're going to do." She rose. "I'm going to let you drive me to the other side of the island, and we're going to walk off the food and let the sea air clear our heads. Come on." She moved quickly to the front windows, grabbing the keys and sliding them open. "Race you to the car."

Bond picked up his Browning, cocked it and settled it in the shoulder holster, then checked that he had the car keys, and followed her. She had just unlocked the inner gate as he got to the top of the stone steps leading down to it. "Stop. Wait for me!" he called, laughing.

She giggled as he ran after her, heading for the car. Then Bond stopped, eyes widening with horror. The main front gates were drawn apart and he shouted "No!" and again, "No. Beatrice!" as he saw her tug at the car door, hardly believing what his eyes and brain told him. "Beatrice, no! No! Don't open—"

But the car door moved and opened. As it did so, she looked up at him, laughing, happy. Then the ball of flame erupted from inside the Fiat. The wind from the explosion hit him a second later, knocking him backward, making his ears sing, scorching his eyes as the flame leaped from the shattered car.

He reached for the pistol and had it up as someone seized him from behind.

Then life changed. There were cars and people. Men in uniform, others in plainclothes. Some dashed around to the rear of the villa, and through his singing ears, Bond thought he heard barking, then shots, from The Garden.

Somehow he was back in the villa, sitting with the remnants of their Christmas meal still on the table, and a familiar figure was striding through the sliding doors.

"Dragontooth, Captain Bond," Clover Pennington said. "I'm sorry, but it was the only way, and it almost didn't work. Can you hear me, sir? Dragontooth."

Bond looked up at her with loathing and spat out, "Dragontooth, and all the other Demons of the Pit to you!" He even seemed to be cringing back against the chair, as though to get away from her.

9

Northanger

Even though he had seen the ambulance people, firemen, and the police around the twisted and blackened shell that had once been the Fiat, James Bond could not take all of it in. Vaguely, in the far corner of his mind, he realized that he must be in shock, but every time he turned to Clover Pennington he expected to see the trim and bubbly Beatrice Maria da Ricci. He could not believe she was dead, even though Clover was spelling it out to him: slowly, as one explains to a child, and loudly as his ears still rang from the explosion.

"She was either Cat or one of Cat's close accomplices," Clover told him, time and time again. It was like being beaten over the head. Occasionally a plainclothesman came to her, muttered in her ear and received a reply. "M had the staff here checked out. One of our people spotted there had been some kind of a switch when they saw the man called Franco in the gardens. We went on full alert then. Nobody was sure of the situation. That is until I spotted you with her yesterday."

Another couple of men came in through the french windows and spoke to her. Clover's eyes flicked toward Bond, then away. When the men left she said that, unhappily, the two men Beatrice had at the house had been killed in the firefight. "My orders were to be absolutely ruthless, though we had to try and get at least one of the team alive. Unhappily we didn't manage it, and I'm uncertain whether the Ricci girl was the Cat or not. . . . And"—she paused, embarrassed—"and I don't know if we'll ever get confirmation. She must have taken the full blast. There's nothing, or very little, left. Sorry," she added, as though apologizing.

Bond sat, staring into space as though he was taking nothing in. "She gave me the right daily codes," he said, his voice like that of a robot.

"They had the telephone in here wired. Picked it all up at the big villa." Clover, in her pleated gray skirt, sweater and sensible shoes, felt she was still not really getting to him. "Captain Bond? James? Sir?" she tried. But he still sat, staring into space.

Someone switched on the radio in the kitchen. "Have yourself a merry little Christmas," the late Bing Crosby sang in English, and she saw Bond's head lift, cocked to one side.

"Put that off, you clown!" Clover shouted, then turned back to Bond. "They've found the regular staff, and the watchers our people put in. At least they're alive: gagged and bound in the wine cellars. We'll know more when our fellows provide their reports and descriptions. Now, I have to get you out of here, sir. Do you understand? We really do have to debrief you as well."

Finally, Bond nodded, slowly, as though common sense had started to prevail. In his head, whenever someone made a noise, dropped something, or talked too loudly, he heard the deafening double-crump again, and clearly saw Beatrice smiling at him, pulling open the car door, then being engulfed by the explosion. The ringing in his ears had turned into a permanent whine. He looked up at Clover Pennington. "I want to speak, personally, to M," he said coldly.

"Not yet, James—er, sir. Not yet. We *do* have to move you on. And we have to be very careful. M's instructions are that you remain in deep cover. That's essential. We have to drop you out of sight again so that you can re-emerge when you join *Invincible,* in just over a week."

Bond made a gesture that signified he understood. Though this was not borne out by his next question—"If she was BAST, what happened? Did *they* kill her by mistake?"

"Later, sir. Please. I really think it would be dangerous for you to stay on here. We have a helicopter coming in to pick you up. They'll take you to a secure base on the mainland. There's a debriefing team standing by, and they have good doctors in case you need medical—"

"I'm not in need of doctors, First Officer Pennington."

"With respect, sir, you need them to give you the once-over." There was the clattering sound of a helicopter, getting louder as it swept in from the sea to circle above the villa.

"I take the pistol, sir?" from one of the thickset men in civilian clothes.

"Not on your life." Bond was now becoming really angry. "I'm not a child, nor am I about to do anything stupid." He glared around him. "What're we waiting for, then? Let's go."

Outside, hovering directly over the villa, an old Agusta chopper, carrying Italian Naval markings, began to descend.

One of Clover Pennington's men gave hand signals and they lowered a crewman with a harness and winched Bond into the chopper. The last thing he looked at, as the helicopter turned away, heading for the coast, was the black, charred and twisted remains of the Fiat, and local police blockades at each end of the road.

An hour later he was inside a small military base, near Caserta. Bond's local geographic knowledge was enough to follow the route. From the air, the base looked anything but military, with half a dozen oblong buildings and a triple security perimeter: a sandwich of heavy-duty razor wire between two high chain-link fences. The guards at the main gates were armed but did not seem to be uniformed.

He was given a large, airy room, functional, with minimal comfort, a small bathroom and no TV or distracting pictures on the wall. Somehow they had managed to pack his case at the villa and it now stood neatly just inside the door. Bond stretched out on the bed, placing the Browning within reach. At least they had not disarmed him. There were a dozen or so paperbacks in a pile on the night table, a couple of thrillers, one Deighton, a Greene, two thick Forsyths and a little assorted bunch which included James Joyce's *Ulysses* and a copy of *War and Peace.* He knew from his own strung-out state that he needed something to keep his mind working, but this was a bizarre little collection, and he felt very tired, too fatigued to read, but not enough flaked out to sleep. Anyway, he had read the lot, apart from an odd little thriller masterpiece by some unknown author, boasting the title *Moonlight and Bruises.*

He played back the memory which blazed in his head. The Fiat, the steps, the wrought-iron gate, Beatrice smiling and opening the car door, then being blotted out by the ball of fire. No, was it his memory playing tricks? It was not really like that. She waved and smiled. What next? The violence of the explosion throwing him back? No, something else. She was smiling and pulling the car door open. Smoke. There was a lot of smoke with the fireball, wind and crack-thump of the explosion. What kind of explosive could they have used that made so much smoke? It did not happen with Semtex or RDX. This was something he would have to report. It could be that some terrorist organizations were using a new type of explosive: or was it an old mixture which, with age, produced more smoke than usual? Anyway, it had wiped out an unusually cold-blooded terrorist princess.

How many terrorist princesses does it take to wire up a time bomb? Three: one to get the wire, one to get the gold Rolex and one to call the expert. There was a tap on the door and he called "Come," with one hand slipping off the Browning's safety and turning the pistol toward the door.

The man was tall, dressed casually in slacks and a sweater. He had the dark, leathery looks of the Middle East, but his voice was pure Oxbridge English.

"Captain Bond?" he queried, though Bond got the distinct impression that he was merely adhering to some kind of ritual.

He nodded.

"Name's Farsee." He was in his forties, carried himself in an alert military manner, adjusting everything to make it seem as though he was pure civilian to the marrow. His laugh, when it came, lacked real humor. "Julian Farsee, though my friends call me Tomato. Play on words, kind of thing, y'see. Tomato Farsee. *Tomates Farcies*—the old French stuffed tomatos. See?"

"What's bloody going on?" Bond asked, his voice brittle and with undertones of violence.

"The quacks want to give you a bit of a going over. I just dropped in to see if you were feeling okay, and ready for that kind of thing, right?"

"And who exactly are you, Julian? Where are we; what are you; and what's going on?"

"Well, I'm the Two ^{1}/c actually. Right?" Two ^{1}/c was military for Second-in-Command, just like Jimmie The One, in the Royal Navy, stood for First Lieutenant, who could hold the rank of Commander or even Captain, depending on the Captain's rank, which could even be Rear-Admiral. Some people found it confusing.

"You're Second-in-Command of what, exactly?"

"This." Farsee waved a hand in the direction of the window.

It was like prising a grape pip from a peach. "And what *is* this?"

"Nobody told you?"

"If they had, I wouldn't be asking you, Julian."

"Oh, ya; right. We're slightly irregular actually."

"How irregular?"

"Comes under NATO installations, right? Highly classified, you might say. *Very* highly classified. We're not even in the book, as they say, right?"

136

"More!" Bond almost shouted. He could stand Yuppies up to a point, but not Yuppie military.

"CO's American, right?"

"CO of what?"

"We sort of handle things. Hide folk away when we don't want the world to see them—or I should say when some of the Intelligence people don't want the world to see them."

"Such as myself?"

"Ya. Oh, ya. Right, Captain Bond. Look, you ready for the medical wallahs, eh?"

Bond gave a long sigh, then nodded. "Lead me to them."

The doctors spent over three hours going over him. There was a general examination, and a few tests. The ENT specialist said he was lucky. "Eardrums're intact. Miracle from what I hear." This particular specialist was very much in the military mold.

Bond only became angry when they took him to a room in the hospital block that smelled strongly of psychiatrist. You could tell, first, by the pictures on the wall: light-gray skies and calm landscapes. Then there was the abundance of plant life. You could have been in Kew Gardens, and the young, very laid-back young man leaning in his adjustable Drabert chair had about him an air of calm, laced heavily with deep anxiety. But it was the Rorschach test that clinched it. In his day, Bond had seen experts play with psychiatrists when they brought out the ink blots. He also knew the crazy and clever answers that gave an analyst the Rorschach protocol.

"Just look at each one and tell me what you see." The young man laid the ink blots on the desk one at a time. A butterfly that could be a praying mantis if you were dangerous enough; a kissing couple, which might just be a nasty weapon. Each time Bond told him the blot looked like a woman's breasts, so when they finished the psychiatrist smiled—"You're extracting the urine, aren't you, Captain Bond?"

"In a word—yes. Look, doc, I've been through worse traumas than this in my time. Yes, I feel as most men do, after the sudden, destructive loss of a woman I'd come to care about. But I do know that it was all quick. Too quick. Immediately afterwards there was sorrow, and a little self-pity. Shock, if you like. Now I just feel very angry. Angry with myself for being such a pratt. Angry with them, for setting me up. Natural, isn't it?"

The psychiatrist smiled and nodded. "On your way, Captain Bond. Anger's the healthiest reaction, so let's not waste each other's time."

Bond did not reveal that he had a sneaking suspicion that another few strands of wool were being pulled over his eyes. That would come out in time. Give them enough rope, or wool for that matter.

Julian was waiting for him. "CO would like a word, I think, sir."

"A word, or several sentences?"

Julian whinnied like a horse. "Oh, ya, jolly good, Right. Ya."

The buildings were quite long, brick structures, set as though some designer had just thrown six models at random inside the perimeter fencing. They were single-story and, while there were windows down each side, Bond had noted that the interior rooms had no windows at all, the natural light flowing only into corridors. In both the living quarters and hospital there had been notices in several languages commanding people not to talk in the corridors.

The conclusion was obvious. The inner rooms were shielded against all types of sound-stealing.

As they crossed the compound, he tried to identify the various uses of the buildings. One for staff; one for senior staff; the hospital; one sprouting every kind of antenna known to man, therefore the communications center; a possible guest suite (the one in which he was quartered) and, at the furthest point from the entrance, the executive offices.

It sounded about right, as Julian was leading him toward this last building. Julian, Bond thought, was not such a stupid idiot as he had first appeared.

The Commanding Officer had a large room tucked neatly in the center of a nest of other rooms within the executive offices. Julian tapped at the door and a voice, distinctly American, possibly southern, called "Okay." The voice was as slow and smooth as molasses.

"Captain James Bond, Royal Navy, sir," Julian brayed. Bond painted a smile on his face and found himself alone in the room with the door closed and Julian left on the outside.

There were no potted plants here; and no soothing paintings. Two maps covered one large wall—one of the local Italian area, and another of Europe. The second was highly detailed and contained a lot of military symbols. The remaining pictures were very United States gung-ho. Blackhawk and Chinook helicopters figured largely, and the Chinooks had combat-ready troops pouring out of the doors, while mortar bombs burst nearby.

"Come on in, Captain Bond. Pleased to have you here." As he came around the desk, the CO looked as though he had stepped straight out of a glossy ad from some very smart magazine which sold clothes in the megadollar bracket. The beige suit had the look of a genuine Battistoni, which you cannot buy on Army pay, and certainly not on what you get from any of the Intelligence Services; the shirt was identifiably Jermyn Street irregular; the silk tie was probably made up specially, maybe by Gucci, in the stripes of some United States Army Regiment. The shoes needed no second-guessing: hand-stitched Gucci. No guessing, one hundred out of a possible fifty.

The man inside the clothes was short, sleek, balding, and, as they say in the subtitles, some tough hombre, even though he was surrounded by a hint of Hermès cologne. "Real good to see you, Captain. Sorry about your trouble earlier today. Not exactly the way to spend the holiday season, but I guess in our business we work, even a few hours, on Christmas day. I once heard some author say *he* did that, but maybe he was exaggeratin'. Anyways, welcome to Northanger."

"Northanger?" Bond repeated, his tone suggesting disbelief.

"That's what the secret guidebooks call us. Name's Toby Lellenberg by the way." In spite of his stature it was like shaking hands with a gorilla. "Sit down, Captain, we have a couple things to talk about."

Bond sat. The chair had been converted from an F14 pilot's seat, and he had to admit it was comfortable. "What kind of things, Mr.—er . . ."

"No rank. Langley don't really like rank. Just call me Toby. Anyways this is one of those sideways career offers—Officer Commanding Northanger. All I do is sit on my butt, shiver in winter, sweat in summer and view the passing spies. You, Captain, are one of our VIP passing spies."

"I really need some evidence of that, Toby. People can get burned by being identified as passing spies."

"No problem. I call you James, by the way?"

"Why not."

Toby went behind his desk and tackled a large, solid-steel filing cabinet which appeared to require three keys and two digital touch-pads to open it. For a moment of sheer hellishness, Bond had the urge to sing "I did but see a passing spy" to the tune of "There was a lady sweet and kind." He managed to quell the urge. The whole setup in this place was so interesting, and unlikely, that it helped to banish any pain that might still be raging in his emotions.

"There you go. Both versions. Cipher and the *en clair* I punched out on my own little gizmo in that safe."

He took the two proffered sheets and saw the double-check fail-safe on the original cipher. It was, undoubtedly, straight from M. The fail-safe was unfakeable. The text read—

FROM CSSUK TO OC NORTHANGER BASE MESSAGE
CONTINUES THANK YOU FOR ASSISTANCE
REFERENCE OUR PREDATOR STOP WOULD
APPRECIATE A DEBRIEF COPY ME ONLY STOP THIS
OFFICER MUST BE KEPT IN DOWNLOAD UNTIL
JANUARY TWO STOP WILL SIGNAL HOW HE IS TO
PROCEED AND JOIN HIS SHIP ON JANUARY THREE
STOP. CSS FINIS.

"Happy about that, James?" The smooth little man was smiling.

"You obviously have the facilities for a debrief."

"I don't get the best men in the business, but we do have

a representative team here, yes. One of your own guys: fella called Draycott, know him?"

"Heard of but not known."

"Well, out to grass, like the two guys we got from Langley. One of them's called Mac—built like a fireplug—and the other one's just known as Walter. Walter knows where all the bodies're buried and won't tell a soul. Guess that's why they've sent him here. When you get a posting to Northanger don't expect to see any further active duty. Backwater. But you'll get a good debrief."

"Fine, as long as Julian's not involved."

"Ha!" Toby put a brown hand on the corner of his desk, raised his head and barked out a one-note laugh of derision. "Julian Tomato. Ha!" He pronounced it "Tom-ay-toe" like any other red-blooded American, so the play on words did not really work. "That Julian. Y'know he couldn't pour piss outa a boot, even if th'instructions was written on the heel. You fancy some chow, James? We're havin' a full old-fashioned Christmas dinner tonight. Turkey 'n' all the trimmins, plum pudding, the entire works."

"Sounds fun." He looked at his watch. "But first I should make a call."

"Yeah?" Was the suspicion imagined?

"Change of contact code for the day. It's past time."

"Of course it is. Sure, use the phone here." He pointed to one of five different-colored telephones on his desk. "You want me to leave?"

"Oh, I don't think that's necessary." Bond was already dialing.

This time London picked up on the fourth ring. "Predator," said Bond. "Day three."

"Catclaw," the voice said from the distant line. "Repeat. Catclaw."

142

"Acknowledge." Bond was about to put down the receiver when the distant voice asked, "Is everything smooth?"

"They tell me it is."

"Acknowledge." And the line went dead. So they *were* still being clever. But this time the code was very much tied to the situation. Dante's lines once more went through his head—

Front and centre here, Grizzly and Hellkin . . .
You too, Deaddog . . .
Curlybeard, take charge of a squad of ten.
Take Grafter and Dragontooth along with you.
Pigfusk, *Catclaw,* Cramper and Crazyred.

"You want an okay from me?" Toby was adjusting his tie in a wall mirror overprinted with the cover of *Time* magazine, so that you got on that coveted cover every time you looked.

"Be mighty civil of you, Toby."

Lellenberg gave him a little leer. "You bein' funny, son?"

"Yep."

"Good." He grinned. "My money today's on Catclaw."

"And you'd be right." Bond laughed, and they left the office together.

The party was held in a large room which was obviously used as the officers' canteen in the senior ranks' hut. They had it decorated with the kind of stuff you picked up for a small fortune at stores in the U.S. with names like 𝕮𝖍𝖗𝖎𝖘𝖙𝖒𝖆𝖘 𝕿𝖔 𝕲𝖔 or 𝕭𝖒𝖆𝖘 𝖎𝖘 𝖀𝖘. It all looked lovely and unreal. Magnificent angels held unknown wind instruments to their lips as they shimmered on trees dripping snow; piles of gifts were heaped under the largest, and most magical tree, which had "Victorian" trimmings hanging from it, and electric lights that looked like real candles with moving flames.

Clover Pennington was the only woman present and, when she saw Bond, she detached herself from a handful of young officers and came over to him.

"Forgive me, sir," she said, kissing him, a little hard and on the lips. "It's allowed." She pointed above him at the dangling mistletoe.

"You're going to do sterling service tonight, First Officer Pennington." Bond smiled but did not unbend.

"Catclaw," she said quietly.

"Correct. Catclaw."

"They've put me next to you at dinner, sir. Hope you don't mind."

"As long as we don't talk shop."

She nodded, bit her lip, and together they moved into the crowd.

During the meal he did not do much talking. In his time, James Bond had learned around four hundred ways of killing: four hundred and three if you counted gun, knife and strangling rope. He was also *au fait* with the art of paper-tripping—supplying oneself with necessary documents to survive in a foreign country. Now he figured out what he could recall of the number of ways he could fake a death. Die, yet not die, at home or abroad. Privately or in full, plain sight. They added up to around a score, though he was in two minds whether he now knew the twenty-first way of doing it. Or was it still wishful thinking?

The dinner was excellent, and Bond watched his intake of alcohol, though others did not. Julian Farsee was well away, while one or two of the other staff became rowdy.

One couple of heavy, battered men even had a row which almost led to a full-scale fight until Toby Lellenberg stepped in, his slow drawl taking on a whiplash quality.

"Just like Christmas at home," Bond said, unsmiling, to Clover. "You staying here long, by the way?"

"I leave on thirty-first to get the Wren draft ready."

"Back to RNAS Yeovilton?"

She nodded. "I thought this was a no-shop evening." Then, quite suddenly, "Can't we make it up, sir? Sort of start again . . . James? Please."

"Maybe, when it's all over. Not yet though. Not until you-know-what's out of the way."

She nodded and looked miserable, though not as miserable as some of the faces Bond saw at breakfast the next morning. The party, they told him, had gone on quite late.

Braying Julian came over during breakfast and said it would be nice if he could be in Suite #3 at ten-thirty. "The debrief," he explained.

So, at ten-thirty on the dot Bond met the two American officers—Mac and Walter—and the man from his own Service, Draycott, who was not quite what he expected.

The debrief was exceptionally thorough. Much more so than he had anticipated. Walter was elderly, but had the knack of slipping off into tributary questions which suddenly ended up becoming very searching. Mac, who was, as Toby had suggested, built like a fireplug, had one of those faces that remained permanently impassive. Though he did smile a great deal the face and eyes remained blank, and rather tough: impossible to read. Mac was inclined to chip in with subsidiary questions which turned out to add a lot to Bond's testimony. Draycott was also deceptive, in the mold of the legendary Scardon: a man who looked very ordinary, as though he would be happier in the English countryside. He smoked a pipe, used to great effect—to add in pauses when he fiddled with it, or to break questions in two halves when he smoked.

They took Bond back to the beginning, telling him the stalking-horse theory of the operation, just so that he would know they were pretty well briefed themselves. On the fifth day, the trio walked off with practically every second Bond had spent in Ischia accounted for: naughties and all.

When the debrief was complete all three of his interrogators seemed to vanish. At least Bond did not set eyes on them again.

On the thirty-first of December, Clover came to his quarters to announce that she was leaving. He did not keep her long, though she obviously wanted to linger. "See you on board, then" was his final, sharp, word, and he thought Clover's eyes were moist. She was either very much for real or had become one hell of an actor.

Two days later it was Bond's turn. Toby showed him M's latest signal and he repeated the contents so that Northanger's CO was satisfied he was word perfect.

They took him in the elderly helicopter to Rome where he went to the Alitalia desk and they provided him with tickets and a baggage claim check.

The flight from Rome to Stockholm was uneventful. He had one hour's wait for the military transport that ferried him to the West German naval base at Bremerhaven where he stayed for one night.

On the morning of January 3rd, James Bond, in uniform, stepped aboard a Sea King helicopter which took him out to *Invincible* and her gaggle of escorts which lay twenty miles offshore. By the following night they were one hundred miles into the North Sea, cruising slowly and waiting for the orders to be opened which would start *Operation Landsea '89.*

·　　　·　　　·

They were loading staff at Northanger into innocent-looking buses within four hours of Bond's departure. Julian Farsee, dressed in olive drab trousers and a military sweater complete with reinforced shoulder and elbow pads, walked into the CO's office, not even knocking. The CO was shredding documents and hardly turned to look at his second-in-command as he came and sat on the desk.

"Well. You think they bought it?" asked Ali Al Adwan, Farsee's true name. In the hierarchy of BAST, Adwan was the "Snake" to Bassam Baradj's "Viper."

"Of course. All the incoming signals were dealt with. Nobody queried a thing."

Adwan scowled. "Except me. I query *your* judgment."

Baradj smiled and fed more paper into the shredder. "Yes? I thought you were unhappy, though you played your part to perfection. What *really* worried you, Ali?"

"You know what worried me. Bond should have been killed. Here, on the spot, while we had him. What was the point of bringing him here at all, if not to kill him?"

"Already we have made two botched attempts on Bond's life. The first was one of those things that just went wrong—the wrong kind of missile, the fact that Bond is obviously a good pilot." He shrugged, a wide, unhappy gesture. "Then, Ali, we tried again, and that was disaster. We went for Bond and killed . . ." This time his lips clamped together as though he had become upset at the thought. Then, throwing it off, he spoke again. "*I* made the decision, Ali. No more assassination attempts until we get nearer to our true targets. There will be plenty of chances then. His sudden death, after the wretched Ischia business, might even have jeopardized the entire operation. They could even have called it off."

"Then why bring people like him here at all?"

Baradj smiled, patiently. "It was necessary. After Ischia they would have moved him here anyway. They would have wanted him close and confined. We want him confident, so that the blow will fall very unexpectedly. This has been excellent psychology. We have had a chance to know him and be close. Don't you think that *you* know the man better?"

"I know he's dangerous, but yes. Yes, I think I know him now. But have we really deceived everyone?"

"All who had to be deceived *were* deceived. Nobody from any other base, or from London, showed any sign that they were concerned. The other regular staff will wake from their enforced sleep in the morning, and I don't suppose they will question the strange loss of time they will all have suffered. They will eventually realize that in some strange way they all missed Christmas and the week after, but the hypnotics Hamarik supplied should keep the true facts at bay for a week, maybe even ten days. By then, my dear friend, we will have the Superpowers, the United States of America and Russia, together with the United Kingdom, on their knees begging for mercy."

Adwan, whose leathery dark complexion seemed now more apparent, smiled and nodded; his attitude changing. "Yes, you are right. In the end of it all we will have a great deal to thank you for, Bassam."

"What is money compared to this?"

"Ah, but you proved to be a fine actor also."

Bassam Baradj chuckled. "You were very convincing yourself."

A smile crossed Adwan's face. "Oh, ya. Ya. Right," he said.

10

Monarchs of the Sea

James Bond felt the slight tremor under his feet, and with it the old frisson returned. There was nothing in the world like being at sea in a capital ship: the ordered routine, the feeling of men working as a quiet, well-trained team, the regularity of events, even in a crisis. To Bond, all this returned in a warm shower of nostalgia. No, it was better, because of the very special feeling of serving in *this* ship.

HMS *Invincible* was a relatively recent addition to the Royal Navy's history. In some ways she had already become a legend: certainly the first kind of ship of her type—nineteen and a half thousand tons of platform from which to launch practically any type of operation, including the nuclear option with the Green Parrot variable yield weapons, capable of being carried by the Sea Harriers, to the 1-kt versions, which could be dropped by Sea Kings as antisubmarine bombs. *Invincible* could also carry a Commando for armed assault, and, at this moment, 42 Commando, Royal Marines, was on board.

The ship's air group consisted of ten Sea Harriers, eleven antisubmarine-warfare (ASW) Sea Kings, two antielectronic-warfare (AEW) Sea Kings and one Lynx helicopter, configured for Exocet-type decoy duties. *Invincible* was a very full ship, though officially, and technically, it was not even classed as an aircraft carrier. *Invincible* was a Through Deck Cruiser (TDC).

Back in 1966, the then British government had canceled a new building program that would give the Royal Navy a number of conventional carriers for fixed-wing aircraft. In the following year a new program went into action. What they required were light command cruisers with facilities for a number of helicopters. The whole political subject, mainly involving costing and pulling back on defense expenditure, was sensitive, but the success of the V/STOL Harrier aircraft changed things in a dramatic manner.

Plans were again changed, though the politicians still clung to the name TDC as opposed to aircraft carrier. Three such ships were commissioned, and the success and lessons learned during the Falklands War had made for even further alterations. The exercise, *Operation Landsea '89,* was to be the first chance for *Invincible* to show her paces following the extensive refit, which included new armament, electronics, communications and the 12° Harrier ski jump which had replaced the original 7° ramp.

The "Through Deck" principle remained, for practically all the ship's equipment was carried belowdecks, apart from the complexities in the long, almost conventional island which ran along the center of the starboard side, using over half of the main deck's 677 feet, bristling with tall antennae, radar dishes, and other domed detection devices. Most of the information required in the island was accessed from electronics buried deep below the flight deck.

Invincible, and her sister ships *Illustrious* and *Ark Royal,* were powered by four mighty Rolls-Royce TM3B twin-shaft gas turbines, designed on a modular principle, making maintenance and repair a simpler job. *Invincible, Illustrious* and *Ark Royal* were quite simply the largest gas-turbine-powered ships in the world.

Once more he felt the slight tremor and rise under his feet. Bond sat down on his bunk, took out the Browning 9mm and began to clean it. Apart from the Royal Marine detachment on board, he was the only officer who carried a personal handgun: though he was most conscious that two armed Marines stood only a few feet for'ard of his cabin, stationed there, on the port side, as a guard on the series of cabins that would be used by the visiting VIP brass, and already partially inhabited by the Wren detachment.

As he sat down, there was the telltale click all seagoing members of the Royal Navy recognize as the Tannoy system about to broadcast either one of the many routine orders, or bugle calls, which told off the time in a similar manner to the religious "hours" in a monastery.

But this was not a normal message. "D'ye hear there! D'ye hear there! This is the Captain." Throughout the ship, Bond knew that all ranks would stop everything but the most necessary duties to listen.

"As you all know," the Captain—Rear-Admiral Sir John

Walmsley—continued, "the land, sea and air exercise called *Operation Landsea '89* will commence at 23:59 hours. You will have already been briefed about this exercise by your divisional commanders, so you know it's not in the normal run of similar training such as *Ocean Safari.* I want to remind you that, as from 23:59, we will be operating under actual rules of war and rules of engagement, apart from using the big bangs, of course. This message is to be relayed to all other ships in what is to be known as *Taskforce Kiev,* and we will darken ship at exactly 23:59. You are also aware that this evening we will be receiving aboard three very senior officers and their staffs. There will be women among the staffs, and there is a detachment of Wrens aboard at this moment. I have no reason to repeat what your divisional officers will have already told you, though I will: fraternization with the female officers and ratings aboard, apart from normal and obvious duties, is strictly forbidden. Anyone either attempting to, or actually fraternizing can expect the harshest possible penalty. Apart from that"—there was a long pause: the Rear-Admiral had a quirky sense of humor—"good luck to you all."

Bond smiled to himself. The entire message had been blandly understated, for this certainly was a different type of exercise, if only for the strange mixture of who were *Red Side,* and who were *Blue.* To inject an even deeper-than-usual "fog of war," some units of the NATO powers remained in their real-life situations; while others were split in half—some *Red* and some *Blue.* For instance this very task force consisted of ships of the Royal Navy, but were *Red,* other ships, particularly submarines of the Royal Navy, were *Blue.*

Bond had read his own sealed orders, after coming

aboard, and had sat in on Walmsley's briefing to the Executive Staff.

The exercise briefing was in three parts. Political situation; Current strategic situation at the commencement of *Landsea '89;* Objective of all parties involved, with an accent on their own powerful *Taskforce Kiev.*

The fictional scenario was shrewd and complex: shortly before Christmas there had been a major military attempt to take over Chairman Gorbachev's ruling power in the USSR. This action, spearheaded by high-ranking officers of the Russian Army, Navy and Air Force, coupled with some ambitious members of the Politburo—all disenchanted with Gorbachev's *Glasnost*—had gone off at half cock, but was far from being a failure.

The bulk of the military power remained anti-Gorbachev and now threatened to take their own idealism out of Russia, and draw world attention to the changing events in the Soviet Union, by engaging the NATO powers in a series of tactical operations designed to show they could rattle sabers as loudly as anybody.

The USSR was, as Gorbachev had known from the first, heading toward a huge, possibly catastrophic, financial and economic crash. Gorbachev's way had been a more open system of government which would assist in his begging-bowl diplomacy. The military, and more hawkish members of the regime, still held to the idea that one could bargain only from power. *Glasnost* was, to them, a watered-down version of a great political ideology. The USSR *had* to show strength, and, they argued, the only way to get help from the class-ridden, consumer-oriented West was to show strength and ability. They wanted to threaten the West—blackmail by force to get assistance.

That night elements of *Red Side*—representing Soviet forces—would cross into the West and start aggressive covert military operations against NATO bases, throughout Europe. These actions would be carefully limited and controlled. In reality, the troops would be members of the United States 10th Special Forces Group (Airborne), and two troops of Delta Force—each troop consisting of four 4-man squads. The choices had not been arbitrary, for the units bore a close resemblance to the Soviet Airborne Force, which does not come directly under the Red Army chain of command; and highly trained Spetsnaz—"Forces at Designation"—who come directly under the GRU (the elitist Military Intelligence) and are also known as "diversionary troops."

U.S. Air Force facilities within the NATO boundaries could provide air backup to *Red Side* if things got out of hand, though no USAF bases in the UK were to be used. The Royal Air Force, and remaining British and U.S. Forces in Europe, would act as their real selves, as would United States Naval forces. They would be *Blue Side*—the goodies—while the British 2nd Parachute Regiment; the Special Air Service; 42 Commando, together with *Taskforce Kiev* would be *Red Side*—the baddies.

At 23:59 hours—which is Naval euphemism for midnight—*Taskforce Kiev* would be approximately fifteen miles off the Belgian coast, steaming west. The Force was made up of the flagship, *Invincible;* six Type 42 destroyers; and four Type 21 frigates.

They would, at the start of the exercise, be aware that they had been shadowed since leaving their Russian bases—their main opponents being their own Royal Naval colleagues, the submariners. So *Taskforce Kiev* would be hard-pressed to make their dash through the narrow English Channel, around the Bay of Biscay, heading for Gibraltar, where they were to land 42 Commando and, with their considerable presence, seal off the Mediterranean. All this was a calculated risk. *Red Side* did not believe the Western forces would precipitate matters by escalating the crisis.

The final objective of both sides was to come to a successful cessation of hostilities, not allowing actions to escalate into anything more than a tactical show of force and guerrilla warfare. For the first time, politicians of the NATO powers would be called upon to make true political decisions. The ideal ending would be the withdrawal of all Soviet units, and a move to the bargaining table, where Gorbachev's future—indeed the future of the Soviet Union—would be thrashed out.

The scenario was neat and interesting, apart from one facet. Bond, and some of the Intelligence chiefs, already knew that playing games with real Army, Air Force and Naval units, in this realistic manner, made some form of terrorist intrusion a heady temptation. BAST were poised for some specific action against *Invincible,* and that was no surprise to 007 when he thought of who would eventually be aboard the ship, for this was the tightest secret of all, the final box of a Chinese puzzle of boxes. This last secret of *Landsea '89* was coded *Stewards' Meeting,* and this was Bond's true reason for being in charge of security aboard *Invincible.* Already, his brushes with BAST had proved they were a ruthless and determined organization. What nobody knew was their size, true efficiency in a critical situation, and the final aims of their possible assault on *Invincible.*

•　　•　　•

Bassam Baradj, most recently in the guise of the smooth Toby Lellenberg, station chief of Northanger, was the only person who could have told Bond, or anyone else, the real truth about BAST: its strength, and, more particularly, its true aims.

Baradj was certainly all the things the many dossiers said about him—and they all said the same thing: immense wealth, former close friend of Arafat, ex-member of the PLO; no photographs; could not be tied into any known terrorist operation in the past twenty years. Indeed, that was the sum total of the man, apart from the varied number of descriptions taken from a variety of sources.

True, he was, as they suspected, the Viper of BAST, on the back of which rode the Snake, the Man and the Cat. If it had been possible to ask any, or all, of these last three, each would have given slightly different answers to the questions, What is BAST? What are its true aims?

Only the short, sleek man known as Bassam Baradj was in a position to give the correct answers; though it was unlikely he would do so, for they were locked tightly in his head.

In a couple of words, the answers were Bassam Baradj and Bassam Baradj. He *was* BAST and he *was* its true aim. If you asked the further question—How did Baradj gain his truly immense wealth?—it was plain to see, but only if you had the eyes to see it.

It was not strictly true that there were no available photographs of Bassam Baradj. There were many. The New York City Police Department had several, as did the Los Angeles Police Department, and Seattle, Washington, New Orleans,

Paris and Scotland Yard, London. Most were filed under F—for Fraud; and they carried varied names: Bennie Benjamin aka Ben Brostov, Vince Phillips and Conrad Decca: and those were only for starters in the files of the NYPD.

Over the past twenty years Baradj had gained quite a reputation, but under many different guises and *modi operandi.*

Bassam Baradj had been born plain Robert Besavitsky, in the old Hell's Kitchen area of New York. His father, Roman Besavitsky, was of mongrel immigrant stock, part Russian, part Rumanian, with a strange dash of Scottish via his great-great-grandfather on his mother's side. Eva Besavitsky, Robert's mother, was of a similar mixture: part Irish, part French, with a tincture of Arab—not that you would have guessed it from her maiden name, which was Evangeline Shottwood.

Robert Besavitsky was, therefore, the mongrel product of half-a-dozen other mongrels, and, as such, was born with two great talents: ambition and the ability to sense when it was time to move on.

As a growing boy, Robert was well and truly streetwise by the age of ten. By the time he reached fourteen he knew exactly what one needed to survive in this world—money. For money was the direct route to power. If he could make money, the power would come later. He made his first million by the age of twenty-one.

It started with the seemingly accidental find of an automatic pistol, shoved into a garbage can in a back alley off Mulberry Street in the Italian area. It was a Luger 9mm and had a full magazine, but for one bullet. Twenty-four hours after finding this weapon, Robert had carried out four quick stickup jobs on liquor stores, which netted him six hundred dollars. The following day he sold the weapon for a further one hundred dollars. Then he set about spending wisely. He bought clothes: two good suits, four shirts, three ties, underwear and two pairs of shoes.

While on the buying spree, he also lifted a silver cigarette case and lighter, a pigskin briefcase and matching wallet. This left him with one hundred and fifty dollars. Fifty went into his pocket, the remaining hundred opened his first bank account. What followed would have been legend if the cops and the Feds had ever managed to interconnect him with all the fiddles, some of which were not just fiddles, but fully orchestrated capital crimes.

During the past two decades, Robert had been married twice, under different names. Both women were obscenely wealthy, and both apparently died accidentally within a year of the marriage. The first was a widow. Robert, under the name of William Deeds, had managed to ingratiate himself with a stockbroker called Finestone. Jerry Finestone knew all the tricks of the stock market, and took a liking to young Bill Deeds, who proved to be an apt pupil. After six months poor old Jerry walked into an elevator that was not there, but thirty floors down. Later the coroner heard there had been a wiring fault which had allowed the doors to open. It just so happened that Robert, or Bill or whatever you chose to call him, was by way of being an electrical expert, but who knew? Good old Jerry left three point five million to his widow, Ruth, who, after an appropriate period of mourning married Bill Deeds. Sadly, she followed her first husband within the year: a nasty business which involved a Cadillac and an unmarked road which led to a sheer drop. The contractors, who swore this cul-de-cliff had been well marked, lost the case when Bill Deeds sued them for one and a quarter million.

Thus set up, Bill Deeds moved on. To Los Angeles, where he made the money work for him, and married a movie star. By this time his name had changed to Vince Phillips. The movie star was a big name and the headlines were even bigger when they found her accidentally electrocuted in her Malibu beach house. Another one and a half million passed to Vince Phillips, who had once been Bill Deeds but was really Robert Besavitsky.

Two out of two was enough of that game. Robert altered his name yearly from then on, and was involved in several dozen stock market frauds—hence the name changes—before he turned his hand to buying and selling. He would sell anything as long as he could buy cheap and sell at a profit, and he certainly never asked questions about the things he purchased. That was how he became a good friend to Yasir Arafat, and even a member of the PLO.

It was at the time when the PLO needed a regular supply of arms and, as it turned out, Bennie Benjamin tka (Truly Known As) Robert Besavitsky had made a good friend of an unscrupulous quartermaster with an infantry regiment. This was how Bennie got hold of hundreds of assault rifles and automatic pistols, together with thousands of rounds of ammunition and four large drums of Composition C-4 disguised as drilling mud. Ninety percent of C-4 is RDX, the most powerful plastique explosive in the world, the rest is a binding material. It is known by various names these days, including its Czechoslovak clone, Semtex. All the arms and explosives ended up with the PLO during the time when that organization was branded as a terrorist army.

It was then that Besavitsky saw there could be a possible future in terrorism. He spent time with the PLO and learned a few tips, then went back to buying and selling—

worldwide, under dozens of aliases, dealing in anything from stolen paintings to rare collectors' motor cars. For many years he stayed well ahead of the law. But he was no fool. He liked a luxurious life-style and knew that it was possible the time might eventually come when they would catch up with him. Just as he knew that one really major killing could set him up for life and allow him to retire in exceptional luxury, and never have to look over his shoulder again.

This was in 1985: the year he decided to make international terrorism work in his favor. It was also the year when his name changed to Bassam Baradj, and it was as Baradj that he went out into the streets and hiding holes of Europe and the Middle East in search of converts. He had links with a number of disenchanted terrorists and, in turn, they had other links.

Baradj had always had an unhealthy interest in Demonology. Now he used it to his own purpose and founded BAST, dragging into his net the three very experienced people who would act as his staff—Saphii Boudai, Ali Al Adwan, and Abou Hamarik. Bait for them was twofold. First, a blow of huge dimensions against the corrupt Superpowers, plus the United Kingdom. Second, very large financial gain which would, of course, assist the cause of true freedom everywhere. The Brotherhood of Anarchy and Secret Terrorism had a nice ring to it, but Baradj saw it as one of those meaningless titles that would draw a certain type of person. His three lieutenants trawled the terrorist backwaters and, by the end of 1986 they had over four hundred men and women on their books.

The Viper—Baradj—gave them the first orders. No member of BAST was to take part in any terrorist operation until he had cleared it. He okayed several small bombings, just to get BAST's name on the map. But as far as the overall plan went, there would be one, and only one, operation he would fund. This would take time to mature, but the returns would be enormous: billions, maybe trillions, of dollars.

Bassam Baradj, cheapskate, big-time fraud merchant, buyer and seller extraordinary, spent the next years gaining information with which he could prepare the plan he was about to play out on the international stage. When it was over, BAST could fall apart for all he cared; for Baradj intended to take the proceeds, run, change his name, paper and possibly his face, with a little help from a plastic surgeon. Now he was almost at the most sensitive point in his operation, for he alone—outside of the tiny circle of Navy and Intelligence officers—knew the secret of what they called *Stewards' Meeting.* Apart from the dupe Petty Officer whom his men had enlisted, Baradj had at least two agents aboard *Invincible.* One had provided the essential clue to *Stewards' Meeting,* the other had people who would obey during the plot that lay ahead. Once the clock began to run on his operation, Baradj considered the entire business would take only forty-eight hours, maybe sixty at the outside, for the Superpowers would cave in very quickly. After that, Baradj would cease to exist, and BAST would be penniless.

When he had abandoned Northanger, Baradj had gone to Rome for a couple of days. From Rome he flew into London, Gatwick, as a transfer passenger to Gibraltar. There, Abou Hamarik, "The Man," waited for him at that British home away from home, The Rock Hotel. For once the men did not exchange the BAST password, "Health depends on Strength"—a password taken very seriously by all BAST members except Baradj, who thought it to be gobbledegook, and did not, therefore, realize that it was one of the tiny clues that had leaked to Intelligence and Security Services worldwide, who also took it seriously: to the point of analyzing variations on its possible meaning.

But, this time, for no other reason than laxity, the words were not exchanged, therefore none of the listening post computers picked it up. The advent of a pair of high-ranking members of BAST went undetected in Gibraltar. If they had exchanged this profoundly nonsensical form of greeting, things might well have been different.

•　　•　　•

James Bond saw Clover Pennington for the first time since their meeting over Christmas, in the wardroom of *Invincible*. Certain seagoing regulations had been altered to allow the Wrens and their officer to do their job with ease, and First Officer Pennington was, as the bearded Sir John Walmsley put it, "A delightful adornment to our ship's company." Not one officer in the wardroom missed the slightly lascivious look in the Captain's eyes as he gallantly kissed Clover's hand and lingered over releasing it.

Eventually, Clover escaped from the senior officers and came over to Bond, who was nursing a glass of Badoit, having forsworn alcohol until the operation had been successfully concluded. She looked fit, relaxed and very fetching in the pants and short jacket Wren officers wore, for the sake of modesty, when on harbor or shipboard duty, and aircraft maintenance.

"You all right, sir?" Clover smiled at him, her dark eyes

wide and stirring with pleasure, leaving no doubt that she was happy to see him.

"Fine, Clover. Ready for the fray?"

"I hope it's not going to be a fray. I just want it all over and done with. I gather that I defer to you in *all* security matters."

"That's what the rules say. They also say it to the Americans and the Russians, though I really can't see either of *them* deferring to anyone. The Old Man tells me he's going to make it plain to the whole lot. They might well obey for the first part, but, when we come to *Stewards' Meeting*, I don't see them budging from their respective charges and telling me anything."—The cipher, *Stewards' Meeting*, was, as far as *Invincible* was concerned, known only to Sir John Walmsley, Clover Pennington, James Bond, the three visiting Admirals and their bodyguards, to whom the information was essential. Even when they got to that particular phase, the present circle of knowledge would not be considerably widened. The entire ship's company might see things, and guess others, but would never be formally told.

"We know who the minders are, Jame . . . sir?"

He nodded, glancing around as officers drifted in to dinner. "Our people're easy, just a pair of heavies from the Branch—both ex-Navy and done up as flag officers; the Yanks've got their Secret Service bodyguards. Four of them. As for the Russians, almost certainly KGB, four in all, including a woman who's described as a naval attaché."

"Any names?"

"Yes. All unmemorable, apart from the Russian lady, who's called Nikola Ratnikov, a name to conjure with . . ."

"I've already marked her card, sir." Clover gave him a

wide-eyed look of innocence. "Whatever she's like, I'll think of her as Nikki the Rat."

Bond allowed her one of his neon sign smiles: on and off. "Let's eat," he said. "I've a feeling it's going to be a long hard night."

• • •

One of the Sea Kings hovered off the port bow. This was normal operational practice during flying operations. One helicopter was always airborne to act as a search-and-rescue machine should an aircraft end up in the drink.

From Flight Operations, high on the superstructure known to all as the island, Bond could see the helicopter's warning lights blinking as it drifted forward, keeping in station with the ship.

"Here they come." The Commander in charge of Flight Ops snapped his night glasses up and swept the sky behind the stern. "Our man's leading them in."

You could see them with the naked eye—not their shapes, but the warning lights of three helos stacked from around five hundred feet, at a good thousand-yard intervals, up to about a thousand feet.

"Rulers of their own Nay-vee-s," Bond parodied the Gilbert and Sullivan song from *HMS Pinafore.*

A young officer chuckled, and as the first chopper, another Sea King, came in and put down, taxiing forward at the instructions from the deck handling officer, the Commander joined in, singing, "For they are monarchs of the sea."

The second machine touched the deck, it was a big Mil Mi-14 in the Soviet Naval livery of white and gray (NATO designation Haze) making a din they could hear up on the bridge above Flight Operations. Bond repeated his line, "Rulers of their own Nay-vee-s," adding, "I think that one really *has* brought along all of his sisters, and his cousins, and his aunts."

As the rotors slowed to idle, the final craft did a rather fancy rolling landing, touching down right of the stern threshold. This looked like an update on the Bell model 212, and carried U.S. markings, but no designation and no *Navy* livery. Nobody in Flight Operations had seen anything like it. "I want those choppers off my deck fast," the Commander barked at the young officer acting as communications link with the deck handling officer. Then he turned back to Bond. "We've got two Sea Harriers out there, fully juiced and carrying operational equipment: real bangs, Sidewinders, 50mm cannon, the works. Don't know what's behind it, but the Captain gave the orders. Round-the-clock readiness, with a four-minute ability to switch them for unarmed Harriers. Bloody dangerous if you ask me."

The three helicopters were discharging their passengers with speed, each machine being met by a senior officer, a bosun, and several ratings: the senior officer to salute, the bosun to pipe the Admiral aboard, and the ratings to secure any luggage. Admiral of the Fleet Sir Geoffrey Gould; Admiral Edwin Gudeon, United States Navy; and Admiral Sergei Yevgennevich Pauker, Commander-in-Chief of the Soviet Navy, together with their staffs and bodyguards were aboard *Invincible.*

Half an hour later, Bond was ushered into the Captain's day cabin. The three Admirals were standing in the center of the cabin, each nursing a drink, and Rear-Admiral Sir

John Walmsley greeted Bond with a smile, turning to the assorted brass from the Royal Navy, United States Navy and the Soviet Navy. "Gentlemen, I'd like you to meet Captain Bond, who is in charge of your security arrangements while you're aboard *Invincible*. Bond, this is Admiral of the Fleet Sir Geoffrey Gould." Bond stood to attention in front of the smooth-looking, impeccable officer. "Captain Bond . . ." Gould had a voice which matched his looks: he was one of those people who always look neat and freshly barbered. "I'm sure we'll all be safe in your care. I have two flag officers who have had experience in these matters—"

"Gentlemen, Captain Bond is to meet your personal staff, as soon as I've introduced him to you," Walmsley broke in quickly. "I must stress that while you are guests aboard my flagship, your people will take their orders directly from Captain Bond. This is *essential* to your well-being, and the safety of those who will, eventually, be part of *Stewards' Meeting*."

"Sure, if that's the way you want to play it. But I've got four guys with me." Admiral Gudeon's voice was the unpleasant growl of a cantankerous man who always liked his own way, and was never wrong. "I guess they'll be able to look after me without you doin' much to help them." Bond did not know if the Admiral meant to be rude, or whether it was merely a long-cultivated manner. "Bond? . . . Bond . . .?" the American continued. "I knew a Bond, way back at Annapolis. You got any American relatives?"

"I think not, sir. Many friends, but no relatives—not as far as I know, anyway." Rear-Admiral Walmsley moved a foot, kicking Bond's ankle sharply. But Gudeon seemed oblivious to the tongue-in-cheek answer.

"And," Walmsley quickly pushed Bond along the line, "our most senior officer here. Admiral Sergei Pauker, Commander-in-Chief of the Soviet Navy."

"An honor, sir." Bond looked the man straight in the eyes. Pauker had the rosy cheeks of a Mr. Pickwick, but there the likeness ended. The eyes were gray and cold, showing no emotion. Dead eyes, overhung by frosty eyebrows. He had a small mouth, but it did form itself into a surprisingly friendly smile. The main feature of the face, ruddy cheeks apart, was a huge aquiline nose.

"Bond." He pronounced it "Bound." "I think somewhere I have heard the name before. Have you, perhaps, served in your embassy in Moscow?" He spoke excellent English.

"Not exactly *in* the embassy, sir." Bond gave an almost imperceptible smile.

"But you are known there, I think. In Moscow, I mean."

"It wouldn't surprise me, sir."

"Good. Good." The humor disappeared from his face and the eyes glazed over.

There was no offer of a drink, and Rear-Admiral Walmsley ushered Bond out of the room, like a farmer getting an errant sheep into a van. "The security people are in Briefing One," he whispered.

Briefing One was the primary Air Group briefing room on the port side, amidships and two decks below the officers' quarters. It had been cleared for an hour, so that the security teams could get together, and Bond entered it quickly, going straight into his prepared routine. "My name's Bond, James Bond. Captain, Royal Navy," he began, then stopped abruptly. The one woman among the ten large men was enough to stop anyone or anything. She also spoke before anyone else. "Captain Bond. I am First Naval Attaché to Admiral Pauker. My name is Nikola Ratnikov. My friends call me Nikki. I hope you are to be my friend."

You could feel the unsettling tension spark through the room, and it was obvious that Nikola Ratnikov had been showing the cold-shoulder to the rest of her colleagues, which must have been irritating to say the least. Comrade Attaché Ratnikov would have given a tweak to the loins of even a devout monk, and it would not matter whether the monk was Roman Catholic, Protestant, Buddhist, or Russian Orthodox. She had that indefinable quality about her manner, features and body which made all heterosexual men turn to look twice, and, possibly a third time, if they had the energy left.

Nikki Ratnikov wore a well-tailored Soviet Naval Woman Officer's uniform, which is not flattering to all. There again, Nikki could have made sackcloth and ashes look like Dior. When she moved toward him, hand extended, even Bond felt his knees tremble slightly. She had short ash-blonde hair, cut in what used to be called a pageboy style, but from where he stood it looked like a tempting golden helmet, framing a face of classic beauty. It was not the kind of face that Bond usually went for. He preferred slightly blemished good looks, but Nikki's eyes held his for almost a minute, and it was a little longer before he let go of her hand.

"Hallo, Captain Bond, we've met before." It was one of the Special Branch men, all done up in a lieutenant's uniform, complete with the gold trimmings of a flag officer. "Brinkley," he added.

"Yes, of course. Yes, I remember you. Ted Brinkley, right?"

"On the button, sir." The Special Branch man looked for

all the world like a Special Branch man in fancy dress, as did his partner, Martin—"My friends call me Moggy"—Camm.

He did the rounds of the other security men. Few had resorted to the bad disguises of the Branch men, and they all looked like a very heavy team. The Americans introduced themselves as Joe, Stan, Edgar and Bruce. Bruce was a very tall black officer with an exceptionally bone-crushing handshake, and looked as though he could probably stop a tank with his chest. Joe and Stan seemed to be made-to-measure, off the peg, standard-issue "bullet catchers." Edgar—"Call me Ed"—was in a different mold: lean, mean, tense, with obvious staying power and taut muscles, he had the battered good looks of one who had seen plenty of action in his time. Bond had him down as the brains of the outfit.

The other three Russians were simply Ivan, Yevgeny and Gennady. Three nice boys. The kind of nice boys you saw popping in and out of KGB facilities, looking after more senior officers. Bond had once seen a trio like this coming out of a building after six men had died—none of them through natural causes.

He tried to engage all of them in polite conversation, unveiling a plan that had been set up on an easel, showing exactly where they were to be stationed, in relation to their charges. Outside, three Petty Officers stood by with cards giving details of the several decks, and their geographic relationship to those parts of *Invincible* tagged for the visiting VIPs and the bodyguards. Bond explained this to them, went through the emergency drills, making certain the Russian-speakers understood, then wished them a good night's rest, and began to hand them over to the CPOs.

A light hand rested on his sleeve. "I think, me you take

171

to my quarters, Captain Bond?" Nikki stood beside him, close enough for him to catch the hint of Bal de Versailles she wore.

"You, I think, get special treatment, Comrade Attaché—Nikki."

She gave him a glittering smile and he noticed her perfect teeth and the inviting mouth. "Yes, you're quite near my quarters as it happens. I have to hand you over to one of the lady officers we have on board, but it's a nice little walk up to my cabin." He turned.

"I'm *so* sorry I'm late, sir." Clover Pennington stood by the door, her face looking like the wrath of God. "I have instructions to escort the Comrade Attaché to her quarters. Show her the ropes, sir."

"Which ropes?" Nikki's voice sounded as though she was genuinely puzzled.

"An English saying. Means she's going to show you the way around the ship. This is First Officer Pennington, Nikki. She'll see that you're well looked after."

"Oh, but Captain Bond, I was thinking you could look after me."

"Not in a million years," muttered Clover so that Bond could hear.

"Best go with her, Nikki. Protocol, really. Perhaps we can talk later on."

"I also would like that. In your cabin, maybe, yes?" Reluctantly, she allowed Clover to guide her toward the companionway. Nikki looked back and smiled invitingly. First Officer Pennington kept her eyes to the front.

Bond had just turned in for the night when they darkened ship, right on 23:59 hours. Ten minutes later he realized few people were going to get much sleep while the exercise was running, for the klaxon began to blare while the orders came blasting out of the Tannoy system. "All hands to action stations. Close up, all watches."

Shortly after this, the Captain calmly announced that the whole force had been spread into their approved battle formation, a huge rough diamond shape, as they were entering the English Channel at full speed. "Our escorts report a wolfpack of submarines trying to get inside the screen." Walmsley's voice was calm, dispassionate, and Bond imagined it would be just the same if this was the real thing. "One of our escorts on the starboard side has been challenged by a submarine, and ordered to stop. I'm putting four helicopters into the air on submarine search. If the subs fire on our force, or become more belligerent, our helicopters will go into search and destroy mode."

Bond stretched back on the small bunk, fully dressed. It was almost one-thirty in the morning. He could give it five more minutes before he would need to check out his charges and make certain all was well.

Thirty seconds later he was on his feet, springing to the cabin door, answering the pounding on it.

A flushed Royal Marine sentry stood there, almost breathless. "Captain Bond, sir, you're needed. It's bad, sir. Very bad . . ."

He was about to add more when Clover Pennington appeared behind the Marine. "It's one of the Americans, Jame—sir." She looked as though she was about to throw up. "The one I believe they call Ed. The slim, very tough, good-looking one, with sandy hair."

"Yes? That's Ed. What's wrong?"

"One of my girls . . . One of my Wrens . . . found him. He's dead. A lot of blood. I think . . . I . . . Well, I

173

know . . . he's been murdered, sir. Someone's cut his throat. The heads are like an abattoir."

Bond felt his stomach churn as he reached for the webbing belt with the big holster hanging from it. Then, buckling it on, he nodded, following the Marine and First Officer Pennington into the VIP area. The belt, with the heavy pistol bouncing against his side, made him feel like a Western gunslinger. Unreal. But it was not every day of the week you get an American Secret Service bodyguard murdered aboard one of Her Majesty's ships.

11

Death's Heads

Bond paused for a second before the bulkhead, with its fire door bolted open. Belowdecks there was always a familiar smell, difficult to describe, dry, filtered air, a little oil, tiny mixed scents of machinery and humans. The paintwork was light gray and a mass of piping ran high along each side of the passageway, with electrical ducts carrying wiring down to the deck itself. The air conditioning, plumbing and electronics hummed. This was what always assaulted the senses when the ship was alive and at sea.

Ahead of him there were the other cabin doors, usually used by executive officers, who were now forced to double-up on messdecks and in other areas of the ship. Beyond there was a further bulkhead where another Marine stood on duty. Through there, he knew were the cabins occupied by the Wren detachment, who had ousted the junior officers.

Before stepping over the first bulkhead, Bond gave rapid orders to the flushed Marine who had banged on his door—"I don't care who it is, admirals or special duty staff who came aboard with them, you are to check who is in each of these cabins, and also have a list ready for me. I want to know who was where over the past hour at least. And get one of the doctors as quickly as you can. You'd best get your sergeant down here to give you a hand. My authority. You know who I am?"

The young Marine nodded, and Bond turned to Clover. "Right, the body's where? In the heads used for your Wrens?"

She gave him a sickly "Yes," and Bond brushed past her and started to run down the passageway. Behind him he heard the young Marine banging on the first cabin door with his rifle butt.

At the second bulkhead he told the Marine to stay alert and asked him if any of the officers, or their men, had gone past him into the prohibited area where the Wrens were.

"I've only been here for fifteen minutes, sir. We had to reorganize the guard duties when the Captain called all hands to close up."

"So. How long was the area unguarded?"

"Not sure, sir. Fifteen minutes at the most."

Clover led him through the passageway adjacent to the cabins occupied by the Wrens. A rather startled girl in pajamas poked her head out of one of the doors. "Back inside, Deeley," Clover snapped sharply, and the figure disappeared.

There was a trail of bloody footmarks, ending abruptly

in a spatter of blood, around twelve feet from the closed bulkhead door which led to the heads. For some reason a query ran through Bond's mind. The ablutions and lavatories on Royal Navy ships were always known as the heads—plural—while the U.S. Navy called them "head"—singular. It was the other way around with the HUD in fighter aircraft. The Americans called it the *Heads*-Up-Display; the Brits translated it as *Head*-Up-Display. Any odd thoughts on British and American semantics were cleared from his mind as he opened the bulkhead door.

Clover had been right, the place *was* like an abattoir, awash with blood, and the body on the tiled floor rolled with the ship, giving the horrific illusion that the blood was still pumping from it.

"You touch him?"

Clover shook her head, lips closed tightly as though she was fighting the urge to vomit.

"Better get out. Go back and tell one of those Marines that the doc should bring down a couple of sick bay ratings to help clean up the mess."

"I'll do that from the nearest phone." A tall, gray-haired figure stood behind them. "Surgeon Commander Grant. Let's take a look at the cadaver."

Bond had met Grant for a few seconds in the wardroom on his arrival aboard. The doc appeared to be a no-nonsense man, of few words. He was in uniform but with his trousers tucked into green surgeon's boots. "Leave him to me, then I'll get one of my boys down with a spare set of boots for you, Captain Bond. Blood's the very devil to get off."

Bond nodded and stood at the door as Grant splashed across the gore-swilled tiled deck. He bent over to examine

177

the body, giving a little grunt of disgust. He shook his head, plodded back and picked up the telephone intercom on the wall in the passageway, dialing the sick bay number. "Barnes? Right, get down to 406. Boots and rubber aprons. One spare pair of boots, and rustle up a couple of lads with strong stomachs, squeegees and buckets. Quick as you can."

He turned to Bond. "Whoever did it wasn't taking any chances, Captain Bond. They've nearly taken his head off. Neat slit. Ear to ear. By the look of it, someone took him from behind, grabbed his hair and reached over with something very sharp. Who is he?"

"One of the American security. Head boy, I think. Nasty."

"It would be stupid to ask if he had any enemies, because he obviously had at least one . . ." He trailed off as his two sick bay attendants arrived, followed by a pair of Ordinary Seamen carrying mopping-up gear.

"Oh, hell!" One of the sick bay attendants looked into the heads, then backed away.

"Just give Captain Bond the boots," the Surgeon Commander said quietly. "Keep the cleaning-up people away until he's finished. Best get a gurney while you're at it, we'll have to put this one in the freezer."

Bond kicked off his shoes, pulled on the boots and made his way toward the body. It was Ed, no doubt about it, and he had died atrociously. Bond was even concerned about moving the corpse: afraid the head would part from the body, for the slash across the throat had been long, hard and deep.

Pulling back the sleeves of his own navy-blue RN issue pullover, Bond turned the body onto its side. His hands were wet with blood, but he reached into the dead man's pockets, removing a wallet and two other pieces of ID. He was about to let the body drop back in place when he heard a minute scraping sound coming, it seemed, from under the Secret Service man's right shoulder. Blood up to his elbow, Bond searched with his hand, which connected with metal. He pulled, bringing out a small, battery-operated dictating machine.

At the door again, arms held away from his body, Bond told the Surgeon Commander that he could get the place cleared up. One of the sick bay attendants thoughtfully came forward to wipe the blood from his arms. He nodded thanks and set off back toward his own quarters.

There was some uproar in the section of passageway where the Admirals and their respective staffs were quartered. A Marine sergeant raised his eyebrows as Bond approached. "Captain Bond, sir . . ." Then he saw the blood, and the dripping miniature dictating machine, "You all right, sir? Blimey, that genuine claret, sir?"

"Freshly bottled, Sergeant, I'm afraid. We have a murder on our hands. What's the situation here?"

"All playing up nasty, sir. All three Admirals are on the bridge with the Captain. Admiral Gould has one of his flag officers with him, a Lieutenant Brinkley; Lieutenant Camm wants permission to leave his quarters—"

"Nobody leaves." It was like a whipcrack command.

"That's what I've told them, sir. Posted extra sentries."

"Good. What other problems have we got?"

"Admiral Gudeon has one of his security people with him on the bridge, the other two, Mr. Stanley Hare and Mr. Bruce Trimble, the black gentleman—they're playing merry hell. They say they should be with their man at the whiff of any incident."

"But they're in their cabin?"

179

"Sir," the sergeant acknowledged.

"Okay, keep them there. Tell them I'll see them in due course. The Russians?"

The sergeant sighed. "Very difficult, sir. All speak English, but they're not being helpful."

"The lady?"

"Miss Ratnikov? She seems a bit distraught. Seems as how she walked into the Wrens' heads just after the body was—"

"Did she now. You will inform *all* of them that I'll see them, independently, in my cabin within the hour."

"Aye-aye, sir."

"Just keep them quiet, Sarge, and put one of your men on my cabin. I'll be going up to the bridge soon. Nobody goes into my quarters, and I mean *nobody,* not even your Captain of Marines, without my say-so. Particularly while I'm seeing the Captain on the bridge."

The sergeant nodded. "Good as done, sir."

Bond washed the blood off himself, then cleaned the dictating machine and took a quick look at the victim's ID. His name had been Edgar Morgan, and it was clear that he was the senior officer of the Secret Service team. He shuffled through the wallet and found a second laminated ID card, tucked deep into a zippered pocket. So. He looked at the photograph of Morgan and read the magic words. Mr. Morgan was not regular Secret Service. He was only on attachment from other duties in Naval Intelligence, where he held the rank of commander.

He dried off the dictating machine and saw that the one small cassette had run all the way through. He checked the batteries, then operated the rewind. The tiny tape scrolled back and he pressed the Play button, saw the red light come on, and then adjusted the volume. The dead Ed Morgan's voice came out clear from the tiny speaker.

"Report Four. To be translated in plain cipher and squirted at first opportunity via HMS *Invincible.* No. 23X5. Request all detailed background on following names. First, Russian officers, possible KGB or GRU. Nikola Ratnikov, assigned as Russian Naval Attaché; Yevgeny Stura, Gennady Novikov and Ivan Tiblashin. Also request further information on the following members of the British Royal Navy . . ." Bond's eyes widened as he listened to this particular roll of honor. "If all cleared and genuine," the voice continued, "I suggest *Dancer* cleared for RV as arranged. If not cleared, will definitely advise abort *Stewards' Meeting.* Repeat . . ." Then came the other sounds: the cry, the thump as the small metal recorder hit the floor, the final horrible sounds of Morgan's death, followed by the muffled tape still running, and behind it other noises. A woman's voice, then another. They were unclear, but he also thought he could hear a noise, as though someone was trying to move the body. There was the muffled sound of footsteps on the tiles. Then silence.

The thing that concerned James Bond was the list of Royal Navy personnel that the late Ed Morgan was trying to have cleared with Washington. It was quite obvious that there was some communications arrangement with *Invincible*—probably an American cipher machine had been installed. The whole thing would have been automatic: the dictating machine's tape would be fed onto a cipher tape which would translate it into whatever random jumble they were using, and the entire message would be squirted to Washington in a fraction of a second. That was a secondary business, though. The real worry lay in the list of people Morgan wanted checked out.

Bond picked up the phone and dialed the bridge. A young midshipman came on, and, in a few seconds, following some urgent instructions, Rear-Admiral Sir John Walmsley spoke. "Be quick about it, Bond. I'm trying to get this force through the Channel without *Blue Side*'s submarines blowing us all to hell."

Bond took less than a minute. There was a long silence, then Walmsley said, "Get up here. You'd best break the bad news to Admiral Gudeon himself. Get up here now."

"Aye-aye, sir." Bond stowed away the late Ed Morgan's ID and the dictating machine, grabbed his cap and left the cabin at a run.

●   ●   ●

"I am not pulling out of this exercise, Bond. Not for you, not for anyone. It's all far too important. Particularly what's due to happen tomorrow night when we should be in the Bay of Biscay. *That's* too important, politically." Sir John Walmsley's bearded jaw stuck forward, giving him an awesomely stubborn look. They were in the Rear-Admiral's night cabin.

Bond shrugged. "At least the *Stewards' Meeting* team has to be informed."

"As security liaison are you telling me to do this? Or is it merely a suggestion?"

"I think you should do it, sir."

"I wouldn't need to make any fuss if you nailed whoever did this."

"And, with respect, sir, I'm not Sherlock Holmes."

"I thought you people could be all things to all men—and women."

"Then I'll try to be a Sherlock, sir. I suppose I'd better break the news to Admiral Gudeon, and his man—"

"Mr. Israel," the Rear-Admiral filled in for him.

"Yes. Joe Israel. Both of them together, I think, sir."

Walmsley paused by the door. "Cantankerous old bugger, Gudeon. Even tried to tell me how to run my own ship."

"Doesn't surprise me in the least, sir." Bond gave him a bland smile, and Walmsley did not catch on to the fact that he had been mildly insulted by this officer, who was a "funny."

Five minutes later Admiral Gudeon and Joe Israel arrived at Bond's cabin. Israel was tall, somewhere around six-four, Bond guessed. He had a shock of graying hair and that lazy, cultivated walk and stance so often used by bullet-catchers to disguise their constant alertness. When he came in, leading the way for Admiral Gudeon, he gave one of his special smiles. Joe Israel smiled a lot; a kind of overbite smile which lit up his eyes. He also had a spontaneous laugh: loud, open-mouthed and infectious. Joe Israel did not laugh during the first part of the interview.

"John Walmsley said you needed to see both of us, Bond." Gudeon sounded disgruntled, like a child called away from playing with his train set—which in some ways he had been, as all hell was breaking loose on the bridge as *Invincible* went through fast turns and changes of course. The submarines were still positioning themselves around the task force, warning but not firing.

"I suggest you sit down, sir. I have some pretty serious, and bad, news for both of you."

183

"Oh?" Gudeon sounded as though all news to him was bad news.

"The senior officer in your bodyguard—"

"Morgan?" Gudeon dropped into a chair. Joe Israel stood directly behind him.

"Ed Morgan." Bond nodded. "I'm afraid Ed Morgan is dead."

He noted that Joe Israel looked shocked. Gudeon's mouth opened. "Oh, my God," he said, this time sounding genuinely concerned. "How, in heaven's name?"

"He was murdered."

"Murdered?" They both spoke together, Israel a touch before his boss. Then Gudeon spoke alone. "How murdered? People don't get murdered on one of Her Majesty's capital ships."

"This one did."

"How?"

"He got his throat cut. In the Wrens' heads. Very unpleasant."

Gudeon just stared ahead. Israel made a sound like the word "But!"

"I have a couple of questions for Mr. Israel, here. Then I'd like to talk alone with you, sir."

The Admiral just nodded an okay. He suddenly looked older and shocked.

"Joe? I can call you Joe?"

"Sure, sir."

"Okay. Had you ever worked with Ed Morgan before?"

"Never. He was very new to me. Never even met him before this assignment. But he was sharp." The way he said it, Israel sounded as though he meant Ed Morgan was too sharp.

184

"And he came to a sharp end, I fear."

Israel shook his head. There was just a mite of sadness, or shock. "It's tough." Then he looked down at the Admiral, "Who takes charge, sir?"

Gudeon cleared his throat. "Well. Well, you're senior aren't you?"

"It's why I asked, sir."

"Okay, you take over until we clear it all with *Dancer*'s people." His eyes flicking up to Bond, as though he had said something wrong.

"It's okay, Admiral Gudeon. I *am* in overall charge of security. I know who *Dancer* is, and I know he's not one of Santa's reindeer. Now, I just want to check times with Mr. Israel." He looked up at the big man. "You were minding the Admiral tonight."

"Yep."

"With him all the time."

"Had dinner with him, sir. Yes. Then we both changed and I accompanied him to the bridge."

"What time was that?"

"Twenty-three-forty, around twenty minutes before the war started."

"And you've been with him all the time, since then?"

"Up there until we were asked to get down here."

"Is there anything we should do about getting details back to Washington? You have special procedures?"

"Yes. I'll deal with all that."

"Okay." Bond pretended to be lost in thought for a couple of seconds. "Not straightaway, though, if you don't mind. I want you to wait outside with the Marine guard. I need a little time with the Admiral. Then we'll get the whole of this done officially. Excuse me." This last to

185

Gudeon as Bond went to the cabin door and spoke to the guard, telling him that Mr. Israel would wait outside, and go nowhere else until the Admiral came out.

"Ed Morgan?" Bond phrased it as a question, back again behind his desk. Gudeon looked worried, and he did not seem to be the kind of man who got worried easily.

"What about him?"

"I need some answers, sir. I'm entitled to answers, particularly as I'm going to be handling all this security for *Stewards' Meeting.* I'm not altogether happy about dealing with personal bodyguards on an international scale. Now, Ed Morgan wasn't a Secret Service bodyguard in the true sense of the word, was he?"

"How in hell you know that?"

"It's my job to know it, sir."

"Nobody was supposed to have wind of it."

"I've been in the business some time. You like to tell me about him?"

Gudeon sighed. "Guess so." He now looked truly older and grayer. If it was not for the uniform he could have been just right for some guy sitting in a rocker on the stoop of a house in a Norman Rockwell illustration.

"Ed was my nominee. We'd worked together before, and I figured him as the best man for the job. He was a Commander, by the way. Navy Intelligence—which included some fieldwork."

"Okay. Do you know how he was handling communications with Washington?"

"Yes, I do."

"Was it directly through our communications staff on board?"

A lengthy pause. "No. I have a closed-channel micro-

186

transmitter in my cabin. When Ed wanted to transmit he was to get on to me, and I'd give him the okay."

"How does it work?"

"How does any of this stuff work. All damned magic to me. There's a place for a small tape in the thing. I gather he simply inserted a tape with his message *en clair,* locked on to the FLATSCOM we used, and the message was squirted in cipher to another ship. They would pass it on to Washington. That's the basics anyhow."

"FLATSCOM is generic for U.S. Navy satellite communications, right, sir?"

Gudeon gave a tiny nod, like someone had pricked him on the back of the neck.

"Did he use it when you came aboard?"

"No." A little tight-lipped. "Look, Captain Bond, I'm trying to cooperate, but I have quite a problem on my hands. Morgan wanted to use our communications link around dawn. I said I'd be down to unlock it and put the keys in. He didn't confide in me, but he was concerned about something. Something on board. Wanted it checked out by Washington before he would okay *Dancer* coming in for *Stewards' Meeting.* Now I'm in the cold. I have to make the decision. And I have to make it without knowing what Morgan wanted."

"I really shouldn't worry too much about—" The telephone buzzed and Bond excused himself to take the call. It was Surgeon Commander Grant. "The place is cleaned up, sir; and I took the liberty of having some photographs done—you know the kind of thing: body in situ, face, wound, all that stuff. Seen it on the moving pictures. Can't be accurate about time of death, but I'd say it was within an hour of me seeing the body."

187

"Mmm-huu. It wasn't long before *I* saw it. Just keep everything on ice. I'll see you later." He cradled the telephone and turned back to Gudeon. "Don't bother yourself too much, sir. I'd okay *Dancer* coming in on schedule."

"Easy as that?"

"Just as easy. I think I know what he wanted checked out. I think it was why he got chopped."

"If you know, then it's your duty to share it with me."

"I said I *think* I know, sir, and that's a long way from knowing."

"And you won't even . . . ?"

"Sorry, Admiral Gudeon, but, no. I carry the ball on this one. I *think* I know, and I'll take steps to make certain and even secure matters before *Dancer* gets here. Anything strange, and I'll have *Stewards' Meeting* waved off. In the meantime I'd suggest that you go back to the bridge and take Mr. Israel with you. Also, I'd be grateful if you don't talk to anyone else about this. And I do mean *anyone,* sir."

"If you say so, Bond." Gudeon did not look happy, but 007 wanted to leave it there. There was a lot for him to do before *he* could take definite action about the operation they called *Stewards' Meeting.* First, he had to do his Sherlock Holmes imitation, and see everybody concerned, then it was essential for him to get his own people to check on the names Edgar Morgan had listed on the tape—even the Royal Navy people. He sat back, making quick decisions on whom he would speak to next. It was three o'clock in the morning. Nobody was going to be happy, but he considered it best for him to stick with people he knew were awake. He called the bridge and asked to see Admiral of the Fleet Sir Geoffrey Gould and his Flag Lieutenant, Mr.

Brinkley. They were with him in five minutes, and he broke the news, followed by the standard questions—Had Brinkley been with the Admiral since dinner? Had they parted company at any time? The answers were yes, and no, respectively.

Gould was shaken. "You do *not* get murdered on one of HM's ships," he said, echoing Gudeon.

"It seems that we are the exception that proves the rule," Bond said briskly.

"We be any help, James?" Ted Brinkley asked.

"Possibly, but not yet. I gather all the Russians are English-speakers."

"Yes." Brinkley had got to that information very quickly. "First thing Moggy and I did. Try out their English. Bit funny, though."

"How funny?"

"The leader of their pack—Stura, Yevgeny Stura. Fellow with the scar and the vodka nose."

"What about him?"

"He tried to play silly buggers. Pretended he had no English."

"But he has?"

"He's been up with Admiral Pauker on the bridge all night. Speaks English like a native. Slight American accent, but he speaks and understands. Just wouldn't let on to us when we were with them. The attaché with all the honeypot trappings aimed at you did the translating. Rum."

"Not really." Bond cocked an eyebrow. "KGB games. They often try that kind of thing. It's almost a standard drill."

He asked them to get back on the bridge, talk to nobody and ask the Captain if he would request, *most respectfully,* if

189

Admiral Pauker and Yevgeny, he with the vodka nose, would come down to see him.

They arrived a few minutes later, and Bond went through the same routine. Oddly, Yevgeny Stura went through the charade of being a non–English speaker with the connivance of Pauker until Bond reminded them forcibly that they were on British territory and he, for one, would see to it that the most important part of *Landsea '89,* namely *Stewards' Meeting,* would be called off if they were not honest with him.

Admiral Pauker became belligerent, shouting at Bond, telling him that he was the highest-ranking officer on board—"I am the entire head of the Soviet Navy. I will have you stripped of rank, ground to dust, for speaking like this!" he ended.

"Do as you will, Admiral, but as I am in charge of security for the whole of *Stewards' Meeting,* I can also make demands, and I'm not putting up with Mr. Stura's games. He speaks English and understands it. I know it, he knows it. We all know it. So, no more games."

The Russians disappeared, slightly cowed, and Bond sent the Marine guard to get Mr. Camm.

Moggy Camm bore out his partner's story, and answered all the questions quickly and with no hesitation. They had agreed that Ted Brinkley would take tonight's duty with Gould. Moggy was due to relieve him at dawn. He had seen and heard nothing out of the ordinary until the activity outside his cabin, then the Marine and his sergeant wakening him.

There were other obligatory questions. What time had he turned in? About eleven. Did you see anyone or anything before then? He had taken a drink with the other two

Russians, and Bruce Trimble, the black American. They had a special little messdeck, with alcohol on tap—one of the small CPO messdecks which had been set aside for their relaxation. They had all retired about the same time. You all come down together? Yes.

One at a time he went through the other bodyguards. Bruce Trimble backed Moggy and the two Russians. The Russians backed everybody else.

The other American Secret Service man, Stanley Hare, had turned in early, "At the same time as Ed. We talked awhile; Trimble came back and we all grabbed a few Zs." No, he had not heard Ed leave the cabin. In spite of the noise from the Tannoy system, Stan had heard nothing until the Marine banged on the door. "In our job, you learn to sleep on a clothesline."

Everyone was exceptionally helpful, so he sent for the Marine sergeant.

Sergeant Harvey was your typical Royal Marine sergeant with no time for messing around with excuses.

Bond put it to him straight, and he answered just as clearly.

"I understand there was a problem over who was doing the guard duty down here, Sarn't Harvey."

"Considerable problem, yes, sir."

"How considerable?"

"When the balloon went up, as expected, at 23:59, *all* Marines went to their action stations, sir. I, as duty sergeant, should have spotted the problem at once. I didn't, sir."

"Go on."

"Around 0:20 hours I realized we had nobody down here. We're stretched as it is—42 Commando not having to do anything unless there's a real flap on—so I sent two Marines down with instructions to do one hour, then report to me. I had meant to sort out a couple more, but I didn't, sir. My fault, I take any blame. The two on duty down here were authorized to go back to their normal posts. When I remembered, I gave the orders on the bulkhead telephone. My fault, sir. Easy as that. I've questioned all concerned. Between them they reckon the posts were left without guard for ten minutes. Me, being what I am, would add another five for luck."

"There's no blame, Sarn't. One of those things, but what you're saying is that people would be free to come and go between the prohibited areas for at least fifteen minutes. From around what? One-fifteen and one-thirty hours?"

"About that, sir."

"Right. Thank you."

There were still three people he needed to talk with. Clover, the luscious Nikki, and one other mentioned in the disturbing list of Naval personnel the late Ed Morgan had wanted checked out. He could leave getting reports back on the Russians, but his own kind would have to be looked into now.

He was dog tired, and there was little likelihood of getting any sleep for at least another twenty-four hours, so he stretched, jammed his cap on and went up to the highly secure Holy of Holies, the communications room, set on the first deck, directly below Flight Operations and the bridge. An aggressive Marine challenged him and he showed the pass which had been issued to him, together with other materials on joining *Invincible*. Apart from Sir John Walmsley, the communications staff would probably be the only ones who realized their special security officer

192

was really a disguised "funny." The duty communications officer certainly did, you could tell by his eyes, and the quick flick of his head when Bond showed him his authority for using the Intelligence Computer, which had a direct satellite link with GCHQ, Cheltenham.

They exchanged code words, and a few heads were raised as the communications officer took him across the busy room to the little sealed-off area, opening the door and following him in to boot up the big Cray Computer. Once done, the DCO tactfully left him alone.

The beast's screen shimmered green, and Bond typed in the first set of digits that would wake up the lads in Cheltenham.

STATE AUTHORITY, the computer asked him in large black letters.

Bond typed in MERRYGOROUND.

GIVE BACKUP flashed onto the computer.

26980/8, Bond typed.

TYPE OF INFORMATION REQUIRED? queried the silent machine.

DATA ON ROYAL PERSONNEL SERVING NOW BIRDSNEST TWO, he told it.

WHAT OPS? it asked.

LANDSEA '89 AND POSSIBLY STEWARDS' MEETING

SPECIFICS. STATE FULL DOSSIERS OR RELEVANT SECURITY CLEARANCE

BOTH

INPUT NAMES—SURNAME FOLLOWED BY GIVEN NAME AND RANK IF KNOWN

Bond methodically typed in the list recalled from Ed Morgan's last words on earth.

In a matter of seconds the machine began to throw dossiers at him on the screen. One at a time they came, and he could scroll up and down them, reading the official lives of all those Morgan had requested. He went through six dossiers and selected the "OK" on each when he had finished.

The seventh was LEADING WREN DEELEY, SARAH.

The response came up, fast and flashing—

NO LEADING WREN DEELEY, SARAH ATTACHED TO BIRDSNEST TWO PLEASE WAIT

He waited. Then—

NO LEADING WREN DEELEY, SARAH SHOWS ON RECORD. PLEASE REPORT YOUR SUPERIOR OFFICER IMMEDIATELY

The name had rung a bell. Yes, he recalled the pajamaed figure as he hurried toward the heads with Clover. Clover had sharply told her to get back into her cabin.

So he would now see Clover and Nikki. Then, last of all, the nonexistent Leading Wren Sarah Deeley. There was no way he could report anything to his superior officer.

Bond went back to his cabin and sent a message out that he required to see First Officer Pennington WRNS, immediately.

12
Will You Join the Dance?

He had sent for coffee, and now sat sipping the strong, black brew. Across the desk, Clover Pennington, looking nervous, picked up her cup—white; no sugar.

"Clover, the situation is quite simple. The guards were off for about ten minutes. I know that. Then one of them, with you in tow, came banging at my door just after twenty-five past one. So, in those ten minutes two things happened. First Ed Morgan left the cabin he was sharing with two other American bodyguards and went to the Wrens' heads. We don't know why. Maybe he had a date. Maybe he wanted to be somewhere he was unlikely to be disturbed, the Wrens' heads were the most likely place he could be alone." The second choice, Bond knew, was the most probable truth.

"While he was there, someone came in behind him and slit his throat. Quickly, quietly, and very efficiently. It could have been one of his buddies, or one of the Russians, even Moggy Camm, one of Admiral Sir Geoffrey Gould's Flag Lieueys. On the other hand, it could have been the Russian lady—"

"Nikki the Rat?" She said it with no trace of humor.

"Nikki, yes. Or, First Officer Pennington, it could have been you, or one of your girls. We still have to discuss the question of how Morgan's body was found. You said it was one of your Wrens. Which one?"

"Leading Wren Deeley." Her hand shook, lifting the cup. So much so that she had to put her other hand up to steady it.

"Okay, Clover. We both know whose side you're on, because you came storming into the villa on Ischia, having almost had me killed—"

She suddenly appeared to steady herself. "I saved your life, as it happens. We blew the BAST girl to hell and gone. You were there. We triggered that explosion before you could get close. It was, as they say, a button job."

"Right, Clover. After spending time with me at Northanger you went back to Yeovilton and collected your girls. Girls you'd already worked with."

"Yes."

"Then how do you explain Leading Wren Deeley? The girl who found friend Morgan's body?"

She took another sip of coffee, then said, "James, I just can't explain her. Those last few weeks at Yeovilton were spent going through all the drills with the girls—all the stuff we would have to do for *Stewards' Meeting*. I came back from Northanger and one of my Leading Wrens had

196

gone sick. They had simply put Deeley in her place. I had a bit of a row with the Executive Office about it. I also had to go through the training with Deeley on her own. Thank God, she's smart and a quick study, as they say in the theater."

Bond looked into her eyes. They were steady and nothing stirred or moved within them. "You baby-sat me in Ischia with a team, right?"

"You know it's right."

"And you're still watching my back here, in *Invincible*?"

"Part of my orders, yes. It isn't easy, James."

He let the pause hang between them for almost a minute. "I've checked you out, Clover. You appear to be absolutely clean."

"What d'you mean? Checked me out?"

"I've been onto *our* records in London with a list of names. You come out clean, and you've done all the courses for *my* particular Service."

"Of course I have. Damn it, I've been in the Royal Navy for six years."

"Then why didn't you run a check on Deeley?"

"I didn't think it—"

Bond hit the desk with the flat of his palm. "Who do you think was responsible for Ed Morgan's death?"

She gave a long sigh. "Nikki the Rat. She arrived in the heads very conveniently, just after Deeley found the body."

"Don't be naive, Clover. *You* saw the state of those heads, they were awash with blood. We made one hell of a mess in the corridors just getting the body looked at and moved. Footprints all over the place. When we arrived—you, me and the Marine—there was one set of smudged footprints leading out. Deeley, you say, found the body, followed

197

quickly by Nikki Ratnikov. Deeley actually went into the heads, yes?"

"Yes." A very small voice.

"Nikki stood outside the bulkhead and screamed her head off, right?"

She nodded.

"Then Deeley came out. In a state? You haven't told me any of this, yet. But I'm presuming it. Am I right?"

She took a long sip of coffee. "The screaming woke me. After all, my cabin's almost opposite the heads."

"Yes?"

"I came out and there was Nikki screaming—"

"Standing just outside the bulkhead?"

"Yes."

"And Deeley was inside, with her feet paddling in blood?"

A quick, almost reluctant, nod. "She was in a state. Just standing there looking at the body and the blood. Frozen there. I thought she'd have hysterics. She could have caught them quite easily from the Russian, who was making one hell of a din."

"Then?"

"The Marine guard came running. He said something about reporting to you."

"Which he did, with you on his heels. You got to me a couple of minutes after him. What happened in that couple of minutes?"

"Nikki faded away, sobbing her heart out."

"And you told Deeley to come out?"

"Yes." Again the little nod.

"You saw she was dripping blood all over the place from her feet?"

"I told her to wait a minute and got a towel from my cabin. She wiped off her feet and I told her to get back to her cabin. I said I'd talk to her later."

"And have you?"

"Yes. I've seen her. She seems to be in shock. There are three other girls in her cabin, they're helping to calm her down. Actually I got the doc to give her something. Sedative."

"You realize that, unless the killer got out very quickly, Deeley's your main suspect? One set of smudged, bloody footprints, which ended suddenly along the passage, when we got there. Deeley's, we presume, with her feet wiped off with your towel. What was she wearing?"

"A robe. Toweling robe—most of the girls find those convenient."

"Carrying anything?"

"No."

"Then there's another problem. We haven't recovered the murder weapon. Somewhere, someone's got a very sharp knife. And there's the other matter of you not having Deeley security-cleared when they gave her to you at Yeovilton."

"She was Grade 3 cleared. On her documents. She's been working on classified stuff at Fleet HQ, Northwood."

"It actually says that?"

"You want to see it?"

"Later. It's all a forgery anyway."

"What . . . ?"

He didn't let her finish. "Leading Wren Sarah Deeley does not exist, Clover."

"What d'you—"

Again he stopped her, by completing the question.

"What do I mean? I mean what I say. No Leading Wren Deeley exists in your branch of the Service. I've had it from London. She's a plant, and I suspect that Ed Morgan knew it, or, at least suspected it. He had other suspicions as well."

"This is crazy!"

"No, you've made a terrible mistake, Clover. You were in charge. You should have personally seen to it that all security clearances matched up and were for real."

"Oh, my God." There was no denying the shock in her voice and on her face. "What do we do, James?"

"You mean what do *I* do? I'll tell you." He spoke for ten minutes, saying that he would feel safer if she was out of the way. "I'll arrange a Marine guard and have you kept somewhere out of sight. It'll make matters easier. Then I want to talk to the Captain. After that, I'll see Nikki Ratnikov. I want an independent identification of the Deeley girl. Then I'll question her, and she'll probably be taken into custody and held until it's all over and we're in Gib. I'm not going to bother my people as yet. More secure to do it directly from Gib. Okay?"

"Whatever you say, James."

As he rose, she came toward him, one hand reaching out and grasping his sleeve. "James, my career's at risk. I've played everything by the book, even saved your life from that wretched girl who I'm certain was going to see you dead before Christmas day was out. You owe me—"

"And *you,* Clover, owe me now. I'll do whatever I can for you."

She came closer, her young body thrusting against his.

Bond pulled away, holding her at arms' length. "Later, Clover. When it's all over we'll talk. Just wait." He went to

200

the cabin door, opened it and spoke to the Marine on duty. While they waited, the Tannoy blasted out—the Captain saying that they had now cleared the English Channel. "There are still submarines shadowing us," he boomed, "but they tell me they've been ordered not to attack. The political situation is that both sides are talking, in spite of the fact that seven NATO air bases on the European Continent were attacked, with varying degrees of damage and success, during the night. I'm going to stand down Red Watch for two hours, but you are all on an immediate-response alert. I shall keep you informed of any change in the situation."

The click that ended the message coincided with the knock on his cabin door. It was the Marine sergeant Harvey. The man was tired, like everyone else on board, and it showed. Bond lost no time asking questions and then issuing orders—"Have you anywhere we can stow First Officer Pennington while I make a couple of enquiries?"

"Yes, sir. The duty Marine sergeant's cabin. I'm still there for the next hour or so."

"Right, take her there, and make sure she's under guard. There's the possibility she could be attacked, like our American friend last night—at least until I've finished my job."

"If you'll come with me, ma'am . . ." Sergeant Harvey appeared to be very considerate. To Bond he said, "I'll see she's guarded every minute, sir."

Clover gave Bond a weak smile, the look of someone with a lot on her mind, and departed with the sergeant. Before he could close the cabin door, a young midshipman appeared in the corridor, which, like all the other passageways below the flight deck, was only wide enough for two people to pass by brushing against each other. In the U.S. Navy, Bond remembered, they called them "knee-touchers."

"Captain's compliments, sir. Could you join him in his day cabin as quickly as possible?"

"Tell him I'm on my way. I wanted to see him in any case." Bond turned back into his cabin, opened up the little cupboard which stowed away a small handbasin and mirror. He looked unshaven, but that could be dealt with later. For now, he sloshed cold water over his face, cleaned his teeth and ran a comb through his hair.

●   ●   ●

"You look dog rough, Bond, if I may say so." Rear-Admiral Sir John Walmsley did not look too hot himself, but you don't tell rear-admirals that kind of thing—unless you're a vice-admiral or above. Walmsley was obviously in a foul mood. "Well, you got anything to tell me?"

Bond wondered why a man of Walmsley's station could so easily murder the English language. "Such as what, sir?" He bordered on that armed forces' crime called dumb insolence.

"Such as your detective work; your gumshoeing. Such as whether we can all sleep safely in our bunks? Whether we have a band of Thuggees aboard, or a crew of cutthroat pirates. Have you caught the bastard who cut the American's throat?"

"Not yet, sir. But it shouldn't be too long. Within the next half-hour or so, unless I'm being led up the garden path."

"And, when you've caught this fellow, do you think it's

safe to continue with *Stewards' Meeting*? Last night, early this morning anyhow, you were all for chucking it away."

"I needed to talk to you about that, sir. Might I ask you what arrangements were made with the U.S. Navy about communications?"

The Rear-Admiral nodded, and repeated, almost word for word, what Admiral Gudeon had told him.

"And the Russians?"

"Not quite as cryptic." Walmsley was down to giving shorthand answers.

"Can you expand on that?"

"Yes. They can use our main communications room, but not with much freedom. The Americans had their own gear on board, as you know. The Russians've been okayed to pass *en clair* signals through our transmitters. I suspect their signals aren't quite as straightforward as they appear. I should tell you they've reported Morgan's death."

"What I really need to know, sir, is how long have we got before there's any question of an abort?"

"At the moment we're in a readiness state for *Stewards' Meeting,* Bond. Things are going ahead exactly as planned. It all starts to happen at around ten tonight. If I recommend an abort after six, then I'll get a right old rollicking from the powers-that-be. What's worrying you? The threat by these BAST hooligans? There's no way they can possibly have information on *Stewards' Meeting.*"

Bond took in a deep breath. "Surely, sir, you must *know* they have some intelligence. I was nearly taken out; there was some loose talk at the RNAS Yeovilton. We've had a very serious incident aboard. I really don't know the security risks. . . ."

Walmsley ran a hand across his brow. "I let fly at you after the incident, Bond. I'm sorry about that, but I don't want to abort. As I said to you before, this is of great political importance." He repeated himself with a stronger accent. "Of *great* political importance. Now, give me your Sunday punch. If you get the fellow who killed Morgan, do you reckon we're in the clear?"

"It might be just that little bit safer," Bond said, allowing his tone to take on a graveside seriousness. "But we cannot be one hundred percent sure."

"Give me the odds."

"That an attempt will be made to compromise *Stewards' Meeting*?"

Walmsley nodded.

"Fifty-fifty. If I get the killer or not, sir, it's always been fifty-fifty. We don't know enough about this damned group BAST. We never have. The seriousness of a threat has always been high. I mean, if our people are right, BAST lost men, and spent a great deal of money organizing some form of assault. We've assumed it was aimed at *Stewards' Meeting,* but we can't be sure."

Sir John Walmsley waited for a minute or so. "If you get the person who killed Morgan, and if he can be interrogated, it will help."

"If it's who I think, then I would imagine interrogation isn't going to be of much assistance. If, as I suspect, it's a BAST job, done to protect their own, on board this ship, then the culprit will be highly trained. Won't break under any normal interrogation. And there will just not be time to bring in any specialists. In any case, sir, I would suspect that the killer knows very little. BAST appears to be well-drilled. If so, they'll work in the usual manner of terrorist groups: cells, cutouts, all that kind of thing. It'll all be very much need-to-know.''

Walmsley stood up and paced the small cabin. ''Will you, won't you, will you, won't you, will you join the dance? I'll tell you, Bond. Unless something comes up—hard intelligence, I mean—I shall go ahead with *Stewards' Meeting* once you have the killer under lock and key. I can't afford to abort.''

''As you say, sir. But, if I might suggest that all parties are given some kind of warning—''

''They've already had the main warning, Bond. They already know these BAST clowns might just make some kind of attempt to compromise the operation. All three parties have stated that the risk is calculated. In other words, they all want *Stewards' Meeting* to go ahead as arranged.''

''They know about Morgan?''

Walmsley gave an unspoken ''No,'' shaking his head and pursing his lips.

''Then on their own heads be it.''

''Easy to say, Bond. But people like that tend to lash out if something does happen. And if your worst fears are realized, then it will be our balls they'll cut off. We both know that.''

Bond grunted.

''We're in for it, Captain Bond. Whatever steps we take, they'll have us for breakfast—fried, with a little tomato and bacon, I suspect.''

''Then I'd best get on with putting my one suspect away; then doing some grilling of my own—without bacon and tomato.''

''Let me know.'' Walmsley's tone became belligerent

205

again. "Just let me know the results. But, after five, local, this afternoon all bets are off. We go ahead."

"Aye-aye, sir." Bond left the cabin. Time to see the lovely Nikki Ratnikov, and the Wren who was not a Wren, Sarah Deeley.

●   ●   ●

"James, I can call you James, yes?" Nikki Ratnikov shook her head. The shining ash-blonde hair swirled and settled naturally back in place with not a strand out of place. Bond could see why other women would take a natural dislike to Nikki.

"Yes," he said. "Yes, call me James."

"I am a little détresse . . . distrait . . . Oh, that is French. How you say it in English?"

"Distressed? Upset?"

"Yes, this is so. I, James, have seen many bad things in my time. *Many*. You cannot do my kind of work and avoid these things. But this was like maniac. This was like your old English Jim the Ripper, is right?"

"Jack," Bond corrected. "Jack the Ripper."

"Unnecessary violence. That poor man. He looked as though head had been removed, decapitalized? Yes?"

"Decapitated."

"So. Decapitated. And the blood. It was all so sudden. Frightening."

"Right, Nikki. Tell me. Tell me exactly what happened."

In spite of the protestations of being upset and distressed, Nikki Ratnikov was very lucid: matter-of-fact. "So. Yes. I wake up. I do not look at the time. I just wake up. Not much sleep I am getting with the noise. But I wake

206

up and realize I need to go to . . . I need the bathroom,
yes?"

"Yes."

"Good. I put on my robe and leave my cabin. I am a little
asleep still, James, you understand?"

"Yes, Nikki. Right, Nikki, I understand."

"I get to the bathrooms. I am looking at my feet to climb
over the little step."

"To climb over the bulkhead, yes."

"My foot is lifted even, then I look up and there is red
water on the floor. Then I see the Navy girl and the body.
My God, it is shock. I move back and scream."

"You screamed a lot, Nikki."

"It was so sudden. The horrible wound and all the blood
on the floor. Then the Navy girl start to also scream."

Bond had collected the clues as they were presented to
him. "Tell me *exactly* what you saw, Nikki." The body had
been facedown when he had arrived with the Marine and
Clover Pennington. "Exactly."

"The Navy girl—what do you call them, the Jenny Wren,
yes?"

"Wren will do."

"Okay. The Wren was leaning over this poor man. She
had one hand on his shoulder pushing him back, as if she
had just found him. His head was back and I could see the
terrible gash. Red, and the throat slashed—is that so,
slashed?"

Bond nodded her on.

"It was horrible. She saw me and let go of the man's
shoulder. He fell on his face, then I think she began screaming."

"What was she wearing, the Wren?"

"She had the sleeping clothes on, and a white robe. Like made from towels, yes?"

"Did she not get blood on the robe? If she was leaning . . . ?"

"She was like, how you say, squatting. She had the robe pulled up so it would not get in the blood."

"And what happened next?"

"We were both screaming, and a man came, then the Wren officer. She was telling me to go to my cabin, and the other girl to come out quickly."

"You saw her coming out?"

"Yes."

"Remember anything in particular?"

"No. Then I left."

"Think, Nikki. Did you notice anything else at all? How did she come out? Did she lift up her robe so that it wouldn't trail in the blood?"

"Yes, that I remember. She came out with it lifted up, but it was strange. . . . There *was* blood on it. She had blood on the chest. On the front of the robe. High up."

"Ah. Good. You *would* recognize this girl again, Nikki?"

"Of course. Anywhere I would recognize her."

"Right. Just wait one moment, please."

"For you, James, much more than *one* moment."

He ignored the obvious pass, went over to the cabin door and beckoned the Marine on duty outside.

"I want you to take Miss Ratnikov into the passage. Then go and find Leading Wren Deeley."

"Sir."

"Nikki." He turned back to the Russian girl. "I want you to wait outside until you see this Marine coming back down the passage with the Wren. If it is the girl you saw last night,

208

you will smile at her. If not, look away. You understand?"

"Is not difficult. Smile if I recognize. Ignore if I don't recognize?"

"Right." He turned to the Marine. "When you bring Leading Wren Deeley in here you either say 'Yes' or 'No.' 'Yes' if Miss Ratnikov smiles. 'No' if she doesn't. Get it?"

"Yes, sir. No difficulty."

"Go ahead, then."

Bond laid a hand on Nikki's shoulder. "Go now, and please, Nikki, get it right."

"Is no problem. I smile or look away. Thank you, James." Before he could stop her, Nikki had reached up and kissed his cheek before leaving the cabin. For some reason he thought of Beatrice and the kiss she had first given him. How it had seemed to burn his cheek. A tiny black cloud of depression came into his mind, and he shook his head, as though trying to rid himself of the last picture he had of Beatrice da Ricci. The smoke, flash and explosion that had left very little of her alive.

The picture would not go away, even when he picked up the telephone and asked for the Master-at-Arms—the "Jaundy" as they called him: the senior noncommissioned officer who had almost the power of God over the ratings, for in some ways he was the ship's chief of police. Bond gave him some quick crisp orders and put the telephone down.

It was not until he heard the knock on his cabin door that Bond realized he should really have had Clover present, but it was too late now.

The Marine opened the door to Bond's "Come."

"Yes, sir," he said. So Nikki had identified the girl as being the Wren who was with the body in the heads.

"Leading Wren Deeley, sir," the Marine announced, and the girl came through the cabin door which closed behind her.

"You wanted to see me, sir?" She was on the short side. Stocky and obviously fit. Her face remained placid and her eyes centered on Bond in full contact. He took in the face, not pretty: slightly angular, oddly masculine.

"Yes, Leading Wren Sarah Deeley." He paused. "That *is* your name and rank?"

"Yes, sir." She showed no trace of fear.

"And your division and number?"

"Plymouth, 762845, sir."

"Right. Can you tell me, Deeley, why there is no record of you as a member of the Women's Royal Naval Service?"

"I don't understand, sir."

"Well, you'd best understand, and quickly, Deeley. There is no record of you. Further . . ." He rose and began to walk around the small desk. "I have sent for the Master-at-Arms. You will regard yourself as under arrest."

Her face did not alter. "Under arrest for what, sir?"

"For the murder of Edgar Morgan, a member of the United States Secret Service."

He did not even see her hand move. He was aware only of the quick glint, and the knife flicking upward, raised above her. Even then, all that registered was the hatred in her eyes.

13

Desperate Dan

For Bond it was pure instinct and training. Deeley's movement had been so fast that the flash of the blade just registered. Then he moved automatically. The girl's arm had passed across her body, the knife, blade outward, ready to slash across his throat. As his left arm came up to block the stroke, he even registered that the knife was a U.S. Marines K-Bar with a seven-inch, razor-sharp blade.

Who would have thought a small woman like this would have so much strength? Their forearms met as he blocked the slash, and it was like banging his own arm against a steel rod. She was closing now, stepping right forward into his body, twisting her arm to free herself.

If she managed it, the next knife stroke would come fast, and from another direction. For a second her eyes, blazing with a fanatical anger, locked with Bond's. She pushed in hard, then stepped away, leaving herself free for the second stroke: it was the old close-combat trick, using her opponent's body for leverage, and Bond should not have fallen for it. This time she had turned the blade, so that the knife protruded from the thumb end of her fist, ready to come from below in the classic knife-fighting manner.

She came slowly, weaving in the confined space of the cabin, sidestepping and whipping in from Bond's open left flank.

He blocked her again, with his left forearm, bringing his right hand across, to grasp her wrist, pushing down, twisting the wrist, in an attempt to force her to drop the weapon, but she pulled down on his thumb, her strength so great that his right hand slipped away as though it had been smeared with butter.

Now she was weaving again. Two steps back, a feint with a third step, changing to a jump to her right, then another feint to the left and straight in, bending her knees and springing up.

Bond saw the knife coming in from below and he turned his body to the left—right around, like a matador performing a *rebolera*. The blade must have missed him by inches, Deeley's hand slamming the point against the steel cabin wall.

But the girl whirled back before Bond even had a chance to grab, and she was coming for him again, the knife still low in her strong balled fist. Once more Bond blocked, and, this time caught her firmly by the wrist with his right hand, pushing solidly with his left forearm.

With every ounce of strength he could muster he pulled up, and then down, felt her arm move and heard the gasp

212

of pain as he slammed her hand into the metal wall. The knife dropped, but she was still panting and fighting: her knee coming up to his groin.

He felt the crushing flash of pure pain as she connected, and heard himself cry out, doubling over, grabbing at himself and seeing her hand snake down, fingers reaching for the knife on the cabin floor.

His cry must have been loud, and sharp enough to save him. The cabin door was flung open and the young Marine, dropping his rifle, threw himself on the Wren's back, taking her in an armlock around her neck. A split second later, a pair of burly sailors had the spitting and struggling girl by both arms and were leading her out.

"You okay, sir?" The young Marine helped Bond into his chair. He was still bent double and the area around his manhood seemed to be on fire.

"I think I'll have a short word with the quack," he breathed heavily, then looked up and saw the Master-at-Arms standing in the doorway.

"You'll have to restrain her," Bond panted. "Just put her in the cells, under restraint." The Royal Navy did not use the term "brig," so popular with the United States Navy. "Get the chief regulating officer to charge her."

"With attacking a senior officer, sir?" The Master-at-Arms raised his eyebrows at the end of the query, in a manner that suggested this was a facial expression he used habitually when asking questions.

"Murder," Bond corrected. His voice seemed a long way off, for the pain in his groin seemed to take precedence over everything else.

"Murder, sir? The American?"

Bond nodded. "Just keep her well under restraint. I think

she's some kind of psycho, and well-trained at that. A killer, who would obey orders and take out someone with about as much emotion as any of us would feel in treading on a bug. I'll be down to see her shortly. The murder charge will, eventually, be a police criminal matter." As the Master-at-Arms departed, Bond suddenly thought of his own words, just uttered—"a killer, who would obey orders. . . ." Whose orders? he wondered. Orders from outside, or some given to her on board?

Someone had called Surgeon Commander Grant, who seemed quite amused at Bond's pain. "There'll probably be some swelling," he said examining the damaged area. "I'll give you some pills to reduce the pain."

"As long as they don't make me dopey." In spite of the small agony, Bond put his job first.

"You'll get no side effects. I have a salve as well. It'll deaden the area and you won't feel like playing with the ladies for a day or so, but maybe that's not a bad thing."

Bond realized that he felt a little embarrassed about the whole business.

"You'd be surprised," the doctor continued, "really surprised how many cases of this I have to deal with these days. Lads go ashore, won't take no for an answer and get a hefty knee in the gonads. Serve 'em right. Bloody MCPs."

"I got this defending *myself,*" Bond muttered grudgingly, trying to sort his mind out, deciding what had to be done next.

Half an hour later he stood in front of the entire section of personal bodyguards for the three Admirals. They were gathered in the small messdeck that had been put aside for their use and relaxation—the one in which Moggy Camm, two of the Russians and Bruce Trimble had joined in a drink before turning in on the previous night. Now the place seemed crowded. Nikki Ratnikov sat apart from her colleagues, Ivan, Yevgeny and Gennady; Brinkley and Camm sat together, still in their fancy dress, among Joe Israel, Bruce Trimble and Stan Hare. Their three VIP charges were in the cabins set aside for them, each with an armed Marine at the door.

"Right," Bond began. "We all know what this is about. Our Captain, the Rear-Admiral, is determined to carry on with *Stewards' Meeting.* My job is to coordinate security, and I want to get your feelings on the matter before I make a recommendation to Sir John—not that he'll take my advice, but I'd rather we worked as a team, and a team has to be one hundred percent in accord on a business like this. We've had one death, and we don't want any more."

Nikki spoke up for the Russians. "James, you must advise us. We have a sacred duty here. The strain will be on us as from tonight. Do you think that the killing of the American agent should make us fear for the lives of those we have to guard?"

"It certainly means that this little terrorist outfit—if it *is* them—has managed to penetrate *Invincible* with at least one person. If there is one, can there be others? I must reveal to all of you that Edgar Morgan was a worried man. As far as I can tell, he slipped into the Wrens' heads to record a series of names—names of people in this ship. He wanted a security check run on them. Well, I ran the check through London. The only one that came out badly was the girl we arrested this morning."

Joe Israel looked up with interest. "This is the first any of us have heard of Ed having doubts. Can you be sure he was not just doing a random test? A sampling? Or was he in possession of intelligence not revealed to any of us?"

"I've no idea." There was no point in Bond not being

open and candid. "I still have to talk with the girl we arrested. She was what some people would call a 'stone killer.' It's not an expression I'm fond of. But that's what she was, and is."

"Can you give us the other names Morgan had on his list?" Ted Brinkley asked.

"I don't think that would be fair at this stage. They all came out ultra-clean from London."

Brinkley conferred with his partner for a minute in urgent whispers. Then Brinkley said that, as far as they were concerned, things could go ahead. "It would have been very difficult for any terrorist organization to infiltrate a Royal Navy ship. That they got one in is a kind of miracle. Barring any outside attack, we consider it ninety-nine percent safe. We vote that things go ahead as planned."

Bond nodded. In his head he still remained unhappy. They had thought of BAST as a bit of a tinpot outfit, yet they certainly had resources, and even one penetration worried him. He looked over at Joe Israel. "What about our United States contingent?"

"I guess we go along with you Brits. Sure there's danger, but that comes with the job. We vote in."

"You're one man short."

"I gather that's being taken care of. Admiral Gudeon's been active and we've got another guy on the way."

Bond made a mental note that he should speak with the Captain about this turn of events. Now he looked at Nikki. "You're senior officer of our Russian comrades, Nikki. What do you say?"

"Our people are the best in the world. We say go ahead."

"Then we're all agreed?"

Around the little messdeck there were murmurs of consent.

So be it, Bond thought. They all seemed to be good, tried and tested people. Now he had to speak with Sir John Walmsley. After that there was the girl, Deeley, though he did not have any high hopes of breaking her down.

• • •

"So, you've decided not to fight me on this?" Sir John Walmsley looked pleased, like a man who had won a great battle.

"It's not a question of fighting you, sir." Bond spoke with almost exaggerated calmness. "We weighed up the chances of this being a one-off incident. We're not entirely convinced, but everyone here in the three bodyguard sections seems to think the risk is even."

"A sensible decision," growled Walmsley, who knew he would have overridden any attempt to abort *Stewards' Meeting*.

"I need answers to a couple of questions before I talk to the girl, Deeley . . ." Bond began.

"Yes?" the Rear-Admiral snapped. "If I'm allowed to answer, I'll cooperate. Go ahead."

"First, there's one thing I have to know about Edgar Morgan."

"He wasn't U.S. Secret Service, but I presume you know that already."

"Yes, I realize he wasn't just part of the normal bodyguard service. I'm pretty certain he was Naval Intelligence, and came aboard with a special brief." Bond had not shown all his cards.

"That's true."

"Can you tell me anything about the special brief?"

Walmsley pretended to think for a moment. "Well, he

had authority to go through the records of everyone aboard this ship."

"Was there time for him to do that?"

"Mmmm." It was noncommittal, but the Rear-Admiral was playing Bond. Walmsley was the kind of man who liked showing his authority and, had the truth been known, he looked forward to a very rapid promotion if the operation called *Stewards' Meeting* went off without a hitch. Finally, he decided it would be safer to tell the truth. "He came aboard two days before *Landsea '89* started."

"Two days?"

Walmsley nodded. "He left the ship shortly before you arrived. Then came on with Gudeon and the others. But, in those two days he went through all the files. He was *very* interested in you, Captain Bond. *Very* interested."

"And he carried on looking through the individual dossiers on his return?"

"He did. Now, anything else?"

"Yes, sir. I've been told that the Americans are sending a replacement. True or false?"

"True. He'll be here before *Stewards' Meeting.*"

"We have a name?"

"Dan Woodward. U.S. Naval Intelligence. As you would expect, he's known to his friends and colleagues as Desperate Dan. Now, Captain Bond, anything else?"

"Only a minor point. The Wren detachment aboard—"

"Damned women in the ship, I didn't approve of it."

"Sir, we both know why they're here. We know it'll make things easier when *Stewards' Meeting* gets underway. Until then, could I ask you, sir, what duties have been assigned to them?"

"This because one of them turned out to be a dummy?"

"Partly."

"Why not ask their officer, what's her name? First Officer Pennington?"

"Because I'd rather have an independent source."

Rear-Admiral Walmsley sucked his teeth. "You know they're all cleared at a very high security level?"

"I do, sir, and it worries me. The one intruder came in through them. I know London says they're all cleared, but I want to check it out again."

"Right. We're making good use of them, Bond. They're doing everything they've been trained to do. We've allotted them shifts in Communications; in writers' departments; and, just to keep their domestic hands in, some are daily assigned to galley duties. I made that a condition of the draft coming aboard. Now, anything else?"

Bond shook his head. So, the Wrens were all over the place. In the galleys; Communications, and writers. A writer is Royal Navy for clerk or secretarial duties.

"Good, because we're still very much a part of *Landsea '89,* and we've still got three nuclear subs shadowing us. I have to get back to work. Can't leave it all to Jimmy The One."

After leaving the Rear-Admiral, Bond sought out Joe Israel, who was resting in the cabin occupied by the three U.S. Secret Service men. Bruce Trimble was with him, while Stan Hare had taken over normal bodyguard duties to Admiral Gudeon.

"You know who's taking Ed Morgan's place?" he asked the pair of them.

"Another guy from Naval Int," Israel said, sounding none too pleased.

"Name of Woodward. Dan Woodward." Trimble grinned. "They call him Desperate Dan, we hear."

"You hear?"

"The Admiral sent a signal to Washington last night—after Ed's death. The reply was very fast, I guess Desperate Dan must be in London. He's close by anyhow, because they're expecting him by early evening."

"You know him?" Bond asked.

"The name only. Never worked with him," from Israel.

"You?" to Trimble, who shook his head.

"What about Stan?"

"What *about* Stan?" Israel laughed.

"Does he know the Woodward fellow?"

"No. None of us know him."

"Okay." Bond pinched the top of his nose between thumb and forefinger. "I would suggest, when he does come aboard, that you do a little verbal check on him. Usual kind of things. Americana; people in Washington; people any of you know in Naval Intelligence."

"You don't think he's clean?"

"I've no idea." Bond shrugged. "I just think we should take precautions, that's all."

•   •   •

In his room at The Rock Hotel, Gibraltar, Bassam Baradj was receiving blow-by-blow accounts of what was going on in *Invincible.* His shortwave radio, with a recording device attached, picked up signals from his main source aboard the ship, though the final news, which had come through in the early hours of the morning, made him wonder if this flow of intelligence would last out much longer. He knew of the death of the American NI officer, and of the possible consequences. He also knew that the Americans had signaled to Washington and that Washington's return signal

220

referred them to the Embassy in London. Since then there had been no other signal and he feared the worst. The only other source connected with BAST was one Engineer Petty Officer, and Baradj knew that everything really lay with this one blackmailed man.

Immediately he had listened in to the message concerning the American Embassy in Grosvenor Square, London, Baradj had taken the only course of action available to him. A long telephone call to London was followed by a lengthy meeting with his colleague, Abou Hamarik. Together they decided the risk was worth the final reward, even though Hamarik had no idea that Baradj had no plans to cut him, or any other member of BAST, in on the eventual riches.

It would not have mattered either way, for Baradj had already set the plan in motion, and it was essential for him to use Hamarik. He thought it was a lucky decision that had made him choose "The Man"—Abou Hamarik—for the work in Gibraltar. Ali Al Adwan, his only other possible choice, had been seen already by the man Bond, at the camp they had called "Northanger." In all, Baradj was happy. The two men he had in London were both good, and well equipped to carry out what had to be done.

•   •   •

Daniel Woodward had a pleasant apartment in Knightsbridge. Nothing luxurious, but, with his pay as assistant naval attaché (Intelligence) to the Embassy, he could afford it. He also found it was an address which stood well with the ladies he dated regularly. It was as though they felt quite safe going back with him to the Knightsbridge address.

The one beside him in bed at three in the morning only grumbled in her sleep when the telephone rang. She grumbled even more when he woke her to say he had to report to the Embassy immediately.

"Oh, God, what's the time, darling?" She was a stunning redhead who worked in the Embassy Secretariat.

"It's fifteen after three. I'm sorry, honey, but I'm gonna have to take you home. I don't know how long I'm gonna be away. They said I should bring a bag with me, which means I'm probably going Stateside. Sorry, but I just can't leave you here. You know what Embassy instructions're like about people leaving their properties with all the alarms on if they're out of the country." He was dashing about, filling a small case with clothes.

She was still half asleep when he drove her back to her own apartment off Great Russell Street. The whole business meant that, though he had been alerted at three-fifteen in the morning, he did not get to the Embassy until almost four-thirty.

The naval attaché (Intelligence) was already waiting for him, and that gentleman did not like being kept waiting so he expected a full broadside when he walked into the office. Instead, the attaché was mild. "It's okay, Dan." The Naval Intelligence attaché was a ramrod-straight, tall and silver-gray man. "You've plenty of time. We've already dealt with the documents. All I have to do is brief you. Your flight doesn't leave London Gatwick until ten o'clock, so we have time."

The slow response Dan Woodward had been forced into by the presence of the redhead at his apartment had caused troubles nobody else knew about. A taxi, with its For Hire sign unlit, had already been in one of the parking slots, which run around the center of Grosvenor Square, for fifteen minutes by the time Woodward arrived. The driver appeared to be taking a quiet sleep. Nobody was visible in the back.

"That must be him. Unless his boss is going with him. Got a case and all," the driver said.

The other occupant, on the floor in the rear of the cab, muttered something about the passport photograph.

"If we're lucky we'll have time to take care of that. First sign of movement in the Embassy lobby, my light goes on and we pick him up. If they've laid on a cab for him, we know his name and we'll probably beat their cab. If it's an Embassy car, then we'll just have to do something embarrassingly naughty."

Woodward, having been given the most exciting briefing of his career, came out onto the steps of the Embassy at six forty-five, clutching a suitcase and looking for the cab they had obviously called for him.

The cab that had been parked since the early hours backed out quickly and turned in front of the Embassy, its driver peering out and calling, "Mr. Woodward?"

Dan Woodward responded with a wave and a smile and came hurrying down the steps. There were few people about, and nobody had seen the second man slide from the back of the cab, just as it pulled out, and make his way around the corner into Upper Grosvenor Street.

The driver was very fast, taking Dan Woodward's bag and stowing it away in the front section. "Where's it to, guv'?" the cabbie asked. "Nobody tells me nothing."

"Gatwick. Departures. North Terminal."

"How long we got, then?" The taxi moved away quickly, circling the Square, preparing to head along Upper Grosvenor Street.

"My flight leaves at ten. So, nine-thirty at the latest."

"All the time in the world," said the cabbie, sashaying to the left, where his colleague was walking slowly up toward Park Lane. " 'Scuse me, guv'nor." The cabbie leaned back with the little sliding window open. "There's a mate of mine. I'd like to give him a message."

"Be my guest."

The taxi pulled over in front of the pedestrian, and the cabbie leaned out and called, "Nobby, can you give Di a message for me. I've got to go out to Gatwick. I'll give her a bell from there."

The man came abreast of the cab, as though straining to hear the driver. Then, as he reached the passenger door, he yanked it open, and Dan Woodward found himself staring into the wrong end of an H&K 9mm, modified to take a noise-reduction assembly.

"One wrong move and you're dead." The pedestrian smiled and got into the cab next to the startled Woodward. The cab drew smoothly away. By the time they reached the T-junction which led them onto Park Lane, Woodward was unconscious. He had not even felt the hypo go through his coat and into his arm.

The cab headed toward Notting Hill, where it would need to make a detour to get onto the M25 and on to Gatwick. In the Bayswater Road it turned right into a mews cul-de-sac, and pulled up in front of one of those quiet little mews houses that now cost an arm and two legs in London. The cab parked very close to the door and the driver and his companion got out. A woman in the uniform of a nurse was already waiting, the door of the house open. Within two minutes they had the unconscious Woodward inside, the driver coming out to get his case and carry it indoors.

They dumped the unconscious man on a sofa.

"He'll be out for twenty-four hours," the driver said to the woman, as he went through Woodward's pockets, while his partner worked the locks on the case. "We'll help you get him into the secure room. I need him quiet for around four or five days. Ah . . ." He removed a bunch of papers which included a passport, and an official-looking batch of documents.

He sat down at the foot of the sofa and began going through the papers. Frowning, he got up, went to the telephone and dialed the Gibraltar code and The Rock Hotel, asking to be put through to Mr. Underwood's room. "Very urgent," he said.

In Gibraltar, both Baradj and Hamarik were waiting. "Okay," the man in London said. "You'll need a United States diplomatic passport. Is that difficult?"

"That, we can fix here. Just read off the details."

The London man then went through the rest of the information. "We have one problem. They're supposed to be meeting him off BA 498, which gets in at local 13:45. They actually wrote down a contact procedure, which means they don't know him at that end."

"Is there a contact number?"

"Yes."

"Okay. Give it to me."

The London man rattled off the string of numbers, and Baradj replied, "Okay. Are the documents essential?"

"Yes. They're his orders, and there's a paper he has to show to the guys meeting him."

"Right. Use your own passport, but check in as Woodward. They never know the difference there. As long as the number of passports tallies with the number of people: and it's no offense to travel under an alias—unless you're up to something criminal, which, of course, you're not. You come through into the concourse, it's small and usually busy. On the right side, when you come through you'll find the men's room. It's poky and unpleasant, but my man will be waiting. He'll have a Woodward passport. He'll take the papers and case from you, come out and run through the contact procedure. Now, Bob, *you* do it. Nobody else. I trust *you* to go through all this. Now, you'll have to get a move on. Go."

●   ●   ●

Bond had been correct, the girl who called herself Sarah Deeley simply refused to answer any questions. She sat in the cell, restrained by what amounted to a straitjacket, and looked Bond in the eyes, unflinching, as he poured question after question at her. She even smiled at him a couple of times. After an hour of this, he gave up. Best leave her to the professionals when they got to Gibraltar.

The Rear-Admiral was on the bridge when he reported his lack of success.

"You people got any specialists in Gib?" Walmsley asked.

"Why, sir?"

"I've got a Sea King going off to Gib in twenty minutes. It'll just make it there and back, if they juice her up in Gib. They're bringing in Morgan's replacement."

"Desperate Dan?"

Walmsley seemed to have lost any humor that might have lurked behind his cold blue eyes. "I believe they call him that. You got anyone in Gib?"

"Let me check it out, sir. If the answer's yes, I'll see he's brought back."

"Let me know before takeoff. You only have twenty minutes."

It took Bond fifteen minutes to make contact. Yes, they had an interrogation specialist with the unlikely name, for his skills, of Donald Speaker who would be delighted to have a go.

So it was that when Flight BA 498 landed, slightly late, at two o'clock that afternoon, the Sea King from *Invincible* was sitting, juiced up, on the helipad away from the terminal building. Its crew of three were aboard, plus Donald Speaker, a red-bearded, casually dressed little man with the sharp look of a bank inspector about him.

The Lieutenant Commander from *Invincible*'s Executive Officer's staff waited in the arrivals terminal—which in Gibraltar is also the departure terminal. He did not notice that one passenger from BA 498 came through the gates, lugging his flight bag, and made straight for the men's room; while a few seconds later another man came out, carrying the same flight bag, and with his passport in his left hand, held over his breast pocket. To the Lieutenant Commander this was simply the man for whom he had been waiting, giving all the signals—bag in right hand, passport in left hand, held high just under his breast pocket where his boarding card stuck out almost a couple of inches.

The Lieutenant Commander smiled and approached the civilian. "Mr. Woodward?"

"Yes, I'm Dan Woodward," said Abou Hamarik. "Want to see the ID?"

"Better take a quick shufty. My name's Hallam, by the way." The Lieutenant Commander grinned. "Your diplomatic-status stamp looks damned impressive. Well, welcome aboard, Mr. Woodward."

"Just call me Dan."

They crossed the metaled apron, walking quickly toward the Sea King. As they did so they saw the stoplights come on, and traffic grind to a halt on the road that ran straight across the runway. A Royal Air Force Tornado came hurtling in with its droops and spoilers fully extended. Their ears sang but cleared by the time they reached the Sea King. The crewman helped them up, and Hallam introduced him to everyone. Speaker just gave him a nod, as though he did not approve of Americans being given free rides on Royal Navy helicopters.

"Great," Hallam said, just before the rotors began to turn. "We'll be back in very good time for *Stewards' Meeting.*"

"What's *Stewards' Meeting*?" Speaker asked. He had a slight, unidentifiable accent, and a suspicious nasal tone in his voice.

"I'm sorry." Hallam turned to him with a smile. "If you don't know what it is, you're not cleared for it. Right, Dan?"

"Most definitely right," Abou Hamarik said. Soon, he thought, the whole world will know about *Stewards' Meeting.* And there will be things the whole world will not wish to know.

The Sea King rose from the pad, lowered its nose, turned away from the Spanish mainland, banked and set course out to sea and HMS *Invincible.*

14

Stewards' Meeting

"D'you hear there! D'you hear there! This is the Captain." Sir John Walmsley's voice rang out through the ship's Tannoy system, and, as ever, all ranks stopped what they were doing and raised their heads to listen.

Invincible had slowed down to a point where she was hardly moving in the light sea. Outside, at 22:00 hours, it was black as pitch, but the flight deck was fully lit and an S & R Sea King hovered off the port side.

"I want all ranks to listen out, and listen carefully. We still have the submarine wolfpack with us, though I am assured that they will in no way impede our progress to Gibraltar. Regarding Exercise *Landsea '89* there is a political stalemate, and talks between various countries will restart tomorrow morning. So far no further incidents have been reported within the boundaries of the European Continent, though our forces—*Red Side*—are still known to be operating behind enemy lines. That is the report, and assessment with regard to *Landsea '89*.

"Now I must talk seriously about the real world, and what is happening aboard *Invincible* tonight. I am standing down all watches at this moment, except for officers and ratings who have been given special instructions to be present on the main deck, Flight Operations, and the bridge. This is for security purposes, and anyone not ordered to be on the main deck, in Flight Operations, or on the bridge will meet with stiff penalties if found there. In fact they could well suffer injury. Marines have been posted on all companionways and bulkheads leading to the prohibited areas. They are armed and there is a password sequence known only to those authorized to work on the main deck.

"You will hear helicopters landing and taking off. This is because the VIP officers we've had aboard, since *Landsea '89* began, will be taking their leave of us. However, other VIPs will be coming aboard, and this is now classified information. Until you're informed of its declassification, no officer, Petty Officer, Warrant Officer, rating or Marine will speak of anything seen aboard *Invincible* over the next few days. If anyone *does* talk, outside this ship, I should remind you that to do so will be regarded as a breach of the Official Secrets Act; punishable accordingly.

"To underline the seriousness of this situation, you should know that, until we reach Gibraltar, there will be four Sea Harriers, fully armed and ready to fly, on and around the ski ramp, for'ard. There will be two pilots from the Air Group at five-minute readiness, twenty-four hours a day, starting now. That is all."

In Flight Operations, Bond could see that was not all, for the first two Sea Harriers were not only in place but also had pilots in the cockpits and their engines on at idle. Apart from that, there was a sense of déjà vu in the lights flashing from three helicopters stacked, one behind the other, closing on the stern. The cloud cover was high so he could only see the red and green rotating lights against the darkness. But he knew, from the Commander (Air), that the first chopper was about one mile away, closing at a speed of around fifty knots; and the other two were stacked at one-thousand-foot intervals.

The Sea King was visible now, a shaft of light coming from its nose as the halogen spot came on. It closed, then hovered as the flight deck controller and his men signaled it in to land some hundred yards behind the pair of backup Sea Harriers, parked together well behind the ski ramp.

Nobody approached the Sea King as its rotors gently slowed down. They were still whisking the air as the U.S. Navy helicopter rolled in behind it, followed by the big, twin-finned Kamov-25 which nosed onto the deck with its two huge contrarotating rotors whirling fast and its turbines giving a final dying roar.

Bond just caught a glimpse of the three VIP officers, the British, American and Russian Admirals, being hustled toward their respective helicopters. Then the main deck-lights went out, leaving only dim blue guiding lights leading from the helicopters to the main bulkhead doors in the island.

"Time you joined the reception committee, Captain Bond." The Commander glanced toward him. Bond nodded and with a "Good luck!" left Flight Ops, turning his

231

body sideways, rattled down the companionway, heading toward the section of cabins recently vacated by the trio of Admirals and their bodyguards.

In the hour that had passed since he had last been in this part of the ship, a great deal had taken place. The passageway floors were now covered in thick red carpeting, and three sections of the long corridor, which led from James Bond's cabin to the turning into the Wrens' quarters, had been separated by neat wooden doors, the jambs screwed into bulkhead cross sections.

The doors were open, and he could see right down to the end, where the entire draft of Wrens were drawn up, with Clover Pennington pacing anxiously. In the middle portion, the new Naval Intelligence man, Woodward, was accompanied by two armed Marines. Woodward gave Bond a wink, lifting his right hand and following with a thumbs-up, to which Bond replied in kind. Through the door nearest to him Nikki Ratnikov and Yevgeny Stura were also accompanied by two Royal Marines, while another pair, with Sergeant Harvey in tow, waited patiently to one side of Bond's cabin door.

Bond nodded to the sergeant. "Any minute now," he said, and the words were hardly out of his mouth when he heard the sounds of feet on the uncarpeted section of passageway leading to the spruced-up VIP quarters.

They came at a brisk pace: Rear-Admiral Sir John Walmsley, Ted Brinkley and a civilian who could only be from one Service, for he had all the smooth and tough, alert looks of an officer of the Special Branch Close Protection Squad. At the center of this group, Bond saw the first of the VIPs who had come aboard from the helicopter which had picked up Sir Geoffrey Gould.

The Rear-Admiral stopped in front of Bond. "Prime Minister," he said to the almost regally dressed Mrs. Margaret Hilda Thatcher. "I'd like to present Captain James Bond, who is in total charge of security for *Stewards' Meeting.*"

The Prime Minister smiled and firmly shook Bond's hand. "It's nice to see you again, and congratulations on your promotion." She turned to Walmsley. "Captain Bond and I are already old friends," she said. "I couldn't have better protection, and it's not generally known that Captain Bond was instrumental in saving not only my life, but that of ex-President Reagan, some time ago." Then back to Bond. "I couldn't be in better hands. Just see that we're left alone for a full four days, Captain Bond. We shall need every minute of it, if we're going to get through a tough agenda. And it is a *very* tough, and *important* agenda. I'm sure you are already aware of that."

"Yes, Prime Minister. I'll do everything possible. If your people require anything they should get in touch with me personally."

"Very kind of you, Captain Bond," and with her best electoral smile, the Prime Minister of the United Kingdom marched away with her retinue.

Bond's eyes followed her, and he ignored Sergeant Harvey's muttered, "I wouldn't like to be on *her* defaulters' parade."

From the far end of the passageway, he heard the Rear-Admiral introduce the PM to First Officer Pennington, and then make his excuses.

He came striding back, glaring at Bond. "You said nothing about saving her life! Anything else I should know?"

"She exaggerated." Bond did not smile. "The information's restricted anyhow, so I shouldn't let it go any further, sir.''

"Hrrumph!" Walmsley said—or something very like it—and went off to meet the next arrival.

President George Herbert Walker Bush, surrounded by his Secret Service men—Joe Israel, Stan Hare and Bruce Trimble—and with a small man carrying a briefcase chained to his wrist, had been met at the foot of the companionway by Walmsley. The President was tall, smiling, graying and very open-faced.

"Captain Bond," he acknowledged as the Rear-Admiral made the introduction, "I *know* I'm in good hands. A close friend of mine told me what a help you'd been to him, and I believe we have another friend in common."

"We probably have, sir."

"Yes, Felix served under me when I was DCIA. A good man. Hope to see more of you, Bond, but you'll appreciate the schedule's tight as a drumskin. Good to meet you."

The President of the United States had a firm handshake, almost as firm as Mrs. Thatcher's, and, as he walked away, Sergeant Harvey muttered, "Nor his."

"Nor his what?" Bond said out of the corner of his mouth.

"Wouldn't like to be on his defaulters' parade either."

"If you were, they'd call it a masthead, Sergeant Harvey. That's what the U.S. Navy call defaulters—just as the Royal Navy did a long time ago."

Sir John Walmsley gave Bond another dirty look as he hurried past, again heading for the companionway and the final VIP.

Mikhail Sergeyevich Gorbachev, General Secretary of the CPSU and President of the Presidium of the Supreme Soviet, was dressed in a camel's-hair overcoat that he had not bought at GUM. He held a gray felt hat, which could have been purchased at Lock's in Jermyn Street, and wore a broad smile. He was neat, burly, broad-shouldered and relaxed.

Walmsley introduced them, and to Bond's surprise, Mr. Gorbachev replied in English, "Captain Bond, it is a great pleasure to meet you. I hope you mingle with those who look after me in a true spirit of *Glasnost.*" The short man's handshake was positively bone-crushing and left Bond speechless as the Russian passed on toward his quarters.

"Ho dear, sir," Harvey whispered. "He hasn't brought Raisa with him. Hope *he's* got an Amex card as well."

"Be fair, Harvey. The Prez hasn't brought Barbara, and Mrs. T's without Denis. It's reasonable enough."

Walmsley returned, looking flustered. "Well, at least one of them didn't seem to know you, Bond."

"I wouldn't bet on it, sir."

"No, well . . . All senior officers, divisional officers and the chief regulating officer in my day cabin in fifteen minutes. We're not using the PA to warn you, so tell me now if you're happy about arrangements—I mean happy enough to leave this section of the ship for an hour or so."

"I'll be there, sir. If I'm at all concerned, I'll let you know, personally, and give you my reasons."

The Rear-Admiral gave a curt nod and left, his long, important strides indicating that he was well pleased with the final transfer of probably the three most powerful people in the world to his ship.

Bond thought this was one hell of a responsibility, and Walmsley should not show any cockiness until it was all safely over.

• • •

Petty Officer "Blackie" Blackstone looked at the great turbines whining strongly in the engine room of *Invincible*. When he had first joined the Royal Navy the engine rooms were hot, dirty, sweaty and noisy places. *Invincible*'s engine room was brilliantly clean, and only a few people were actually needed close to the turbines, for they were monitored from a separate room, full of dials, VDUs and switches.

Blackstone was probably the only man on *Invincible*, outside the Captain, senior officers and security people who knew what was going on. He did not question how his two "friends" Harry and Bill had got hold of the information; nor did he have any moral qualms about what he was to do. After all, it would get him off the hook, both financially and domestically. In any case, they had told him it was really a Greenpeace operation, timed to cause great embarrassment to the Americans and Russians, also to the British establishment, and Blackie had always had a lot of sympathy for Greenpeace.

He had thought for a long time about the job, but once he weighed the positive and negative sides, he realized there was no real danger.

Blackie had gone to a lot of trouble in arranging his shifts. The first one just after these nobs come aboard, they had told him. Then the second one would require action in the middle of the following forenoon. Blackie Blackstone would have access to the turbines on both required shifts. He had seen to that, just as he knew the other men on the watch were content to let him do the physical check on the turbines. Even now, just after the visitors had arrived on

236

board, he was alone in the engine room, while a Chief Petty Officer, another Petty Officer, like himself, and a "Killick"—a Leading Seaman, so called because of the anchor-badge he wore: killick being the old slang term for anchor—lounged their way through the watch, occasionally checking the pressures and speeds of the turbines.

The Second Engineering Officer was, as ever, in the officers' caboose, just behind the control room. Nobody would require him unless something went terribly wrong. Changes of speed, and other such things could be accomplished at the touch of a button, or a couple of clicks on the small levers which acted as throttles. So the Lieutenant who was the Second Engineering Officer was left to do a little "Egyptian Physical Training" as they called it. In other words, the Lieutenant was sleeping.

Petty Officer Blackstone quietly moved to the far side of number one turbine. He pulled a screwdriver from a leather tool kit attached to his belt, and tucked away behind his right hip. He then removed a cylinder, wrapped in Kleenex, from his pocket. The cylinder, which was made of strong wire gauze, had an opening at one end, and was rounded at the other. Anyone, from Midshipman to Ordinary Seaman, could have identified the cylinder as a straightforward filter for the turbine's oil system.

Blackstone quickly unscrewed the two lugs that held down a small panel, roughly six inches by six, and lifted it on its hinge. Above the panel the words FILTER ONE were stenciled.

Quietly, he placed the screwdriver on the deck, by his feet, and took an abnormally long pair of tweezers from the tool kit on his belt, at the same time gathering another handful of Kleenex into his left hand. Gently, Petty Officer

Blackstone inserted the tweezers into the open panel of filter one, extracting an identical heavy, dirty, gauze cylinder from within—though this one was hot and dripping with oil. He placed it into the handful of Kleenex and put it carefully on the deck, beside the screwdriver. It would take three minutes for any sign of the change to be registered on the instruments in the control room, and it took less than thirty seconds to slide the new filter into place, and another minute to close the panel and screw back the lugs.

Blackstone next returned the screwdriver and tweezers to his tool kit, picked up the bunched Kleenex which held the recently removed filter, and made his way through the bulkhead door, aft and leading to the engine room heads.

There he unbolted one of the ports, opened it up and hurled the filter and Kleenex out to be whipped away by the wind. He closed up the round port, washed his hands, clearing away all traces of oil, and returned to the engine room, casually walking around all the turbines, taking his time before returning to the control room.

"They all still running, Blackie?" the CPO asked with a grin.

"Difficult to say, Chiefy. I went and had a smoke in the heads."

"You jammy bugger," the other Petty Officer said. "I was just telling them about how you sloped off that time when we last docked in Gib. She was a corker, wasn't she? Black-haired beauty, that one."

"You're full of shit," said Blackie, and the conversation continued on this high intellectual plane for the next hour or so.

The turbines all ran smoothly, but Blackie knew that it

would not be smooth running at about eleven in the fore-noon tomorrow. For one thing, the oil temperature on number one turbine would start to rise spectacularly, and he would be there to deal with it.

.   .   .

"Gentlemen, thank you for your time. I'll be as quick as possible; though it's essential that you all know exactly what's at stake here." Sir John Walmsley was full of himself: sitting back in his chair in the crowded day cabin, with all his senior officers around him, he almost overflowed with his own responsibility. Bond viewed the man with pity rather than awe. Walmsley was a pompous ass, full of self-importance, and therefore, from Bond's viewpoint, not really suitable for the job he had to do. "Now, *Stewards' Meeting*. This is a very clear name for what is happening aboard *Invincible*."

The Rear-Admiral cleared his throat and continued. "You all know who's on board. The three most powerful heads of state in the world, and they see themselves attending a real Stewards' Meeting, for they regard themselves as true Stewards. Stewards in whom the world puts its trust. Two men and a woman who can truly hold the world in their hands." This, Bond concluded, was going to be a sermon, not a briefing. Nor would it be a sermon to the wholly converted.

Walmsley was still talking. "You'll also realize one important factor. They are all here with close protection squads but *without* their normal advisers—apart from the sinister bag man with President Bush who is required to have the nuclear-alert codes with him at all times."

He paused, as though pleased with his own knowledge and the ability for him to share it. Then he continued. "As some of you already know, they are here under highly classified code names. The PM is *Shalott*—Lady of, I presume, not just because she knows her onions." He paused again for the obligatory chuckle to pass around the room. "The President of the United States is *Dancer;* and Secretary Gorbachev is *October.* You will refer to them by those names, both in conversation and any radio messages you might be called upon to give. But, as I have said, the one unique thing is that they're here with no advisers, or assistants. As far as their colleagues are concerned, *Shalott* has a touch of the flu; *October* is resting in his country dacha, and has left orders that he should not be disturbed for five days; *Dancer* has requested no Press, and no calls to his hunting lodge where he is quail shooting."

Again he waited for a laugh, but the jest was, if not dying, at least fatally ill. "The point is that all three chose to meet in secure conditions so that they could carry out four whole days of highly personal, one-on-one—or, I suppose it could be one-on-two—talks without the usual interference from the throngs of experts from both government, military, financial and social levels who often advise more caution over sensitive issues.

"There will be no official statements regarding *Stewards' Meeting.* Nobody is to know, unless they feel they have accomplished some incredible breakthrough that can be announced. Their main objective is to set some ground rules on world finance, security against terrorism, and the acceleration of solving that thorny question regarding the quick phasing out of nuclear weapons.

"Our job is to see they have the next four days to themselves. They will be eating and working together in the forward lecture room, which has been made more presentable than usual. So, with the help of the Wren detachment to see they get decent food, and good service, and the assistance of Security, they will be following a very tight schedule which, even in the midst of *Landsea '89,* we *must* see is adhered to. They have got to be given four whole days, no matter what. If you have any questions come straight to me. Understand?"

Yes, Bond thought. Go straight to him, and he will pass you straight on to me. He left, went back to his cabin and sent for Donald Speaker, the interrogator who had come in from Gibraltar with the new American, Woodward.

He had never met Speaker before, but knew his reputation as a hard investigator who rarely gave an inch, so it was, when the man came into his cabin and sat down without even being asked, that Bond took an almost irrational dislike to him.

If Speaker had made any progress with Deeley he was not going to tell Bond. In fact it was just the opposite, for, within minutes, Bond realized that the interrogator was asking questions of him.

"I don't altogether trust those two Branch men in fancy dress," Speaker said of Brinkley and Camm.

"Oh?"

"Not cut out for the kind of job they're doing on this ship. I'm highly dubious of their motives, Mr., er, Captain Bond."

"Interesting, but what about Deeley?"

"I'll report when I have anything to report."

The gingery beard, Bond decided, covered a weak chin. The man was, in a sense, hiding from himself. "You have only a very limited time. You realize that?"

"How so?"

"It becomes a non-Service matter, once we get to Gib. She has to be handed over to the civil police."

"What are we, two days from Gib?"

"We're taking four actually. For operational reasons which don't concern you."

"Well." The lips curled under the beard. "Well, that's plenty of time for me to whop some kind of story out of her. Don't worry." He rose.

"Sit down!" Bond all but shouted. "Sit down! I haven't said you can leave."

"I didn't know you were *my* keeper on this ship."

"Well, you had better know, Mr. Speaker. You don't move on this ship without my say-so."

"You're not trying to tell me you're SIS?" The leer again.

"I am telling you just that."

"Very interesting, in view of what seems to have happened on board this ship. I think we'll have a little talk when we're back in London. I can be a very suspicious man, Bond, and they trust me at the interrogation center. I can reach into your file and come up with something, I'm sure. Everyone has at least one thing they want to hide. We'll discover yours, then I can embroider it a little and they'll drop you into a well and forget about you. I've broken stronger men than you, Bond. Good night," and he walked from the cabin, leaving Bond floundering. The man was some kind of a nutter, he thought. Best get a signal off to London about him.

He went out and toured the passageway, speaking to all the varied security men, British, American and Russian. All seemed in good order, so he decided to leave the signal until after dinner, which he took quietly in the wardroom.

Later, as he was about to go up to Communications, the

242

Tannoy clicked on. "D'you hear there! D'you hear there! Would Captain Bond please take a message in his cabin. Captain Bond to his cabin, please."

Nikki, looking pale and uncomfortable, was waiting for him.

"What can I do for you, Nikki?"

"Oh, please don't tempt me, James, but I have a terrible concern. A worry."

"That's what I'm here for. Pour it all out."

"This is about the new American. The one called Woodward, Dan Woodward."

"Desperate Dan." Bond smiled. "Has he been desperate with you? He comes complete with a reputation that he likes the ladies."

"No, James. No. This is not funny. I am suspect that this man is *not* American. That he is *not* truly the Dan Woodward he claims."

"What?" He sat up, a little twitch of anxiety deep in his stomach. "Why do you say this, Nikki?"

"How do I tell you? It is difficult. Look, is operational secret, but we must share it. Three years ago, I was assigned to work in Afghanistan. With KGB. We had a dossier on terrorists operating in the Gulf. You know the kind of thing. A mixed bag of names and suspicions. The man who says he is Dan Woodward. His picture was there in dossier. I forget what he was called then. Hamarik, or Homarak. Something. James, you should take a look."

"Keep quiet for now, Nikki. I'll run it through London. Play it gently. I know how we can check it out."

He went up to Communications and went through the same thorough inquisition by a different, armed Marine, then got on with the job in hand. First a cipher concerning

Speaker, followed by a second one to liaison with Grosvenor Square, requesting a photograph to be sent over the wires. When unbuttoned, the text read—

PLEASE HAVE PHOTOGRAPH OF DANIEL WOODWARD
YOUR NI OFFICER STOP SEND MY EYES ONLY
URGENT AND HIGHEST PRIORITY STOP PREDATOR
STOP

It had been a long, tiring day, so he hoped it would come in before he went to sleep.

He had just got into his bunk when there was a tap at the door. He opened up, and Nikki slipped past him into the cabin.

"James, I'm sorry. I feel so alone. So afraid. It is like a feeling of doom. Please don't send me away." She wore a toweling robe which she slipped from her shoulders. There was nothing underneath. Bond's mind traveled back to the villa on Ischia. Once more he saw the doomed and treacherous Beatrice and realized that, whatever she had been, it would take a long time for her to be expunged from his emotions.

Now, looking at the young body of Nikki Ratnikov, he realized that he was also lonely, worried, and in need of comfort. He turned the lock in the cabin door and took her in his arms. For a long time she just clung to him, then, lifting her head, Bond put his own lips to hers, and they moved to the bunk, then drowned in each other as though this was the first and last time they would ever meet.

She left him at dawn, and he lay on the bunk alone, thinking they had both given and taken from each other. It was the most, except for dying, that any two humans could give.

Communications did not come back to him until almost ten-thirty the next morning. There were two messages waiting for him. First, a flash from Regent's Park authorizing him to remove Speaker from the interrogation of Deeley if he was not happy. The second was almost an afterthought, but in cipher.

PHOTOGRAPH OF USNI OFFICER WOODWARD
FOLLOWS PAGE TWO

And, sure enough, there was Daniel Woodward's photograph with a number stamped beneath it. He looked into the face to see clearly that the Americans' Daniel Woodward was certainly not the Woodward they had on board *Invincible.*

Bond went back to his cabin, clipped the holster to his belt, behind his right hip, inserted the Browning 9mm and sent for Bruce Trimble, Sergeant Harvey and four Marines. Trimble arrived first, and Bond wasted no time in telling him they had at least an impostor, at worst a terrorist in the shape of Dan Woodward.

"Was goin' to talk with you anyhow." The massive Trimble looked menacing. "I been worried about that guy. Doesn't mix, won't be drawn. Best get him in the brig."

They went together—four Marines with loaded weapons, Sergeant Harvey, Bond and Bruce Trimble, who looked as though he would rather do the job single-handed.

Stan Hare told them that Woodward was in the cabin they all shared, so they took up assault positions and Bond raised his hand to knock. If possible he wanted to take the man clean, and with little violence, but, before his knuckles could tap on the metal door, the whole ship seemed to tremble under their feet, as though it had suddenly hit unexpected, and very rough water. The jolt was so great that they were all thrown to one side. The explosion was not loud, more like a heavy-duty grenade exploding a long way off.

Then the warning klaxons started to wail.

15

The Rain in Spain

Half an hour earlier, Petty Officer Blackie Blackstone sat in the engine room control module, passing the time with the other members of his watch. None of them noticed that Blackstone kept idly scanning one particular section of the turbine controls—those which would give indications of oil-temperature rise.

They had told him to expect the temperature on number one turbine to start going up rapidly sometime between nine and eleven o'clock.

He spotted the first indicator at nine-forty-five, number one showing a minute rise. By ten o'clock it was really going up, and at 10:05 Blackie was able to give a startled cry—"Oil temp on number one going into the red!" He moved toward the controls, checking off item by item, trying to locate any obvious fault. In fact he let his Chief Petty Officer discover the problem. It took less than a minute.

"It's the bloody filters. Change filter one on number one turbine, Blackie."

"Done." Blackstone went into the little storeroom behind the control room, signed for one filter and took a sealed package from the spare module rack.

"Want some help, Blackie?" the Killick asked.

"Nah. Take me a couple of minutes." Blackie went on to the engine room, making his way to the far side of the first turbine. In case of accidents, he had already put the new, but doctored, filter, in its packaging on the shelf which held filters in the storeroom. As it was first in line, the filter would, naturally, be the one to be used if any emergency arose. They had told him that this filter would produce, within five minutes, thick smoke and do a very small amount of damage which would cause the turbine to be shut down. The small pencil mark he had inscribed to identify this doctored package was there, so he had no worries. Change the filter, he thought, then go back and wait for the panic.

Petty Officer Blackstone went through exactly the same sequence of events as he had done on the previous night: unscrewing the lugs and lifting the filter out with his long tweezers. He took the second, doctored filter in the tweezers and dropped it in place.

There was a great deal of smoke, then an explosion which lifted Blackstone off his feet, hurling him against the metal wall behind him and removing parts of his body as it did so. His last thought before his final sleep descended on him was, *They said it would only be smoke. They said there was no risk.*

•   •   •

Orders were coming through the Tannoy system, spoken calmly but giving essentials—all fireproof doors to be closed up; damage control to their stations; all firefighting crews to the engine room. "This is not a drill! This is not a drill!" the disembodied voice repeated several times.

James Bond and his party were thrown around the passageway in front of the cabin door where they were preparing to take the the substitute Dan Woodward into custody. Bond had been knocked off his feet by the lurch of the ship, and was just picking himself up, when the cabin door opened to reveal Joe Israel, looking puzzled. "Hey, what the hell's going on? . . . Was just—" He was cut off by Dan Woodward's arm snaking around his neck.

"I think they want to have words with me, Joe." Woodward was pressing against Israel. "Tell them I have a gun in your back." He spoke loudly, but with confidence.

Israel let out a long sigh. "Okay. Yes, James, he's pushing a large piece into my back, and I've no doubt he'll take me out. I presume he's not really—"

"Desperate Dan Woodward? No, I'm not," Abou Hamarik hissed. "This is most unfortunate, because I must now get off this ship alive. I would suggest Captain Bond takes me, unless he would like to see this wretched man blown apart. Now, just put down your weapons, all of you. Gently does it. Just put them down on the deck. This is really most inconvenient."

"Okay." Bond's face was like stone. "Just do as he says. I don't want to endanger Joe in any way."

As he bent at the knees to place the Browning on the carpeted deck, he caught a slight movement out of the corner of his left eye. Someone pressed against the bulk-head in the Russian section of cabins.

Around him the Marines and Bruce Trimble also put down their weapons.

"Okay," Hamarik whispered. "Now move away from the door. I'm bringing the American out."

Bond did not dare to even allow his eyes to flicker in the direction of the Russian section. He did not know which way this fake Woodward wanted to go, so he simply stood back against the far wall of the narrow passageway. "Do as I do," he told the others. "Backs against the wall here." They obeyed—a line of seven men against the wall, and a small arsenal of weapons on the deck. They felt stupid, and there was not one of them who felt he should make some kind of move. Bond sensed it, and said loudly, "I don't want any heroics. Don't do anything stupid." Then, to Hamarik, "Where do you want to go?"

"Off this ship, but I would like to take another guest with me. You have a girl called Deeley in custody, I think."

"Yes."

"I will take her also, and you, Bond, will lead us."

"Okay." Bond shrugged. "If you want to get Deeley you'll have to turn left out of the cabin door. You want me to lead you?"

"I want all of you in front of me. Move, the lot of you."

"Do as he says." It was a risk Bond had to take. Someone would now be behind the so-called Woodward, so maybe they could do something, even though in the confined space it would be a risk.

"Wait!" Hamarik snapped. "Just shuffle along the wall. When I'm out into the open, with Israel, I'll tell you to turn and go in front of me. I shall want you in file so you block off the entire passage ahead of me. Okay! Move!"

They shuffled along the wall, leaving the area in front of the cabin completely free. It made things easier for Bond, for he now had an excuse to turn his head toward the cabin door, his eyes seeking the movement in the Russian section.

He had hardly moved his eyes when everything happened. Hamarik pushed Israel in front of him and came into the open, turning left. As he came out, he glanced to his right and saw what Bond had already spotted.

Standing in the doorway separating the Russian and American quarters was Nikki Ratnikov, her legs apart and a small automatic pistol held in front of her with both hands.

Hamarik gave a little curse, pushed Israel around, trying to get his body between himself and Nikki. Keeping Israel in a hard neckchoke, he pulled in hard, pushing him to the left and realizing he had no option but to fire at the girl.

The shots crashed out, echoing like cannon blasts in the confined space. Both fired twice, and both hit their marks. Hamarik's left arm dropped from Israel's throat as he cried out, took a pace backward, tried to lift his pistol again, but was forced to clutch at his right shoulder, which had suddenly spouted blood. He cried again, dropped the pistol and sank to his knees. It was Bruce Trimble who got to him first, snatching his own weapon from the deck and holding it at arms' length. "Stay where you are, you damned honky fraud!" But Hamarik was already unconscious, keeling over and sprawling onto the deck.

Bond moved forward toward Nikki. She stood like a statue in the doorway, pistol still extended, arms rigid, and feet apart. But the white rollneck sweater she wore had turned crimson: a great, ugly spreading stain.

Bond was only two paces from her when he heard the

ghastly rattle from her throat, saw the blood gush from her mouth and her body crumple to the deck. He knelt over the girl, his fingers feeling for a pulse in her neck. Nothing. "She's dead," Bond said bleakly. He had liked Nikki, in spite of some suspicions, and all sudden deaths of young people were sad moments, particularly in this case, for Nikki Ratnikov had put her own life at risk for their lives.

"Well, this bastard's still alive, and I reckon he can be patched up and made to talk." There was no bitterness in Bruce Trimble's voice as he walked toward the nearest bulkhead telephone to call the sick bay. Over his shoulder he said they would need a Marine guard around the clock.

Bond got to his feet. "Take care of it for me, Bruce. I've got to see what's going on." Even in the few minutes of stand-off and death, they were all aware that there had been some serious problem on the ship. The Tannoy had been active, and Sir John Walmsley, himself, had been issuing some orders. Bond made his way along the passage, turned the corner and climbed the companionway. Whatever else had occurred, he now had to break the news of Nikki's death, and the fact that they had a second presumed terrorist on board.

•　　•　　•

Bassam Baradj scanned the sea with his binoculars. All being well, the operation would have started by now, and soon he expected to hear what course of action the Captain of *Invincible* would take.

He refocused the glasses on the freighter, *Estado Nôvo*, which was at this moment passing through the Straits of Gibraltar. The large crate was still in place on the main deck, shielding the stolen Sea Harrier from view, and he knew the pilot, Felipe Pantano, was also aboard.

The freighter had followed instructions to the letter and Baradj had been in constant, ciphered contact with the ship since it had made its short visit to Oporto. From there the *Estado Nôvo* had passed through the Straits and headed for Tangier, where, with much bribery and considerable ingenuity, Baradj had arranged for other cargo to be taken on board: mainly four AIM-9J air-to-air Sidewinder missiles and a large quantity of 30mm ammunition, belted and ready for installation for use by the two Aden guns already resting in their pods on both port and starboard of the Harrier's fuselage. They had also taken on a considerable amount of fuel.

By tonight, Baradj thought, the freighter would be in place. If needed, the stolen Sea Harrier could be airborne, by using the vertical takeoff technique, within five minutes of an order being received.

Baradj took one more look, then put the glasses in their case, turned and began to walk quietly back to The Rock Hotel. Earlier he had looked down on the airport to make certain his private helicopter had arrived safely. The pilot was to stay with the craft and Baradj knew it would take part in the final piece of his plan—the recovery of the huge ransom he expected to pick up from the sea. Of course the pilot had no idea that he was doomed, just as all members of his brainchild, BAST, were doomed, to the extent that they would have done the dangerous and difficult work with no reward. Twenty-four, maybe forty-eight hours. . . . Baradj smiled. After that he would have a veritable king's ransom. He would also have disappeared from the face of the earth. He actually laughed out loud, thinking of the fanatics who would have given their souls for an opportunity like this, and how they would have wasted the money on guns and bombs, bringing more danger to their lives. He, Bassam Baradj—or to be truthful, Robert Besavitsky—would use it for a really decent purpose: his own pleasure and security. Not yet, but in a year or so, he would emerge, with a new face and identity. He would own houses, estates, cars, yachts, private jets, companies which might even do some good for the world. He would make gifts: a new library here, or a museum there; maybe even scholarships. Yes, that was a new idea. Some good things must come out of the great crock of gold that waited for him. This would only be fair.

The sun shone and Baradj was happy. The sun was set fair for Gibraltar, though the weather report for the rest of the Spanish coast was not so good. Never mind, it would be good enough to do what needed to be done.

●   ●   ●

"I for one, Sir John, do not care about what has happened. This is a unique meeting, and we *do* need a clear four days to complete our talks. Do I have to make it plain again? Four . . . clear . . . days. That is what was arranged, and that is what we all expect." The Prime Minister looked toward the President of the United States and Secretary Gorbachev. An interpreter whispered the translation in Gorbachev's ear. He nodded gravely, the birthmark on his forehead coming into view as the head bobbed and he repeated, "Da . . . da . . . da."

"Prime Minister," George Bush spoke quietly. "I understand the problem, and I see you're anxious because we are your guests. I *agree wholly* with you. We should stay aboard, we've lost almost one hour already. But I'd like to hear the options again."

Sir John Walmsley gave a tiny sigh and nudged James Bond, who stood beside him. "I think Captain Bond should give you a little rundown," he said, his voice that of a desperate man. "He is in complete control of your security, so he, as it were, carries the can."

Oh, yes? Bond thought before he spoke. "I think Sir John's explained it very clearly." He kept his voice deliberately low, and slow enough for the translator to do his work for Chairman Gorbachev. "This morning one of the main turbines which drive this ship had a serious malfunction. One man, a Petty Officer, was killed and there was no further damage. The turbine has been inspected and, so far, there are no signs of sabotage. One thing is clear, though—we should not attempt to make Gibraltar without getting the turbine running again. Also, because the other turbines were produced at the same time as the one which blew, it is essential that they have a complete overhaul. This will take several days." He paused to let all this sink in, and Mrs. Thatcher showed slight annoyance, looking at him as if to say, "Get on with it, man."

"There is a U.S. naval base, near Cadiz, and within a few hours' sailing time from here, but there are problems about this place. . . ."

"You're talking about Rota?" the PM asked.

"Precisely, Prime Minister. Until a few years ago Rota was a base for U.S. ships. In particular for the nuclear submarine fleets. However, this was discontinued at the request of the Spanish government. Now it is solely used for Spanish ships, though the United States use it as an airfield—to support the U.S. Navy, as a staging post for

U.S. personnel returning home, or going to other NATO bases in Europe. It is also, I am told, used for more sensitive matters."

"So what are you telling us, Captain Bond?" President Bush asked a little sharply.

"Permission has been given for *Invincible* to put into Rota. In fact it has now been included in the exercise in which we are supposed to be engaged, *Landsea '89*. A new turbine is being flown out, in several sections, and a special team of engineers are coming in from Rolls-Royce. The problem there is that we shall be called upon to allow more civilians on board—"

"Can they not wait for the four days, which, I must remind you, Captain Bond, are shrinking fast?" The Prime Minister was getting more irritated and Bond already knew that it was unlikely they would budge her from her avowed intention of spending the full four days with President Bush and Secretary Gorbachev.

"There is one other problem," Bond continued. "Yes, I expect the engineers can be kept at bay, but *I* am concerned for your safety. While we cannot prove the gas-turbine accident was an act of sabotage, we have had two incidents since we commenced *Landsea '89,* both, we suspect, are connected to a little-known terrorist group called BAST. One took place before you joined us—that concerned murder, and the resultant discovery that one of the Wren detachment on board was not what she seemed. She was a very definite penetration agent, we think, linked to BAST. Also, this morning, one of your protectors, Chairman Gorbachev, was killed while we were trying to arrest a second man we think is also a BAST penetration."

The Russian leader spoke a few words to the interpreter

256

who said, "Mr. Gorbachev is already aware that Nikola Ratnikov has given her life for his personal protection. She is to be posthumously awarded the highest honor the Soviet Union can give to a brave soldier."

Bond acknowledged the statement, then continued, "I have also been threatened by BAST. Over Christmas I was personally attacked, and my car was bombed on the island of Ischia. This was definitely a BAST operation, which seems to indicate that the whole of *Stewards' Meeting* is known to them.

"Our only option is to limp into Rota tonight, and get you all off the ship, under cover of darkness. The USNB at Rota has agreed to take people off but, as yet, they do not, of course, know who you are."

"Then that will take up a little time, Captain Bond," Mrs. Thatcher said frostily. "I would suggest that you get on with moving us into Rota, and arranging for us to fly back to our respective countries *under the utmost secrecy.*"

"Thank you, Prime Minister. That's what we see as the most viable course—"

But the PM had not finished. "This will, of course, *not* be possible to accomplish in the next four days. We started our talks this morning. We will leave, secretly from Rota, in *four* days. I am sure we'll all be quite safe in your hands. Thank you, Sir John, thank you, Captain Bond. Now we must really get on with our work."

"It's like trying to argue with an Exocet," Sir John Walmsley said angrily once they were outside. "So be it. We make for Rota. The rest of the task force will have to stay outside the harbor, as a defensive wall, while we, Bond, will just have to make the best of it. How's the fellow that got shot this morning?"

"He'll be okay, but we can't even think of questioning him yet."

"Come up to the bridge with me." The Rear-Admiral had already set off at a brisk pace. "When'll you be able to interrogate the man?"

"Probably sometime tomorrow. I have an armed guard on him—round the clock."

"You going to leave him to the tender mercies of the inquisitor you had flown in from Gib?"

Bond sighed. "As it happens, I was going to have him relieved because I didn't think him suitable for the Deeley girl. He's got a paranoid personality, and jumps at every shadow. He's not the most pleasant interrogator I've met, and he sees plots behind every uniform and every bulkhead, though I think he might just be the type to deal with this joker."

"Your province, Bond. Your province. You must do as you see fit." They had reached the bridge. "Oh, merciful heavens, look what we have here!" Walmsley exploded. Outside the weather had closed in, with low cloud and driving rain.

"It'll take me until tonight to get into Rota. Maybe late tonight. You get on with what you have to do, Bond, and I'll try and make it in the shortest possible time. The task force will have to close up, and that's not going to be easy in the circumstances. We'll talk later. Right?"

"Aye-aye, sir." Bond went below, found the sick bay and spoke to Surgeon Commander Grant.

"He's weak and unconscious," the doctor told him, "though one of the Flag Lieutenants guarding Mrs. T came down and shot off some photographs to send to London for identification. The Marines will keep an eye on him, and I assure you that, unless he's subject to a miracle, there's no way he can get out of here. Lost too much blood."

Next, Bond summoned Donald Speaker to his cabin. The man showed no sign of relaxing his near paranoid unpleasant stance and arrived late, without knocking at the door.

"Sit down." Bond knew he sounded like a headmaster who had summoned a recalcitrant boy to his study.

"What is it now? More shady business?"

"In a word, yes. But you'd better know that I had London's clearance to have you taken ashore and sent home, after last night."

"Really?"

"Yes, really. But another job's come up that might just be right for your unpleasant talents." He instructed the interrogator regarding the wounded prisoner. "You'll have a word with the Surgeon Commander tomorrow morning, and you will take his advice, and his advice only, as to when you can start. Now, I don't want to see hide nor hair of you until you've got a result."

In the wardroom at lunchtime, Clover Pennington came over and said she was sorry to hear about the Russian girl. "You'd grown quite fond of her, hadn't you?" she asked.

"In a professional way only, Clover. She was good at her job."

"And aren't I any good at mine?"

"You're excellent, Clover. But let it all lie till we've got the next few days behind us."

They made Rota just before midnight. A boat went ashore with Rear-Admiral Sir John Walmsley, who stayed on the U.S. base until three in the morning, having made all arrangements for the base to house the inbound Rolls-Royce technicians.

The ship's routine went on as usual, and, after doing his rounds of the secure areas for the heads of state and their bodyguards, Bond turned in a good hour before Walmsley was back in the ship.

His bedside communications telephone woke him at just before six. "Captain's compliments, sir. Could you go to his night cabin immediately." It was the officer of the watch.

Bond shaved and dressed at the speed of light, and presented himself at the Captain's night cabin ten minutes later.

Walmsley was in his bunk, looking tired, propped on one elbow, sipping a large mug of coffee with one hand and holding a signal in the other. "They give me no peace," he said. "This is, I think, for you, Bond." He waggled the flimsy signal. "Coffee?"

"No, I'll get some later, sir." Bond quickly read the report.

> FROM OC USNB ROTA SPAIN TO CAPTAIN HMS
> INVINCIBLE STOP IF YOU HAVE A CAPTAIN JAMES
> BOND ON BOARD HE IS REQUESTED TO COME
> ASHORE IMMEDIATELY TO TAKE URGENT
> INSTRUCTIONS FROM HIS SUPERIORS STOP PLEASE
> ADVISE SO HE CAN BE MET STOP CAPTAIN BOND IS
> ADVISED SONGBIRD STOP

"I trust this was in cipher, sir?" The use of the word Songbird authenticated the signal for Bond.

"With you fellows it's always in cipher. My writer unbuttoned it under absolute security. Gravestone security."

"I think I'd better go, then, sir."

"Thought you might. I've got a boat standing by. Only

one rating to take you in. I don't want to send a lot of people off the ship at the moment. Should he wait for you?"

Bond thought for a moment. "No, sir. But, as a precaution, I'll signal you when I'm ready to return and I'll use the word Songbird. If everything is normal, could you use Tawny Owl at the end of your signal?"

"Oh, lord, must I, Bond?"

"My signal to you will assure you of my safety. You should also respond in kind."

"Very well. Off you go. Your boat's waiting at the forward gangway, port side."

"Thank you, sir."

As Bond left the cabin, the Rear-Admiral leaned forward and began to write on the pad by his bed.

The rain had eased off, but Bond had muffled himself in his greatcoat, and was pleased to have done so, as the wind still carried rain and it was bitterly cold at seven in the morning. Also the Leading Seaman who steered them in did not seem to be completely awake. Altogether, Bond was glad when they reached the jetty. A civilian car was parked nearby and, as he came up the stone steps, a United States Navy Commander stepped from the driving side.

"Captain Bond?" He saluted.

"The same."

"Anything else to tell me, sir?"

"Predator," Bond snapped back.

"Fine, sir. My name's Carter. Mike Carter, and I'm acting on behalf of Songbird. If you'd like to get in, we have someone waiting for you on the base, sir."

They drove through the early-morning mist, and the rain started up again.

Finally, the American Commander stopped the car by a

well-guarded gateway. A black guard stepped forward and scrutinized the laminated card proffered by the Commander, looked at Bond and asked who he was. Commander Carter handed him another piece of paper which, to his amazement, Bond saw had his photograph attached to it.

"Okay." For the first time the guard saluted, and they drove on.

It was like any other base, apart from an area in the distance which contained two huge communications spheres, made from angled panels, making them look like humongous white golf balls. From between them other equipment sprouted—a very tall aerial and three rotating dishes.

Over to his left, Bond saw another communications ball with some of the panels missing.

"That one not functioning?" he asked.

"Hell, no." Carter smiled. "We share this place with the Spanish Navy. That was going to be for them, so we built the sphere, then they couldn't afford the gizmos that go inside. Tell you what, though, on Halloween we put lights in it and move the panels around. It looks great as a pumpkin."

They pulled up outside a low office building which had a Marine armed guard at the door.

"Okay, here we are. Terminus, as they say. Just follow me, sir."

He showed the ID to the Marine and they went through a small reception area and along a passage. "In here, sir." Carter opened a door. "Can I get you anything?"

"I haven't had breakfast and I'm pretty dry."

"Bacon, eggs, coffee."

"Why not?" Bond smiled.

"Be back in a few minutes then, Captain Bond, sir."

Bond nodded and went into the room.

"Hallo, my darling, I thought I'd never see you again," said Beatrice Maria da Ricci, who was sitting at a table with a large mug of coffee in front of her.

16

Batsblood

For once, Bond was lost for words. "But . . ." he croaked. "You're . . . Beatrice," pronouncing it as she had done, Beé-ah-Treé-che. As he did so, he realized that he had been mourning her since the terrible moment on Christmas afternoon when he had seen her blown to pieces in front of him at the Villa Capricciani, on Ischia.

Instinctively he reached out to touch her hand. It was flesh and blood, and he really did not care if she was the "Cat" of BAST.

She smiled up at him, the smile lighting her eyes and the whole of her face. "It's okay, James. I am real, not a ghost. Also I am on your side. I am not the Cat."

"But how . . . What? . . . I saw . . ."

"You saw a very good illusion. Like a magician's trick,

like David Copperfield in America, or Paul Daniels in England."

"How?"

"Your life was saved. So was mine, and we owe our lives to Franco, who we can never repay, because he is dead. I pleaded with M to let you know before this, but he said no, not until you could be off the ship for a little time."

"But, how, Beatrice?"

There was a knock at the door and Carter reappeared with a tray. Bacon, fried very crisply, the American way, two eggs, sunny-side up, a plate of toast, preserves and a huge pot of coffee.

"Don't forget, Miss da Ricci," Carter cautioned as he left. "There isn't much time. Your boss said it had to be done as quickly as possible."

"Haven't forgotten, Mike. Thank you."

Carter left and she told Bond to eat. "I will talk. Just like old times, eh?"

He nodded, and again asked how.

"There are two things you should know, James. First, you only met Franco and Umberto, who both gave their lives for all this. We had more people watching out for us. Four more men, all well concealed. They were our real watchers. Second, while we showed you around the villa we did not quite show you everything. Maybe that was wrong. I don't know anymore."

"What didn't you show me?" He swallowed the orange juice in one draught, then tucked into the bacon and eggs. As fastidious as he was about breakfast, this was heaven. He had not realized how hungry he was, nor how thirsty. Unnaturally thirsty.

"You recall the turning space for the car, near the lily pond, just inside the main gates?"

He nodded.

"Well . . . the wall to the right, before you came to the second gate and the steps—"

"What of it?"

"Describe it to me."

Bond frowned, munching on a piece of toast. "It was a wall." He thought again. "A wall covered with ivy."

"You got it. A wall covered in ivy. But it was a wall that was not a wall. There was also a gate in the wall. The ivy was always clipped regularly, so that the gate could be opened and closed. The same on the other side, but when you were through the gate you were in a little metal room, like a tall box. It was used as a watchers' point, or for quick escape and concealment. One of our other watchers spotted people getting in through the main gates in the early hours of Christmas day. The locks and devices seemed to make no difference to them. They were very skillful people. But you know they are skillful."

"And they . . . ?"

She nodded. "They tampered with the car. Put a bomb underneath."

"Yes?"

"Franco was alerted. He told me on Christmas morning. Also, you should know that they had already put in a bugging device. I blush, James. They heard everything."

"*You?* You blush?" He leaned across the table and kissed her.

"Listen, James, there is not much time. Our other watchers saw that the intruders, the people from BAST, were lazy. They knew we would not come out, or go near the car until either late on Christmas day, or even the next day. They left all things unguarded. They just went away."

"And Franco had a look-see?"

267

"More than a look-see. It was not easy. They used C-4 plastique, with a remote detonator. A button job, as they like to call it."

"So what did Franco do?"

"It was dangerous. Very dangerous. He bypassed their remote control and put in a different one. He also added a few extra things for luck. The door had been left open, and their remote simply operated a little light bulb on the steering wheel. That was the first thing Franco put in." She poured herself a cup of coffee, and the building shook slightly as an aircraft took off from the base.

"We had our own button job. When they operated their button, I pressed our button and this made for a great deal of smoke. Very thick smoke, and a flash, which went off four seconds after the smoke. A big flash. The smoke was dense. It covered the whole parking area."

Bond remembered, and saw it all again. First there was smoke. Then the flash, followed by the terrible detonation.

"This is why I dashed ahead. We thought that if they believed I was dead they would make a move—which they did. As soon as I pressed our button I was able to run through the smoke and get to the other side of the wall. In the tall metal box, there, we had another remote, linked to the real detonator. With these things there is often a time lapse. They all thought, like you, that I was blown to pieces. . . ."

"But you were. They found remains."

She did not look him in the eyes. "Yes, that was most unpleasant, and a terrible thing to do. I shall have to make many novenas. Franco's people robbed a grave. I don't wish to talk about that."

"You're alive, Beatrice, my darling. That's really all that matters."

"Actually, James, it *does* matter, but there is something more important. You have to get back to the ship. Even now, terrible things could be happening. We have people watching but we don't really know what they're going to do. Or how they'll do it. You were followed, by the way. . . ."

"Followed here?"

"No, after the bomb. To the place they had set up on the mainland. We managed to get our first good photograph of Bassam Baradj, who we think is the 'Viper' of BAST. The leader, who is going to do something pretty terrible to those three important people you have on your ship." She pushed a photograph across the table. It was the man he had known as Toby Lellenberg, the Commanding Officer of Northanger.

"That's Baradj?"

"Yes."

"Well, if all that was phony, why in heaven's name didn't anyone do something about it? Why didn't you get me out? Come to that you could have scuppered Baradj at the same time. Why, Beatrice?"

She gave him a wan smile. "Why, indeed? I tried, James. I tried very hard. To me it seemed the obvious thing to do."

"Then why didn't you . . . ?"

"M overruled it. You were monitored very carefully. The whole Northanger setup was kept under close surveillance, but M said we were to let them play it out. His argument was fairly sound. He wanted to use the information regarding your hijacking, and, come to that, the hijacking of all the Northanger staff, as a lever."

"What kind of a lever?"

"He thought the Prime Minister, the U.S. President, and Gorby would abort the whole thing if they smelled danger. He—M, that is—laid it all out to the PM; went through the dangers, and the difficulties we might have with security. But—"

"But she wouldn't listen," Bond supplied.

Beatrice nodded. "She waved aside everything. Even called the U.S. President while M was there. Their argument was that this was urgent, important, and couldn't be rescheduled. I rather gather that she just waved aside the danger, and the others followed her, like sheep."

"That all figures. Do we know where Baradj is now?"

"We're not sure. Maybe on Gibraltar. Maybe even nearer. Now you know this, you have to get back. You also have to get Mrs. Thatcher, the President of the United States and Mr. Gorbachev off the ship in time. Off and away from it."

An expletive suddenly burst out of Bond's mouth.

"What?" Beatrice asked.

"If you're not the Cat, then—"

"Of course. Did you not realize that before? It's one of the reasons you have to get back. If we pinpoint Baradj, then I'll be near him. Look for me near Baradj." She had risen and pressed a button set in the wall. Mike Carter appeared in the doorway. "Time to go?" he asked, almost gratefully.

"I have told him all we know, Mike."

"Your boat didn't wait for you." Carter looked at Bond.

"No. No, I have a code sequence with Walmsley. Are you in touch with the ship?"

"Sure. No speech, just the electronics."

"Okay, send this—Songbird requests boat to come aboard. You should receive a response with the words Tawny Owl in it. If they don't send Tawny Owl, then I guess we're in for a shooting match."

He rose, and she came around the table to him. For the first time, Bond noticed that she was wearing the gold and diamond clasp, shaped like a *scutum,* that he had given her for Christmas. He held her close, and kissed her hair, then her lips. "If you're going to be near Baradj, you take care, Beatrice, my darling."

"You just get those important people off *Invincible.* Then we'll go for Baradj together. I want another Christmas with you, James."

"Maybe a lot of Christmases."

Carter had returned and coughed, delicately, by the door. "You're okay, sir. The message read, 'Am sending boat for Songbird stop The Tawny Owl is waiting.'"

"Thank God for that." Bond kissed her again, then left quickly, not looking back. He rarely looked back in a situation like this. In some ways he thought it might bring bad luck.

The little boat, with its engine throbbing, was already waiting at the steps. In the bow a Leading Wren waited to help him aboard.

"The Captain's apologies, sir. He couldn't send the same seaman back for you. The man has had to go to the sick bay. He wasn't too well."

Bond remembered. "He didn't seem all that brilliant, on the way in." He jumped down into the boat and waved to Carter, who waited until they were clear of the jetty and then walked to his car.

Ten minutes later, Carter was back at the low building inside the base. Beatrice was waiting outside, looking frantic and agitated.

"Oh, my God, Mike." Her voice had risen to an almost hysterical pitch.

"What in God's name . . . ?" he began.

"They've got them."

"Who?"

"Thatcher, Bush and Gorbachev. The Foreign Office in London received a telephone call ten minutes ago. They've been told to pass it on to their opposite numbers in Washington and Moscow. The call was from a man. They think from London. He gave them a code word—Batsblood—and said that the three heads of state were being held on *Invincible*. There will be no release to the Press and their demand is six hundred billion dollars: two hundred billion for each of the heads of state."

"Just money? Nothing else? No prisoners to be released? Nothing like that?"

She shook her head, biting her lip. "That's it. They have until three o'clock our time to agree. If nothing by then, they'll show us some kind of firework display. If the task force makes any attempt to approach *Invincible,* they'll kill one of the three." She drew in air. "How? How could they have . . . ?"

"We tried to contact the ship?"

Again the little nod. "Absolutely no vocal response. Nothing except the electronics. *Invincible*'s already signaled to the other ships, ordering them to keep station."

The little boat puttered up to the companionway let down from the main deck, for'ard, on the port side. The Leading Wren held the craft steady with a boathook, while Bond made his way up the shaking steps.

As they had approached *Invincible* he seemed to sense something eery about it. Something wrong that he couldn't put his finger on. Now, he reached the main deck and saw it was deserted except for the aircraft and helicopters.

His intuition was either correct or playing tricks with him. In any case he reached behind him for the Browning. He had not even got a hand on the butt when a familiar voice said, "I wouldn't do that, James. Just take your hand away."

He turned to see Clover Pennington, with a Wren on each side, coming from behind one of the Sea Harriers. All three girls carried automatic pistols.

Stay cool, he thought. Stay very cool.

"Hallo, Cat." He smiled.

17

Operation Sleeping Beauty

One of the girls walked forward, reached behind him and removed the Browning.

"Cuff him, while you're at it," Clover told her. "Well, James, did Tawny Owl give you the go-ahead?"

"Yes. How did you manage that?" he asked, surprised that his voice appeared to be steady.

"The silly old fool made a note of it and left it on his night table. It was so easy."

Bond felt the cuffs go on; the cold steel biting into his wrists. He was still puzzled by the silence. "How, Clover?" he asked.

"Bring him down to my cabin," she ordered the two Wrens, who shoved him like men, leading him to the bulkhead and down the companionway, along the knee-touching passages to the Captain's day cabin, where they roughly pushed him into a chair.

Clover told the two girls to get on with their other duties. "I'll call for you in about five minutes. I want this one nicely locked away in the cells." She went behind the Captain's desk and sat, looking at him. "You see how easy it is for women to do the job of men?" The smile was still attractive, without menace or phony evil. The snarl and leer were strictly for the movies. Clover looked like any other nice, well-brought-up girl with a future.

"There's nobody around, that's obvious." Bond's mind hovered between thoughts of what he could do, and how in heaven's name had First Officer Pennington managed to take over the ship. "There are over two thousand people on this ship." He tried a winning smile. "How do fourteen girls manage to take over, as you appear to have done?"

"Two thousand and eighteen to be correct. Oh, and fifteen girls. We sprang Sarah Deeley. She's a psycho, of course, but useful if it comes to any really distasteful jobs."

"How?" he asked again.

"Because it was very well planned, and we were in a prime position to pull it off. My girls had jobs everywhere—including complete access to the galleys."

"The food?"

She nodded. "And drink. You should not really have got off the ship, James. I was a little cross about that. Didn't you feel very thirsty this morning?"

He remembered chugalugging the orange juice on the base, and the unusual need to drink. "Ah."

Again the nice-girl smile. "Ah, indeed. Every morsel of food, every beverage, yesterday contained a substance that would make every man jack feel thirsty this morning. A craving thirst."

"And this morning?"

"This morning you had nothing to drink before you went off to Rota. If you had taken a swig of coffee you would have become disoriented within twenty minutes and dropped asleep within the half hour. We called it *Operation Sleeping Beauty.* There were minor problems, of course—you were one of them—but my girls had ways of dealing with it all. Everyone, but you, is cosily tucked away. Fast asleep."

"How dangerous is this stuff?"

"Stuff? Oh, the Mickey Finn we popped into the food and drink. Kick like a mule, James. Knocks people out cold. There's a lot of that old standby chloral hydrate in it, but it's been refined, the smell removed, also the aftereffects are negative. The Viper put a lot of money into having the stuff made to the highest standards— Oh, and there's little or no danger."

"The Viper sounds a right little charmer."

"He is, as it happens. Anyway, James, the whole company of this ship will be out cold for at least three days."

"And the object of the exercise?"

"Money. Money to continue putting the world, and society, to rights."

"A lot of money?"

"Two hundred billion for each of the VIPs—"

Bond started to laugh. "Clover, is Bassam Baradj *that* naive?"

"What d'you mean?"

"Doesn't he realize that this isn't the ultimate hostage situation?"

"Why not? Three of the world's most powerful politicians—"

"Quite. You want money for them, and there's no way you'll get it. Sure, the countries concerned will probably

277

chase all of you to the ends of the earth and back, but nobody's going to pay that kind of money to get politicians back. Don't you see that? It'll be *Et tu, Brute?* time. Night-of-the-long-knives time. The Russians will shrug their shoulders and the anti-*Glasnost* team'll be in. The Americans will do something stupid, like letting the Vice-President in for a while and then starting the circus again. The British? Well, Mrs. T has her supporters, but . . . Well, the Cabinet will hold little crisis meetings. Then they'll just announce a new PM. America and us Brits *never* give in to hostage situations anyway, and a lot of powerful people will see it as a God-sent opportunity for a change in leadership." Bond shrugged, thought for a moment and added, "But, then, perhaps not."

She had gone a little pale, he thought. Well, he was only telling her the truth. "Eventually, death. Yes. We have a few aces up our sleeves. If the governments don't meet our requirements by fifteen hundred hours this afternoon, our time, we'll show some power. If anyone tries an assault on the ship, Sarah will deal with them. One at a time, of course. So far it's between us and the governments, but I don't see that lasting if they miss our first deadline." She looked at her watch. "Three hours to go. I don't know what's planned, but we've all been told to stay off the main deck and the island."

"You can't win. There's no way. Clover, how in God's name did someone like you get into a situation like this?"

"Don't talk to me like a cleric patronizing a whore!" she shouted. Then very quietly she said, "Because the world's a rotten place, run by rotten people. Our kind of anarchy is positive. We want a fair and open society throughout the globe—"

278

"You're just like all those pipe dreamers, Clover. There'll never be a fair, free and open society in this world. You see, people get in the way. Ideals are for idealists, and all idealists fall from grace. No ideal works, simply because human beings cannot cope with it. The man said it all—Power corrupts; absolute power corrupts absolutely. Lord Acton, wasn't it? Said it all."

"You don't think . . . ?" she began. "No. No, you're trying the old hostage-rapport trick. Time for you to go quietly on your way, James." Even before she had said it, there was an urgent knocking at the door. She called out and one of the Leading Wrens who had taken him on the main deck came in. She was a tall, angular blonde, but with the unfortunate fire and fervor of belief in her eyes. "All three countries have turned us down, ma'am. Viper says everyone is to stay below at fifteen hundred hours. He thinks that by going public we'll force their hands."

Clover nodded, then cocked her head toward Bond. "You can take him down to the cells. Lock him up tight."

"I don't have to keep the bracelets on, do I, Clover? I mean, the cells are pretty secure."

She gave it a moment's thought. "Make sure he's banged up tightly. Take one of the other girls down with you—armed. The cuffs can go."

Bond went quietly. He knew his only hope would be to get up onto the main deck, and, with luck, get off in the first Sea Harrier which was on the ski ramp, juiced up and heavy with weaponry. When in this kind of situation, go along with them. The entire business was crazy anyhow, for he fully believed all that BAST had done was to present an unexpected political bonus to those who opposed Gorbachev, Thatcher and Bush.

Another Wren joined them, cradling an H&K MP5 SD3, with which she prodded Bond. He could not but admire the organization. Baradj might have chosen a stupid, negative target, but the operation and its methods had been excellent.

The cells were a little cluster of six barred cubicles, deep within the ship. In a world of technology they were a tad old-fashioned. The barred doors slid back by hand and they were equipped with straightforward dead locks. Nobody else occupied the cells and they just pushed him into the first one available.

"What about the handcuffs?" he asked, as the Leading Wren seemed about to lock him up.

"Oh, yes. Frisk him, Daphne." The blonde with the feverish eyes had that tough, rather butch manner that you often found in servicewomen. It did not mean that they were different from other females, but it came with the job. Soft girls hardened under military discipline.

Daphne frisked him. Very thoroughly, Bond thought, for she lingered around his crotch. A genuine FCP, he said to himself.

Finally they unlocked the cuffs, slid the bars in place and locked him away.

"Someone'll have to bring you food, I suppose," the blonde said, her voice irritated at the thought. "Don't know how long that'll be, we're pretty heavily stretched."

"I can wait," Bond said politely, knowing that whatever they brought him would be well laced with their new concoction of basic chloral hydrate.

Alone now, he had decisions to make. This time he really was on his own. Up the proverbial creek without a paddle. No hidden weapons; nothing spectacular from Q Branch.

Just himself, his skills, and the absolute necessity to get away.

●   ●   ●

About one hundred miles to the northwest of Rota, the freighter *Estado Nôvo* had stopped her engines, and the sides of the fake crate were being lowered to display the stolen Sea Harrier.

Felipe Pantano fussed around. There was a lot of arm-waving, and a good deal of shouting and talking, as he supervised the arming and refueling of the jet. He was being given his chance. Today he would see action for BAST and the thought never occurred to him that he just might not get back to the freighter alive. After all, the whole thing was foolproof.

Nobody on any of the other ships from the task force would challenge a Royal Navy Sea Harrier, and by the time he had done his work, he would be streaking back to the *Estado Nôvo* with the throttle fully open. It was certainly a great day for him. The one-word message, *Dispatch,* which had come in clearly by radio, had changed the entire pattern of his life.

To put it simply, Felipe Pantano was an excited man.

●   ●   ●

In Gibraltar, Baradj had been loath to send the *Dispatch* signal to the *Estado Nôvo,* but the American State Department, the British Foreign Office and the Kremlin had left him no alternative.

Fools, he thought, they do not know what they're dealing

with. So he sent the signal—a telephone call to London, as before, another telephone call from his people in London to the registered owners of the ship in Oporto, and the signal sent buried in a longer message, direct from the owners.

Altogether, Baradj was pleased with the way in which he had organized the messages, by short phone calls from himself, to longer calls from his London people, who used pay phones and stolen credit cards—recently stolen: which meant purloined less than an hour before the calls went out. The communications were untraceable, which, once more, put him in the clear.

Baradj sat in his room at The Rock Hotel, just five minutes or so from the famous monkeys which inhabited their own territory of the Rock and were all known by name to their keepers. All of the monkeys had names, and were identifiable. Baradj found it a strange and unnatural trait in the British that they allowed one pair of them to be called Charles and Di, and another twosome, Andy and Fergie. This was almost treason to the British Royal Family, Baradj considered. He had a great love of the British Royal Family—which meant that Baradj would really have liked to have been born into a different kind of background. It also meant that he was trying to buy himself into the aristocracy: via terrorist activities.

Well, he thought, the balloon would go up soon enough. They would see, in less than two hours now, that they weren't playing with any old terrorist outfit. Oh, he thought, the books are correct: it is very lonely at the top of the chain of command. One of his great troubles at this moment was that he had nobody to talk with. He had, in fact, been reduced to making quick, almost nonsensical calls to other members of the organization, uninvolved in the present operation.

Finally, Baradj decided to call in his last lieutenant, Ali Al Adwan, whom he had left quietly in Rome. The call was to be his undoing, for the monitors in the whole area of Spanish coastal waters, had, as the jargon would say, un-waxed their ears: which meant they were listening out with extreme diligence.

"Pronto." Adwan answered the telephone in his Rome hotel.

"Health depends on strength," said Bassam Baradj.

They picked up Ali Al Adwan an hour later outside the hotel, on his way to the airport.

It was decided, at very high level, to let Baradj remain as a sleeping dog. After all, they could monitor his telephone calls, and even run complete surveillance on him.

•   •   •

James Bond had decided his only chance was to make a move when they brought his food. If he ate or drank anything it would be curtains, or at least some heavy gauze that would leave him junked out for a few days.

It was going to be very dangerous, for they would never think of sending a girl down on her own. There would be a guard, and he would have to deal with the situation on the hoof. Time ticked away: half an hour; an hour. Then, at 14:30, he heard the lock on the outer door click open.

"Room service." It was the unpleasant voice of Donald Speaker, who, a second later, appeared in front of the bars, a tray in one hand, keys and a Browning 9mm in the other.

Bond thought it was probably his own Browning. On the tray was a plate of cold cuts and salad, with a large mug of steaming coffee next to it.

"I might have known you'd turn coat."

"Oh, I had it turned a long time ago, James Bond. Money isn't everything, but it helps the world go 'round. I'm not a political traitor: just avaricious." He skillfully operated the key in the lock, and Bond relaxed, trying to work out the best, and safest, move.

"Anyway," Speaker continued, "you can't expect these girls to do it all. Girls can't do a man's job." He slid back the barred entrance and stood in the opening, the tray held by his left hand and balanced on his right wrist, the Browning held tightly and pointing directly at Bond, a mite too steadily for comfort. "Just step right back against the wall. Move fast if you like. It would be a great pleasure to kill you."

"I'll do it slowly and correctly," Bond smiled. "I'm not quite ready for the chop yet." He took one short step backward, then made his move. Swiveling to his right, out of the Browning's deadly eye, he turned and brought his left leg up in a shattering kick at the tray.

His aim was slightly off, but the effect was what he wanted, for the kick lifted the tray at almost the correct point, bringing the steaming mug of coffee up in a scalding spray, straight over Speaker's face.

The interrogator's reaction was one of the most natural things Bond had ever seen. First, he dropped both tray and gun; second, his hands flew up to his face; third, and concurrent with the first two, Speaker screamed—loudly and painfully.

Bond stepped in, grabbing at the Browning, twisting as

he did so, aiming a heavy chop with the gun butt at the base of Speaker's skull.

"Coffee," Bond whispered to himself, "can instantly damage your health." He was outside, sliding the gate closed, locking it and removing the keys.

He went through the outer door with care. There was nobody in the passageway, so he locked the door and moved along the passage until he came to the first companionway, which he went up at speed. He had one great advantage over the Wrens: one of the first things any officer does when reporting aboard a new ship is to make certain he knows the layout, and the best and quickest route to follow between any two points. Bond had spent almost an entire day learning the passages, bulkheads, companionways and catwalks of *Invincible*. He knew the way to the nearest heads that had ports above sea level, and he made this his first stop, unscrewing the lugs on one of the ports and hurling the key to the cells far out into the sea.

He moved as quickly as possible, taking great pains, stopping from time to time to listen for any sign of life. Wrens, he thought, should normally be identifiable at distance, but Clover Pennington's Wrens had obviously been subjected to special training. There were also only fifteen of them, and they would have to be well spread out across the ship.

He was making his way to the crew room in the for'ard part of the island, at maindeck level. He moved by the fastest means, bypassing the more obvious places where Clover would have people posted. It was now 14:45, so with luck they would all be below the main deck and off the island, as they had been instructed.

It was as though the entire ship was deserted, for he saw nobody in his journey, and it was only when he got to the crew room that he realized Clover had left one girl on deck, though, he figured, she would have to get below on the dot of three. The door to the main deck was open, and the girl had her back toward him. It was the tall, tough blonde Leading Wren who had taken him to the cells, and it was obviously her turn with the H&K MP5 SD3. She held it as though it was her child, which was a bad sign with terrorists. Women of this persuasion were taught to regard their personal weapon as their child: and that was not just terrorism according to the top people's espionage novelist. It was for real.

He looked around the crew room and finally found a G-suit and helmet which were roughly his size. Two-fifty in the afternoon. From the bulkhead door he could still see the Leading Wren, and behind her the Sea Harriers, the first of the four aircraft right on the ski ramp, with one machine behind it and a pair of others parked abreast. They were all obviously ready and armed, for the ribbons hung from the Sidewinders slung under the wings.

Standing to one side of the bulkhead, his back to the deck, Bond put up the visor of his helmet and whistled loudly.

There was movement from the deck, so the Leading Wren had heard and been alerted. He whistled, shrilly again, and heard the answering footsteps as she crossed toward the crew room door. The footsteps stopped, and he could imagine that she was standing, uncertain, the H&K tucked into her hip and the safety off.

When she came, she moved quickly and was inside the crew room almost before Bond was ready for her. The only piece of luck that came his way was the fact that she moved to the right first, which is normal in right-handed people, and exactly why Bond had placed himself to the left, from her viewpoint on the main deck.

His arm went around her neck. This was one of those times when it did not pay to be squeamish, or to even think about what he was doing. He only wished that it had been the psycho, Deeley.

She dropped the machine pistol, trying to claw at his arms, but Bond had already done the damage. Left arm around the neck from behind; push in hard; reach over and grasp the left biceps with the right hand, so that his right forearm went across her forehead. Now the pressure: fast, very hard, and lethal. He heard the neck go, and felt her weight in sudden death. Then he grabbed at the H&K and ran out onto the deck, slipping the H&K to Safe, ducking under the wings of the aircraft until he reached the one on the ski ramp. He went right around the aircraft, checking all control surfaces were free, nipping the warning ribbons from the Sidewinders and pulling the caps off the front of the Aden gun pods.

The generator was in place, plugged in. He paused for a second, undecided. He could leave it in and be certain that he could start the engine first time, or unplug and hope to hell there was enough charge on board. If he took the first option, there was danger in the takeoff, with the generator cable still attached. He took the second way and unplugged the cord, then ran around the aircraft, climbing into the cockpit. As he lowered himself into the seat he imagined he could hear the sound of another aircraft. He clipped the straps on and hauled down so that he was tightly secured. He lowered the canopy, and pressed the ignition, going through the pre-takeoff drill in his head.

As he pressed the ignition, there was a huge roar. Flame

speared up from somewhere behind him, and he could hear
the heavy thump of 30mm shells hitting parked aircraft and
the deck around him.

As the engine fired, the shape crossed directly over him.
A Sea Harrier, very low, almost hugging the sea as it did a
tight turn, pulling a load of G, to circle and come in again.

18

In at the Kill

He did not really know if this was a full, coordinated attack on *Invincible,* but, in the last seconds logic told him exactly what it was—the fireworks promised by BAST if the fifteen-hundred-hours deadline was not met.

Takeoff checks: brakes on; flaps OUT; ASI "bug" to liftoff speed. As always, the aircraft was alive, trembling to the idling of the Rolls-Royce turbofan.

Nozzle lever set to short takeoff position at the 50° stop mark; throttle to 55% RPM; brakes off; throttle banged into fully open, and there it was, the giant hand pressing at his chest and face.

The Sea Harrier snarled off the ramp. Gear "Up." ASI bug flashing and beeping; nozzles to horizontal flight; flaps to IN. The HUD showing the climbing angle, right on 60°, and a speed of 640 knots.

Bond broke left, standing on one wing as he pulled a 7G turn, the nose dropping slightly, then coming up with a twitch of the rudder. One thousand feet, and to his right he saw *Invincible,* the aircraft and helicopters on her deck ablaze. Gas tanks going up to produce spectacular blooms of fire, and the other aircraft, low, almost down to the water, then putting her nose up and pulling into a hard left turn.

Bond reached the outer edge of the turn, flipped the aircraft into a right-hand break, harder this time, his left foot pushing down on the rudder to keep level, then back on the stick to gain height as a bleep started to pulse loud in his headphones and the trace on the radar showed another aircraft locking on behind him—behind and above.

He pulled back on the stick, put the nose toward the sky, and heard the rasping noise that warned a missile had been released. His mind grabbed at the recent past, and the missile fired at him near the bombing range close to the Isle of Man. That could have only been an AIM-9J Sidewinder. As close as this, a superior AIM-9L Sidewinder would have followed him to impact.

He punched out three flares, set his own HUD to air-to-air weapons, and flung the aircraft onto its back, easing up on the stick and feeling the redout as the horizon disappeared below him and the sea came rushing up to meet him as he took the Harrier through an inverted roll.

The rasping beep disappeared and the horizon came up again. The flares had done their job, but he could not see the other Harrier and he was down to 2,000 feet again.

Turning in a wide full 360°, Bond searched sky and sea with his eyes, flicking to and fro between the view from his cockpit to the radar screen. In the far distance *Invincible*'s

deck was still littered with burning aircraft, and he thought
he caught sight of a yellow fire-bulldozer being handled in
an attempt to clear the deck of the ravished hulks of planes
and helicopters. Then he caught the flash, on the radar, far
away, thirty or so miles out to sea. The flashing dot began
to wink and he adjusted his course, losing height and slamming the throttles to full power, trying to lock on to the
other Sea Harrier, obviously intent on making its getaway,
and evading chase.

He was pushing the Harrier to its outer limits of speed,
making a shallow dive toward the sea and keeping his
course level with the flashing cursor on the radar screen.
Without any conscious thought he knew who he was up
against: knew it was the Sea Harrier that had gone missing
on the day he had nearly had a missile up his six. The pilot
could only be the Spaniard, though, at this moment, with
the sea flashing below him and his eyes flicking between
instruments and the horizon, he could not have named
him.

In seconds Bond realized he was in fact gaining on the
other Harrier, which was about twenty miles ahead of him
now. He armed one of the Sidewinders, waiting for the
lock-on signal for he might soon be in range. Then the
blinking cursor vanished.

There was a slight time-lag before Bond realized the
other pilot had probably pulled up to gain height, rolled
over and was high above him now, heading back toward
him. He lifted the nose, allowing the radar to search the air,
and, sure enough, the second Harrier was above and closing.

He put the aircraft into a gentle climb, all his senses
jangling and ready for the rasp or the beep which would tell

him Pantano had released a second missile the moment he came within range—the pilot's name returned to his memory without any conscious thought.

Fifteen miles, and the aircraft were closing at a combined speed of around 1200 knots. Seconds later, the marker on the HUD began to pulse and the beep in his ears told him he had locked on.

Bond released the Sidewinder and saw the flashing cursor break to his left. The rasp came into his own ears, and he knew they had both fired missiles at the same moment.

He punched out four flares and turned left, climbing. Seconds later there was an explosion behind at about a mile. Pantano's missile had gone for the flares. Then, without warning Bond's aircraft shuddered and cracked as 30mm shells ripped into the fuselage behind him.

He stood the Harrier on its left wing, then reversed to the right. Pantano had Viffed, slightly above him and at a range of around a thousand feet. Bond armed another Sidewinder, heard the lock-on signal and pressed the button. As he did so, another withering hail of 30mm shells ripped across his left wing and the Harrier juddered again, wallowed, then seemed to leap forward toward the great blossom of fire as the Sidewinder caught Pantano's Harrier.

It was like a slow-motion film. One minute the aircraft was there, firing a deadly swarm from its Aden guns, then the white flash filled Bond's vision and he saw the plane break into a dozen pieces.

He overshot the destroyed Harrier, and saw only one complete wing, twirling and fluttering down like a deformed autumn leaf. He reduced speed and turned, to set course for the coast, and as he did so, his Harrier grumbled, juddering and shaking. He fought the controls, realizing that he had no true stability. The shells from the Aden guns had probably ripped away part of his elevators and a section of tail plane.

Altitude 10,000 feet and falling. The Harrier was in a gentle descent and Bond could just about hold her nose at a 5°/10° angle. He was between twenty and thirty miles from the coast and losing height rapidly, hauling back continuously on the stick to stop the nose from dropping and the entire aircraft hurtling into a dive from which he could never recover.

The engine sounded as though someone had poured a ton of sand into it, and he had switched on the autosignal which would allow the base at Rota to track him in. He was down to 3,000 feet before he saw the coast in the distance, and by then the whole Harrier was shaking and clanking around him as though it was about to break up at any minute. The sink rate was becoming faster, and Bond knew there was only one thing left. He would have to punch out and pray that the shells from the other Harrier had not damaged the Martin Baker ejector seat.

He wrestled with the stick and rudder bar, just desperately trying to get the aircraft closer to the coast before getting out. The voice in his head started to repeat the procedure, and what was supposed to happen.

The Martin Baker was a Type 9A Mark 2 and the firing handle was between his legs, at the front of the seat pan. One pull, and, provided everything worked, the canopy would blow and the seat would begin its journey upward at minimum velocity before the rocket assist fired and shot the pilot, restrained in his seat, well clear of the aircraft.

The comforting words of some instructor at Yeovilton

came back to him. "The seat will save you even at zero height, and with a very high sink rate."

Well, he had a very high sink rate now, down to about a thousand feet and at least seven miles from the coast. The Harrier wallowed, down to around eight hundred feet. His port wing dropped alarmingly, and he realized that he was at the point of stalling. Almost at that moment he caught the glint of helicopter blades and realized it was now or never. Yet, in the few seconds before reaching down to the ejector handle, Bond pushed the port rudder hard, in an attempt to swing the aircraft away from the coast. He did not want this metal brick, still carrying dangerous weaponry, to plow into the land. The nose swung wildly, then dropped.

He knew the nose would never come up again, and he felt the lurch forward as the Harrier began what could only be a death dive.

Bond pulled on the ejector lever.

For what seemed to be an eternity nothing happened, then he felt the slight kick in his backside, saw the canopy leap upward. The air was like a solid wall as the rocket shot him clear of the falling, crippled Harrier. There was a thump and the sudden slight jar as the parachute opened and he was swinging safe and free below the canopy.

Below to his left he saw the white churning water which marked the spot where the Harrier had gone in. Then he heard the comforting sound of the U.S. rescue chopper nearby.

He was now separated from the seat, and seemed to be dropping faster toward the sea, which came up and exploded around him. The buoyancy gear inflated and brought him to the surface as he twisted and banged down

on the quick-release lock which freed him from any parachute drag.

The helicopter plucked him out of the sea five minutes
later.

•   •   •

It was early evening and the weather had picked up, the sun
red, throwing long shadows across the USNB Rota.

Bond sat in a small room, with a U.S. Marine Corps
Major, a Royal Marine Special Boat Squadron Major, Commander Mike Carter and Beatrice. On the table in front of
them lay a complete set of plans showing the layout of
Invincible.

An hour before, he had received a complete briefing, on
a secure line from London. BAST had given them until
dawn, around six in the morning. Then they would kill the
first of the VIP hostages. They knew the message had been
relayed to London from Bassam Baradj in his suite at The
Rock Hotel, Gibraltar.

Varied options had been put forward. The Rock Hotel
was well-covered. They had members of the SAS and local
plainclothesmen, plus one senior Secret Intelligence Service man watching out in case Baradj made a move. At first
it had been thought they should make a full frontal and pull
Baradj, for they knew he had a helicopter and pilot standing
by at the airport. Nobody had attempted to alert Baradj or
his pilot, and the final consensus of opinion was that trying
to take Baradj alive was dangerous.

"Remove their leader and those women will almost certainly kill." That was M's personal view, and one shared by
Bond.

Baradj had given them a latitude and longitude, a precise point at sea where the money had to be dropped and marked. If anyone approached him during or after the pickup, which was to be by helicopter, all three hostages would be killed.

"Whatever else," Bond had said, "he's thought out the operation, and we just cannot risk taking the fellow on the Rock. If we couldn't get him alive, it would be curtains for Mrs. T, Gorby and President Bush."

It had now been agreed that a rescue attempt had to be made long before anyone tried to get hold of Baradj. "We can con Baradj that we're meeting the deadline, let him relax, then make a bid to get the hostages off." Bond's was the last word. The Ministry of Defence, SIS, the Pentagon and the Kremlin had agreed to a last-ditch rescue attempt. The local forces had also agreed that the planning and logistics should be left to Bond. "Has anyone figured out how Baradj is communicating with *Invincible?*" he asked.

"He isn't," Mike Carter had said. "I suspect he'll flash them a code word. A one-time break in silence. Probably on a shortwave from Gib. It'll mean either they're to stand by because we've agreed, or kill, we've not agreed. Then there's the other one—kill, we've double-crossed him."

"All we can do is listen out." Bond's jaw had set, and his eyes turned to that dangerous stonelike look as he tried to gauge how many things could go wrong.

Now, in the low hut on the USNB Rota, he was going through possible strategy and tactics. "It has to be a small force." He looked around the room. "I took out one of these harpies, which leaves them with fourteen—fifteen if the wretched man Speaker is active; sixteen if Baradj's side-kick, Hamarik, is able to function, which I very much doubt.

The situation will almost certainly be that their tame psycho, the woman posing as Leading Wren Deeley, will be locked in with the hostages—or, at least, close to them, with orders to start killing on a given signal. So our first job will be to get down here." His finger moved to the briefing room one deck down from the main deck. "This we must do without being detected if possible." Then he gave a worried sigh. "I want you all to realize that I'm really only guessing. That briefing room is the place where they were having the conference meetings. I'd stake money on the three of them being kept in there, possibly with a guard on the bulkhead door. But it's still only a guess. If I'm wrong and they're being held somewhere else, then it'll go wrong and I'll take the blame."

"But you believe that's our main target?" the SBS Major nodded.

"Yes. We have to take the risk. The quickest way down is through the flight crew room—which is here." He pointed to the bulkhead door he had used to get to the Harrier. It seemed days ago now, not just a handful of hours.

"So, before we decide on tactics, how many people do you think we need?" The SBS Major was putting on a little pressure, and Bond knew it. Behind the dedication of elite forces there was always a desire to be in at the kill; to take credit. They were really in the hands of the United States Navy, so Bond had to make a very careful choice. He also had to make it with confidence and speed.

"They're fourteen, maybe fifteen. I don't think we have to go by the odds." He locked eyes, first, with the U.S. Marines Major and then with the Royal Marine Major from the Special Boat Squadron. "I lead. We draw up the main plan together. I want five of your Marines, Major, and five SBS, Major," turning to each man as he spoke. They both nodded solemnly. "As for weapons, well, there's likely to be killing—regretful, but I see no other way—and I think some of that killing's got to be silent. Have we any hand-guns with silencers?"

It was Mike Carter who answered. "We can provide Brownings and H and Ks with modified noise-reduction units."

"Right," Bond nodded. *Everyone* will carry either a Browning or an H and K. I want one man from each unit to be armed with a submachine gun. Any H and K MP5s, Mike?"

"MP5s, 5Ks, Uzis, you name it, we got it."

"K-Bar knives for the U.S. Marines; usual Sykes-Fair-bairn for SBS. Flash-bangs?" he asked Carter, meaning stun grenades.

"Whatever you need."

"Two each, and some tear gas grenades. We'll go in with masks on. Now, the actual tactics, and here we're going to have to guess a lot. We have to ask where we would put people on that ship to keep watch. I know the girl in charge, and she's no fool. But she'll probably act predictably."

"Then she'll let some of the girls rest for part of the time," the SBS officer said.

"Maybe. They'll be highly stressed, whatever, and there-fore more dangerous. I'd say she'd only let three of the girls rest at one time. That gives her eleven—twelve with Mr. Speaker, and I really don't know how good he'll be in a tangle."

"She'll stay on duty all the time?" the U.S. Marine Corps officer asked.

Bond nodded, with a smile. "Clover is probably able to keep going without sleep for another forty-eight hours. So, if you were her, where would you put your troops?"

They talked it out carefully, using logic, then going back and looking at it in the most perverse manner. In the end they decided that Bond had been right about the psycho being with the VIPs, plus a guard outside. They put two more on the main deck, one patrolling for'ard and one aft. Two on the bridge, probably armed with submachine guns, and two, similarly armed, in Flight Operations. This way they would have the whole main deck covered, fore and aft.

There was a total of five companionways leading down from the island to the first deck, where they thought the VIPs were being held. "One at the foot of each companionway?" Bond asked.

"Either at the foot or nearby," the SBS officer agreed. The USMC Major nodded.

"We can probably pinpoint what kind of defense they've got on the main deck, even possibly in the island and down on the first level." They all looked up as Mike Carter suddenly revealed this information.

Bond saw it at once. The base, he suspected, was now used for major intelligence-gathering: the electronics and the massive golf balls had told him that. "You can scan the ship for us?"

"We can try." Carter tapped a pencil against the table. "We've got several nice four-fanned P36s here stuffed full of the latest reconnaissance hardware. We can do a recce about an hour before you go in. They can see through anything—and it's going to be dark tonight: low cloud. We should at least get a clear idea of where the sentries are posted on deck and who's in the island."

299

"I wish you'd said that before," Bond snapped. "What'll you do? Overfly and then do a square to cover all sides?"

"Something like that. I need to know a time."

"Oh-three-forty-five. Quarter to four in the morning. Nice and dark. Time for births and deaths. Lowest ebb for those under stress. Okay?"

They all nodded.

"See what I can do, then." Carter left and they began getting down to details. Bond asked if they still had the companionway down to a boat dock, at sea level.

"They took it up after clearing the mess off the main deck," the USMC man said. "That Harrier pilot knew what he was doing. They said fireworks and he gave us the Fourth of July."

"Or Guy Fawkes day," the SBS officer added, not wanting the Brits to be left out.

"Well, he won't do it again," Bond said a shade huffily. "Now, down to cases."

They went into the operation in great detail, covering all contingencies: agreeing, disagreeing and finally compromising on one or two matters. When they had the whole business sorted out, Beatrice asked why she had been left out.

"You'll be in Gibraltar, my dear." Bond gave her a long look. "When we've done the daring rescue bit, if we succeed, I'm coming to join you—providing I'm still alive. Then, together we're going to finish the job and take Baradj in."

"Dead or alive?"

"Alive if possible. Enough folk will die tonight, and I am slowly coming to the conclusion that too much killing is bad for the health."

"If you say so, James. But I bet Baradj isn't one who'll give in easily."

"Let's get this little show out of the way first." Ignoring the others, he leaned over and kissed her on each cheek, then on her lips.

•   •   •

The P36 had brought back some very pretty pictures with its sophisticated equipment, a lot of which relied on infrared, which picked up the heat of human bodies.

They had been almost right. There were three guards on the main deck, one for'ard, one aft, and a third amidships. They also knew that there were three, not two, people on the bridge, and two in Flight Operations, and at least one in Communications. They agreed that they had been blind to that one. There *had* to be someone in Communications.

Clover'll be the third bod on the bridge, Bond thought. It was three o'clock in the morning, and they were all gathered by two matt-black inflatables. One for the USMC contingent and one for the SBS. Bond would travel with the SBS, and they had arranged some distractions to go down at zero hour, 03:45. All were dressed in black and with blackened faces, the weaponry slung about them from black webbing harnesses.

They made their approach on the ship's relatively blind side, the port quarter. It took half an hour of steady, quiet paddling to bring them under the darkness of the ship's hull, keeping close together, only parting company, moving fore and aft, once they reached the ship.

The men in both inflatables now put on their respirators, and readied the other equipment, waiting, glancing at their luminous watches, for the distraction to start. The first huge flash and thump came right on time from about half a mile away, in the direction of the other members of the task force. The explosions were made to cause maximum glare and minimum noise. They were very bright, and a lot of magnesium was being used up. The U.S. Marines and SBS people kept their eyes down, but calculated that nobody either on the open deck, bridge, or Flight Ops of *Invincible* could possibly keep their eyes off the flashes.

There was hardly any sound from the spring-loaded launchers which fired a total of four grappling hooks, each wrapped and swaddled in sacking, from the inflatables. Each hook had heavy knotted rope attached, and the irons thudded up onto the guardrails with little or no noise. It was merely luck which caused the irons to be fired at the same time as another of the explosions out at sea.

Bond was the first up the for'ard rope. He knew the whole invading party could make it to the main deck in less than three minutes, so he moved, at speed, but silently, keeping low, seeing the girl on watch near the bows outlined against the sky. There was no time for sentiment. The girl would kill him as soon as look at him, so Bond put her down fast and efficiently, using the blade of a Sykes-Fairbairn knife, taking her in a choke hold and letting the blade slice through the side of her neck, at the prescribed place. She went down without a sound.

At the same moment, the other two girls on deck watch went down—one by knife, the other by a vicious karate chop that broke her neck.

Bond joined two of the SBS men who were standing on either side of the crew room bulkhead. He entered first, the other two covering him, and moved through into the pas-

302

sageway, deep inside the island, turning left to take the
companionway up past Flight Operations, then along the
catwalk leading to the bridge.

They reached the top of the companionway and were
about to move onto the catwalk when quick clicking footsteps came from their right. All three men sank into the
darkness as a Wren hurried past them, obviously on her
way to the bridge.

Bond motioned them to follow him and they moved, like
silent shadows behind the hurrying Wren. By the main
bulkhead to the bridge, they paused.

"They've really agreed?" It was Clover Pennington's
voice.

"The message says *Scratch,* ma'am. You said that was
agreement, and that we should stand by. If they try anything funny when Viper moves in, we'll get *Desecrate,* and,
once he's picked up the money, it'll be *Off Caps,* which
means we get out as planned."

"Well . . ." Clover began. Then Bond nodded, tossed a
stun grenade onto the bridge, waited for its disorienting
but nonlethal flash and bang, and then sprang in, the two
SBS men at his heels.

The girls over by one of the open screens, covering the
deck below, whirled around, their machine pistols coming
up, as though, in spite of the flash-bang, they had reacted
automatically. There were four *phud-phud* sounds, and both
girls dropped their weapons, reeling back against the
screen before falling heavily on the deck.

The Wren from Communications took two bullets in the
neck, and Bond was on Clover, spinning her around and
jamming his pistol in her side. "Right, Clover. You take us
to them or you're meat like the others. The whole ship's

covered. We're everywhere.'' He pushed her toward the bulkhead, catching the glint of sudden fear in her eyes as she nodded, and at that moment all hell broke loose.

The tear gas grenades had gone down the companionways as they had arranged, and the remaining members of the assault force were sweeping the passageways clear. Bond pushed Clover along the catwalk. There was a U.S. Marine standing by the Flight Ops bulkhead, and you could glimpse a body on the deck. The Marine nodded and followed up Bond's party.

"You lead. Tell me where they are," Bond muttered as they went down the companionway.

"Probably dead," Clover choked. "My orders to Deeley were to chop them if anything happened."

"Well, get a move on."

At the bottom of the companionway, an SBS man loomed out of the tear gas, motioning them to avoid the body that lay sprawled across the narrow passageway. Bond had to push Clover on as she was fighting for air in the stinging, choking, tear gas, but there was no doubt of their destination. They were heading for the briefing room in which the secret summit had been held.

"Watch for the next corner!" Bond shouted, knowing it would angle around into the area which led to the briefing room. There would be at least one girl on watch there.

One of the SBS men leaped forward and fired twice with a silenced H&K. They followed to see that another Wren had gone down, directly in front of the briefing room bulkhead.

They were halfway down the passage when there came a crack and thump from the far end. One of the SBS men was flung against the metal wall, along which he seemed to spin three times before sprawling on his back. But before the casualty even hit the deck, the American Marine fired, four times in quick succession. Peering through the smoke, Bond saw that the unspeakable Donald Speaker had said his last word.

They were at the briefing room bulkhead door now, and Bond signaled a cover from both sides. Then, his hand slammed down on the heavy doorhandle and, as the metal swung back, he pushed Clover inside.

"No! Sarah! No. It's—" She was thrown back by a burst of fire from inside, then the Marine leaped forward and aimed two precise shots.

Bond came from behind him, just in time to see Sarah Deeley catapult back against the metal wall, hitting it with a thump which must have broken bones, and sliding down it, taking a smear of blood with her.

Lying on camp beds, set in a neat row in front of where Deeley had been standing, were the silent, still figures of President Bush, Chairman Gorbachev, and Prime Minister Thatcher.

Bond moved forward and felt each neck in turn. They were alive, and, it seemed, unharmed. M. S. Gorbachev was actually snoring.

The U.S. Marine Corps Major came into the room. "We have control of the ship, Captain Bond," he reported.

"Well, you'd best wake up Rear-Admiral Sir John Walmsley and organize some way of getting these rather important hostages off the ship and back to their own countries without any Press interference. I've got a date in Gibraltar."

19

Tunnels of Love?

Bassam Baradj had not slept well. The telephone call had come in at around three in the morning, and he had gone out onto the balcony, feeling elated.

For the first time since the operation started he broke radio silence with his wonderful girls on *Invincible*. Even then, he did it by tape on the shortwave, high-frequency transceiver which had stood by his bed since his arrival at The Rock Hotel.

He tuned to the correct frequency, and then chose the right tape. The *Scratch* tape, which would tell them that the three countries had accepted his terms and ultimatum. The girls would still listen out, and remain very alert, for had he not told the Americans, Russians and British that should he be double-crossed, or if anyone

307

showed themselves near to him, he would have Bush, Gorbachev and Thatcher exterminated with exceptionally extreme prejudice immediately?

He stood on the chill balcony, repeating the tiny signal, *Scratch-Scratch-Scratch-Scratch* again and again. They would have it by now, so he went back inside, closed the balcony windows, pulled the curtains, destroyed the *Scratch* tape, and put the little transceiver into its imitation leather case, then made certain the other two tapes were there, ready for use.

He placed the machine back on his bedside table, then changed his mind, opened it all up again and inserted the *Desecrate* tape, just to be on the safe side. If they did double-cross him, make an attempt on his life, try to arrest him on the way to the airport, or come thundering down on him with jets as he picked up the money, he would at least have time to press the button. This was a very high-quality machine, and, if anything went wrong—even though the thought was remote—he would be able to see things through to the end.

But how could anything go wrong? They had agreed. These people did not normally agree, but, in these special circumstances, it was the only thing they could do—give in to his demands. He lay down on the bed, but only dozed, waking again at six in such a state of elation that he might as well have been high on some drug.

He calmed down, drifting into a light sleep, waking again at seven-thirty. Outside, the sun was shining. An omen, he thought.

Baradj rang down for breakfast, which came within twenty minutes. He ate heartily: grapefruit juice, toast, bread rolls, preserves and coffee. Then he showered, toweled himself off and looked at himself in the mirror, turning this way and that to admire his physique. He was not a vain man, nor a stupid man. Far from it. But he had come a long way, and part of his success had been to keep fit. He might lack a six-foot stature, but his muscle tone and high degree of fitness made up for that. Nobody could deny that Bassam Baradj—who, by tonight, would have the name and identity of someone else—was very fit for his age.

He sat, naked, on the bed and put a call through to Switzerland. At the clinic, high in the mountains above Zurich, they confirmed his booking. Even the timing had been immaculate. He began to dress, thinking he had been foolish and paranoid yesterday.

Yesterday, when he had gone out for his walk, he thought they were watching him. There was a man in the foyer who followed him a little way, then another, different, man appeared behind him. When he got back to the hotel there had been a woman who seemed to be observing him with almost nonchalant care. Or had he imagined it?

He dressed, the lightweight beige suit made for him in Savile Row; the cream shirt, from Jermyn Street; and the gold cuff links he had bought in Asprey's; the British Royal Marine tie. He laughed as he knotted the tie. This was the supreme two-fingered gesture.

Last, he took the soft pigskin shoulder holster out of the drawer and strapped it on, adjusting it so that it lay comfortably just under his left arm. He put on his jacket and picked up the 9mm Beretta 93A, slammed a magazine into the butt and worked the slide mechanism. He did not leave it on safety. Baradj had more than a passing acquaintance with pistols and he knew that, as long as you were safe, careful and practiced often, there was no point in putting the weapon on safety. A man could lose precious seconds by using the safety catch. He was wrong, of course, according to the manuals and instructors, but he always played things *his* way.

The Beretta was comfortable under his shoulder, and he hummed a phrase from *My Way* as he slipped three spare magazines into the specially built pockets in the jacket. He picked up his wallet and credit card folder, dumping them in the pockets he always used for them, then slung the transceiver's thin strap over one shoulder and his camera over the other. He was ready. The maid could keep the pajamas, and there was nothing to incriminate him. Another pigskin shaving bag would cost him a great deal less than the hotel bill, so why pay the hotel bill?

It was hard to believe this was February. The sun shone, and the sky was blue. A faint breeze stirred the flowers. But all was well with the world, and he had spotted no familiar figures in the hotel foyer. It must have been his imagination. So he could walk. Walking was good, and, in the end, faster than facing the crammed Gibraltar traffic.

He started away from the hotel, with the sheer rock face on his right. Bassam Baradj was less than three minutes into his stride when the hair at the nape of his neck began to prickle. There were steady footsteps behind him. Not just the footsteps of idle tourists, but official footsteps.

He glanced over his shoulder and saw them: a man and a woman in jeans about ten paces from him. The man wore a leather bomber jacket, the woman had a short canvas jacket. Then he made eye contact with the man. It was a face he knew. A face from the files. He had ordered this man dead on at least three occasions. The man was James Bond.

•   •   •

Bond saw that Baradj had made him, so he acted quickly, his hand going for the Browning behind his right hip, covered by the bomber jacket, his legs moving apart to take up the shooting stance. But he was not quick enough. By the time the pistol was out, Baradj had leaped up the low rock face and clambered out of sight.

If I am to take this man, Baradj thought, then I shall do it on my own terms.

Back on the narrow road, Beatrice also had a pistol out and was speaking rapidly into a walkie-talkie, calling up the police and SAS reserves. Bond had insisted on going in alone. "I want to bring this guy back alive," he had said.

"Careful, James!" Beatrice called as he jumped from the road into the rocks. Boulders like sculpture, huge and rough, were strewn everywhere up the slope, but he could see no sign of Baradj.

Beatrice joined him and they fanned out, watching each other's back. In this terrain it would be relatively simple for Baradj to outflank them and take a shot from behind. But, when the shot came, it was from high up, and nothing thumped or ricocheted near either Bond or Beatrice.

Still spread out, they moved forward until they came to a wide arched opening, like a man-made cave in the face of the rock. It had been barred by a large iron gate, fastened with a padlock. The padlock had been shot away, and one of the gates was half open.

"The tunnels!" Beatrice whispered, and Bond nodded. "Yes, the tunnels—and we have no idea how well he knows them."

"What about you?"

Bond shook his head, whispering, "I've only ever been in the galleries open to the public. But where he goes we'll have to follow."

The phrase "As Solid as the Rock of Gibraltar" is a misnomer, for the great Rock is, in reality, like a huge, a giant, ants' nest of tunnels. All of them were military in nature, and the public were allowed to see the first true feats of engineering—the Upper and Middle Galleries, built under the instruction of Sergeant Major Ince of the Sappers in the 1780s. These faced Spain, were installed with cannon, and were largely responsible for holding the Rock during the Great Siege. But that was far from the end of the story. Later, tunneling played a key role during World War II, and sections of the tunnels were still very much in use now. Unless you knew the way, you could get lost very easily inside the Rock of Gibraltar.

Bond and Beatrice edged their way in, trying not to allow their bodies to be highlighted against the exterior.

Inside, the lights, drilled into the ceiling, were on, and they found themselves in a high curved vault, big enough to take a three-lane highway.

They spread out, one taking each side of the rough chiseled wall, their eyes straining ahead for any sign of movement. There was none, and the lights seemed to go on forever.

They stopped beside two curved Nissen huts, built into a cavern carved from the rock face. But they were locked and empty, so they continued, moving slowly, very aware of the fact that should Baradj find a hiding place—some dugout in the rock—he could pick them off as easy as shooting fish in a barrel.

The tunnel branched off, and within a hundred yards

Bond and Beatrice found themselves in the remains of what had once been a field hospital. Parts of tiled operating theaters remained, the sluices and lavatories were intact. But the hospital led nowhere, and in minutes they were back in the wide main route.

Bond remembered now that these tunnels were once full of men, tanks, lorries, field guns and jeeps. Indeed, they had been used as one of the main staging posts for *Operation Torch,* the Allied invasion of French North Africa in 1942, the force commanded by Eisenhower, way back when he was still only a lieutenant general. There were many ghosts in this dank and cold place, and Bond could feel them all closing in on him now as water dripped from the roof of this incredible stone highway.

"Over here," Beatrice whispered, and he saw that there was another tunnel leading off, only large enough to drive a jeep into, and possibly reverse out again. They stopped, listened and went down the branch tunnel. The far end was blanked off by a high metal wall, into which a door had been set. Bond tried the door and it swung open easily. Beatrice covered him while he leaped inside and was met by such an incredible sight that he almost forgot to follow the routine. He heard Beatrice gasp as she passed through the door, then the shot, echoing through this incredible place, and the bullet shattering only inches from Beatrice. They both dived for cover, and there was plenty of that.

They appeared to be in natural light, on what could have been a large movie set, only the place as it appeared was so real it would be easy to imagine you were dreaming. There were streets, houses, shops, even a church in the distance.

It took Bond a few moments to realize what it was, for he

had heard of this place, though never seen it before. Graffiti was daubed on walls. Jibes at the police and military.

It was all so real that it took time for the truth to sink in. This was a training ground for troops resting in Gibraltar. A place where they could practice street fighting: the kind of work that was so often required in times of civil unrest. He had heard a rumor that some members of the quick-response teams, police and army, were sometimes flown here for training.

They were lying on a pavement, sheltering behind a wall which was part of The King's Head, a pub that looked so real you could almost smell the beer.

Bond tried to assess where the shot had come from. "You work left," he whispered. "I'll cross the street and go right. Yell if you see him or he fires at you. Give it ten minutes." He held up his watch. "Then we meet back here."

She nodded, and crouching low, scuttled along the wall, while Bond readied himself and made a crouching run for it, across the street to the far side, along the blank wall of JACK BERRY, FAMILY BUTCHER. The shop front, in the main street, decorated with lifelike meat, carcasses hanging inside. He was almost at the angle of the wall on the far side when two bullets came down, flinging shards off the pavement. He thought he saw the muzzle flash, from a doorway, three houses up the cramped, terraced street, and, still running, he fired, two lots of two shots, from the hip. Bond was sure he had seen a figure duck back in the doorway.

He was panting, his back flat against the wall, working out the next move. If he went behind the butcher's shop he should be able to make his way down the back of the parallel street, and head for the rear door opposite the house from which he thought Baradj had last fired.

314

Keeping his back against the wall, he edged himself behind the shop and along the backs of the terraced houses. One. Two. He tried the handle on the mean little door of the third house. It moved and he stepped into a long dark passage. There were stairs going up to the right. He leaned his right shoulder against the stairs, listening, wondering if he should try the front door ahead of him, then decided to move left, into what would be the little front room. He heard nothing before the door crashed open and two shots ripped against the stairs, one of them clipping his Browning, sending pain dancing up his arm and the pistol flying.

He waited for death to come quickly, looking up at the figure of Bassam Baradj, silhouetted in the doorway.

"Captain Bond," Baradj said. "I am sorry about this, but in other ways pleased that the honor of being your executioner falls to me. Good-bye, Captain Bond." The pistol came up in the two-handed grip, and Bond winced at the shot, but felt nothing. Tense, unable to move, he stared at Baradj, who still appeared to be looking at him, his arms outstretched, the gun aimed.

Then, as in a dream sequence, Bassam Baradj buckled at the knees and toppled forward into the narrow passage.

Bond let out a deep, long, breath and heard Beatrice's sneakers thudding across the road. She stopped in the doorway. "James?" she asked. Then, again, "James? You okay, James?"

He nodded, his arm still shaken from the thump when the bullet had caught his pistol. "Yes. Yes, I'm okay. I guess I owe you another life, my dear Beatrice." He stepped forward, over the dead body of Bassam Baradj, and took her in his arms. "It's one hell of a way to make a living," he said.

"James?" she whispered. "Love me?"

He held her close. "I love you very much," and he realized that he meant it.

Together, they walked back down the unreal-real street, to the door which would take them to the tunnels and finally to the light outside.

20

Some Die

It was summer, and an hour before dusk: hot and pleasant. The Villa Capricciani looked lovely at this time of day. Lizards basked under the foliage, the flowers were in full bloom, and the lilies burned yellow from the pond below the house.

James Bond came onto the terrace and plunged into the pool, swimming strongly, doing a couple of lengths before climbing out, rubbing his hair with a towel which had been thrown over one of the garden chairs, into which he now sank, stretching his body like a cat.

Cat, he thought, suddenly shivering. It was the word in his head. He had noticed that, since the business earlier in the year, he had a tendency to tense up at certain words: cat; viper; snake. The shrink had told him it was not surprising. "You went through a lot during the BAST thing."

317

Yes, he supposed he had gone through a lot. He thought for a moment about death. Not the quiet friend that comes to old and worn-out human beings, but that which comes suddenly and with a terrible violence.

He thought of the Fiat down in the turning circle below. There was a little BMW there now, but, in this contemplative state of mind, Bond saw it as a little Fiat. For a few seconds he was aware of Beatrice, smiling and holding the door open, then the fearful flash and smoke, and the agony of knowing he had lost her. But there was joy also, for he had not lost the girl who could quite easily, if he did not take care, become the love of his life.

As the lights began to come on, the sun went down and the night animals began to come out. The bats started to flit to and fro, and geckos came from the daytime hiding places, strangely seeming to bask in the electric lights around the pool.

His head began to fill with other horrors. Poor old Ed with his throat cut, head almost severed from his body; Nikki, who had sought comfort from him, then tried to save his life and had her own life taken from her; then all those girls who could have lived really useful, happy, long lives: the ones he had personally taken to their graves, and Clover Pennington, whose relations he had known, cut down by her own triggerwoman.

He shivered again in the warmth, feeling the goose bumps coming up on his skin. Behind him the lights came on in the villa, and he heard Beatrice flip-flapping out toward the pool.

"You okay, darling?" she said, kissing him and looking hard into his face and eyes. "James, what's the matter? It's not us, is it?" Almost a frightened tremor to her voice.

"No, my dear, not us. I was just having what the shrink would call a touch of the horrors."

"I wondered if we should come back here."

"Oh, yes, this was the right place."

"Good. Let's go out to dinner. I enjoy it here." She squatted down beside him, looking up into his face, shadowed by the lights and the night. "James, darling. You know, some you win and some you lose."

James Bond nodded. "Yes," he said quietly. "And some die."